Love Lost Adventure

The Lie

Roseann Gargiulo

IMAGINE MEDIA CONCEPTS
FLORIDA

Copyright

Love Lost Adventure — The Lie

Acknowledgment & Credits:

In two areas of the book, I showcase lyrics written by independent songwriters Diane Ward (Chapter 33) and Marianne Flemming (Chapter 41). If you have a chance, please check out their music on the web.

"When I'm Needing Someone" by Diane Ward from the album "Mirror." © 1995 Diane Ward (ASCAP). Lyrics used with permission from the artist.
www.dianeward.com

"Fly Away" by Marianne Flemming. Lyrics used with permission from the artist. © 2021 Marianne Flemming Music (BMI).
www.marianneflemmingmusic.com

"Rawhead & Bloody Bones" by Unknown Author. The original Rawhead and Bloody Bones, also known as Tommy Rawhead or simply Rawhead, is part of an old traditional nursery rhyme from England (Yorkshire, UK). The Oxford English Dictionary cites approximately 1548 as the earliest written appearance of "Bloodybone."
https://en.wikipedia.org/wiki/Bloody_Bones

Additional Editing by Laura Wilkinson, London, England, United Kingdom

Facts & Historical Content:

The story of "Love Lost Adventure: The Lie" takes place in parts of Florida, New Jersey, and New York during the late nineties. While some aspects are based on historical data found on the web, primarily on Wikipedia, such as locations, The Fat Black Pussycat, the 1994–95 Major League Baseball strike, the Pro Bowl, and the history of Fort Brooke, most of the tale is entirely made up, such as the Blood & Bones Society and The Olustee.

www.lovelostadventure.com

Dedication

For my Mother, Vinny, & Thomas...
You live on through my words & in my heart.

Diane Ward... for all your brilliance, lyrical knowledge, and words that always seemed to elude me, but mostly for your love and unwavering support.

Marianne Flemming... for our friendship, music, and stories we've shared that ignited this journey twenty something years ago.

Eric Smith... for your brilliant mind, competitive spirit, and our silly little bet that became a new passion—*AND* yes, you won!

A BIG special thanks goes out to... My Father, Suzette, Billy, Dee, Momma Shirley, Gail, Suzanne, Sarah, Darrell, and to all of my other wonderful family & friends who have given me a lifetime of love and support. I am truly grateful.

(((Big Hugs)))

Contents

Love Lost Adventure

The Lie

1

Prologue

January 23, 1998
Friday, 11:30 pm
Tampa, Florida

"Oh, the glory of being a Senator's wife."

She stood by the windowsill in her bedroom dressed in a black silk robe with her reddish auburn hair tied up in a bun, watching as the limo pulled up the driveway.

The traitor is home…

Three sheets to the wind, the fifty-four-year-old woman turned around, clicked off the evening news, and threw the remote on the bed. She then headed over to the small bar in the corner of the room. It was a stunning rare Civil War piece of furniture currently occupied by empty vodka bottles. She grabbed her cocktail and took a sip.

At the sound of the front door latch clicking open, her face flushed red, bags dropped to the floor, a set of keys clanged on the foyer table, and then the slow dance of footsteps creaking up the grand staircase that led to her bedroom.

How dare he...

Sarah Prescott would have given Scarlett O'Hara a run for her money. She was a proud, shrewd, cunning, calculating woman—a real ol' Southern bitch. The meticulous woman took pride in making sure that everything in her life was perfectly in place, and if it wasn't, she'd make it appear so.

Just a few sacrifices here and there, that's all... some big, and some not so, but it was worth it, right?

She took another sip of her drink.

Daddy knows best...

A memory of her father swept over her, and suddenly she was just eleven, sitting in her mother's parlor room wearing her favorite dress. The Prescott family had just left the house, and her father, Frederick C. Jenkins—a short, stout, opportunistic man with ambitious dreams for his beautiful daughter, came rushing back in.

"I have wonderful news," he said, beaming with joy. "Today, I made a deal that will bring us a lot of money, and set you up for life, my sweet darling." He kissed the top of her head, then locked eyes with her. "But first, there are a few things you must do in order to achieve Daddy's li'l goals. Can I count on you, my love?"

Her father often spoke those words whenever he needed to justify the horrible things he wanted her to do, and just like the good girl she was, she did them.

Daddy's little girl...

A pained expression twisted her beauty. Her perfect world was in turmoil, and Daddy wasn't there to make it right. Hints of the Senator's infidelity had been all over the news, and tonight's headlines were especially bad. A questionable video of the Senator and his secretary filled the airwaves.

The door handle turned.

Speak of the devil...

Sarah braced herself like a boxer readying for a fight, and with one big swig, she emptied her glass as the door opened.

"How could you?" she blasted.

Andrew Blake Prescott, a six-foot-three distinguished-looking man in his late fifties, dressed in a suit and tie, entered.

"You're drunk," he snapped in disgust.

"You and that *WHORE* were all over the news again. I hope you are happy with yourself, mister."

"Gimme a break, Sarah. You always do this. Just stop it." Contempt oozed from his lips as he walked over to the bar and grabbed one of the empty bottles. "For God's sake, how much have you had?"

Sarah eyed her empty glass. "Not nearly enough." Then tossed it into the wastebasket.

"I see. It's going to be one of those nights, huh?"

The Senator took off his jacket, revealing a shoulder holster and gun, which he unstrapped and placed on the bar, then reached into the cabinet, pulled out a bottle of Jack, and poured himself a drink. Like daggers, her eyes followed his every move.

"I can't stand to even look at you," she hissed. "You destroyed everything... everything we've worked so hard for." Her upper lip curled in disdain. "And now it's all gone, down the drain... and for what, a piece of ass?"

"Calm down, Sarah, nothing happened. That video is misleading." He looked at his reflection in the mirror. The burn of satisfaction smiled back as he undid his tie. "Trust me, nothing is going on—

3

she's married, for Christ's sake."

"Oh, really?" Sarah's eyes grew wide, her expression crazed as she got up in his face. "Do you think I'm that stupid? The world is *that* stupid?" She raised a hand, wanting so bad to slap him, but stopped herself and stepped back laughing.

"Mr. Big Shot Politician… you're so smart, aren't you? You thought you'd get away with everything. You didn't care who you'd hurt as long as you got what you wanted. Nope, it's all about you, and you just couldn't stop, could you?"

"Oh, bullshit, you don't know what you're talking about. It was just a friendly kiss… none of this is true. Just calm down. It'll all be fixed by the morning, I promise. Now come here and stop this craziness." He pulled her into his arms. "Don't worry, Paddy will take care of it. He'll make things right." He brushed his lips softly to hers. "You know I love you—"

"Not this time, Blake!" She jerked out of his arms. "No matter what you do, you can't fix this. It's done. You blew it! Kiss your chance at the presidency goodbye, mister—Kiss. It. GOODBYE! It's *OVER!*"

Sarah rushed to the front window and stared out into the darkness. The cold rage she felt terrified her. She had heard about Blake's affairs in the past and discounted them as boys being boys, but this time was different. The indelible images couldn't be erased, and just like a strobing celluloid projector, the many scenes from the evening news of her husband and the tall blonde kissing in the elevator flashed before her eyes.

"Everything is destroyed," she muttered to herself as she tried to make sense of it.

All of Father's dreams are gone… they're gone forever. Everything that I have worked so hard for is RUINED! The sacrifices that I have made, all of them, WASTED! And all because of this son of a bitch and that two-bit whore!

Sarah spun around.

"How dare you!"

And with all her might, she grabbed the heavy cast iron lamp off the nightstand and hurled it at the Senator's head, hitting him dead center. He flew back against the wall and slid to the floor.

"Get up! Get *UP*," she shouted, rushing over.

"Be a man, you *COWARD*—Get *UP!*" She kicked his leg. He didn't move. Staring in disgust, a twisted look appeared on her face. "Mr. Wonderful Handsome Blake, look at you now… you're pathetic."

Blood streamed down his face from the open gash on his forehead. She hovered over his limp body and whispered, "I only married you because Father said you'd be something… ha, you're something, alright."

She kicked him again.

"A no-good-lying-cheating-piece-of-shit something—pfft, you dirty bastard."

She grabbed his drink and saluted.

"Cheers, my love."

Dazed, he began to move, his eyes struggling to focus.

"Mr. Big Shot… you thought you were the only one who had dreams," she sneered, pacing back and forth. "I had DREAMS—*I had dreams too,*" her voice trailed. She appeared to be searching for meaning. "Things that I wanted to do, but *YOU*… and Father, you stole my dreams… you stole my love."

She stepped behind the bar to pour another drink.

"*ALL* that I gave up… for *YOU*… for *him*…"

She threw the glass.

For nothing!

Her face contorted from the honesty of her words, the ugly truth she had never wanted to admit, and her breath hitched.

"So much loss…"

She reached for the holster, undid its clasp, then took the gun out and pointed it at the Senator's head.

"Never again."

Blake's eyes grew wide.

"No, Sarah… *DON'T!*"

All the lies…

Sarah pulled the trigger.

"The lie."

2

The Whirlwind

Tuesday, 8:00 am
Hollywood, Florida

Four days later…

The golden morning sun poured in through the kitchen window of the two-story house. Cleo stood by the sink, watching the neighbor's cat chase a squirrel up the mango tree. A crack of a smile appeared on her face. She loved this time of the year. The weather was cool, the humidity low, and the crazy northerners paraded their fur coats up and down the aisles at the local market.

Silly New Yorkers…

A quiet chuckle slipped from her lips as she gathered the dirty dishes from the table and placed them in the sink. The kids had just left for school, and the house was quiet—*and oh, how she loved her alone time.* Yet as peaceful as it was, she knew it wouldn't last because today was a Teddy-day.

PLOP!

"Cleo-*O*, where's my plane ticket?"

A headful of dark wavy locks popped up from a large black leather handbag that was spread out on the countertop, and within seconds, make-up, hair ties, gum wrappers, and other girly things were scattered about.

"I don't know, Teddy. What did you do with it?"

"It was right *here* next to my wallet—*WAIT,* where's my wallet?" Frantically, she eyed the room, then rushed over to a neat stack of papers in the corner and sifted through them, tossing several to the floor.

"Dammit, I just cleaned that!" Cleo swatted at her, but she just ducked and continued on her path of destruction. Teddy often short-circuited on her adventure days, and within seconds, the entire kitchen was upturned. "You know, Theodora, you'd lose your mind if it wasn't locked inside that thick skull of yours!"

"I love you too, my dear sweet sister." Teddy blew her a kiss and reached for the next pile. "Now, where could it be? Hmm, maybe *upstairs?"*

The Hayes sisters were as different as two people could possibly be. And while they bickered constantly, fought daily, and drove each other nuts, the truth was they absolutely adored each other. Cleo, whose real name was Cynthia, was a new divorcee with three children. At thirty-eight, she was pretty in a simple way, with bright green eyes and natural strawberry-blonde hair. She was overprotective to a fault, and dogs and kids just loved her.

Her younger sister Theodora was single and had been staying at the house to help with the kids. Teddy was a whirlwind of a person, a reckless adventure lover that drama and insanity seemed to follow no matter where she went. At thirty-six, she looked twenty-two. She was tall with dark brown hair and amber cat-shaped eyes that were notorious for catching a heart in just one look.

She often liked to muse that she would never let her love life be decided by the typical boring conventions of marriage, race, color, or sexual preference, for that matter. Instead, she liked to brag that she fell in love with passion. However, on a recent warm September evening, mesmerized by the beautiful harvest moon shining through the bay window, Teddy had an epiphany.

"You know, Cleo, I think I might have made the biggest mistake of my life."

"Oh yeah, how so?" Cleo was seated on the couch, half-listening and half-scribbling her way through a crossword puzzle.

"I think I walked away from the love of my life."

"What's an eight-letter word for extreme foolishness?" Cleo tapped the pen on her lower lip.

"It was my one chance at happiness, and I blew it," Teddy sighed and plopped down on the couch beside her.

"Your *what*—with *who?*" Cleo looked at her, confused. "I can't imagine who you're talking about, Theodora."

"Cole."

"Who?"

"Cole O'Keefe."

"*O*—Who?"

"You know… the artist?"

"Oh, God, not another artist," Cleo sighed. "Why couldn't it be the gym teacher?" Teddy frowned, "I never dated the gym teacher. He had *ALL* those thingies everywhere."

"Those thingies are called muscles, and you didn't like him because he was normal. Heh, such a shame too. He was so nice,

9

and he just adored you."

"Pfft, *NORMAL?* He was *BORING*, bland, and not to mention *CREEPY!*" Teddy shuddered, then laughed. "I told my therapist about him."

"And?"

"Well, I said I'd never sleep with a guy like that, even if he was the last human being on the planet." She bubbled her lips. "I guess that's kind of harsh, huh?"

"And did you tell her about your crazy obsession with out of work artists?" Cleo battered her eyelashes, trying to convey how ridiculous she sounded, but Teddy doubled down with an intensity she had never seen before.

"It's not an obsession, and Cole isn't just an artist. He is a *TRUE* artist—a painter and a brilliantly damned good one, I might add. I've been dreaming about him lately, and I think he may be the one, the *BIG ONE* even."

"The *BIG* one?" Cleo laughed. "I don't ever recall anyone being the one, and especially not the big one."

"Oh, stop, he's perfect for me. He's my equal in every way."

"Well, I don't know about that." Cleo put down the puzzle book. "Okay, refresh my memory. Which one is he again?"

"What? I can't believe you don't remember him."

"Of course, I do."

"No, you don't."

"I *DO.*"

"You *DON'T.*"

"I remember him just fine. So, are you going to tell me about him or what?" Teddy crossed her arms. "Pfft, never mind… why waste the words when you don't hear a thing I say?"

"Theodora don't be like that. It's just that there have been so many I get their names all mixed up."

"So *many?*" Teddy glared at her.

"Yes, but I'm not judging—"

"There have only been five or six at tops!"

"Ha, five or *six?* There were way more than that!"

"*ENOUGH*—you know, Cleo, I don't think I like you very much at the moment." Teddy turned away, refusing to look at her, and, amused, Cleo tapped her on the shoulder and stuck out her tongue. "Come on, Theodora, you know I worship the ground you walk on—now *SPILL IT!*"

"Oooh, you're *SUCH* an asshole!" And with an incredulous smile, Teddy uncrossed her arms and scooted over, eager to tell. "Okay, so remember about ten years ago when I posed for those art classes downtown?"

"Yes, vaguely."

"He was standing in the back all by himself, just watching. So hot. So gorgeous. So brilliant, and just like me, full of passion."

"Teddy, those were nude study classes!"

"Yes, they were," she giggled in delight. "Now you remember, don't you?"

Cleo's eyes grew large, and slowly, she sank back into the fluffy cushions.

"Oh, *that* Cole…"

"Yes, that one."

Teddy fanned her face.

"Heh, the nude study guy?"

Teddy looked down and laughed, realizing the nude factor might take away from the seriousness of the moment, and with her best yup-that's-the-one smile, she uttered, "Well?"

"Yes, now I remember him... he was the one true love, who drove you absolutely crazy, that's for sure."

"Crazy? Ha, I don't remember him being like that."

"Of course, you don't. Geez, Teddy, you only remember the good stuff. It's amazing how quickly you block out the bad."

"Well, I guess the heart wants what the heart wants."

At a loss for words, Cleo picked up the crossword puzzle and uttered, "What's an eight-letter word for extreme foolishness or irrationality?"

Teddy shrugged.

She can't be serious about this guy. She'll be bored after two days, and I hate to break it to her, but no one has ever been the ONE. She's totally—"Hey, that's it!" Quickly, Cleo scribbled in the boxes, mouthing the word:

I-N-S-A-N-I-T-Y

Satisfied, she closed the puzzle book.

"Well, Theodora, I don't know about Cole being the one and all, but I do know that you'll never catch me posing nude and showing my girly bits to the world. That's a sight only seen by the good Lord and my gyno."

"Is that *so?*"

Cleo's eyebrow rose.

"What are you trying to say, Theodora?"

"I'm not *trying* to say anything, Cleo-*O*-patra." Teddy's face brightened. She loved sassing her sister, and the best way to sass Cleo was to talk about her sex life... or lack thereof. "I just know of a few others who have seen those girly bits, that's all."

"Clearly, you're confusing me with someone else."

"Shall I refresh your memory?"

"No, don't you *DARE!*"

Counting on her fingers, Teddy started to rattle off names. "There was Davy and Mikey and Jimbo and, oh yeah, ha—good ol' hunk of burning love, Arturo! Now that one makes me proud."

"What... *how* so?"

"You were so naughty that Mom and Dad blamed me for rubbing off on you, which, of course, I did!"

"Hmph, I don't know what you mean by that."

"Oh, Saint Cleo, give me a break! Don't try to play innocent with me because I know where you've been!" Teddy made the sign of the cross and blew a kiss up to the heavens. "Hallelujah, now can someone give me an amen, please?"

Cleo's face scrunched into a tiny little ball as she tried her damnedest to look pissed, but it backfired. Instead, she let out a hearty belly laugh which caused her to sink deeper into the couch, and the two sisters burst into a howling fit of laughter. Over the next hour, they replayed memories back and forth, each telling a better story than the last. Until Cleo clutched her sides and let out a long whining sigh, "Sis, I must admit that you and Cole did make a beautiful couple. It was like watching wildfire."

"We did, didn't we?" Teddy sat upright, finally feeling gotten.

"Yes, and over the years, you've brought home all kinds, but out of all of them, Cole was just as carefree and passionate as you, which drove Mom and Dad nuts."

"He did, didn't he? Oh, my God, they hated him!" Teddy jumped up and grabbed the phone. "Well, I'm going to give him a call and see what he's been up to. I hope his number still works. Wish me luck!" Smiling, Cleo crossed her fingers.

Insanity at its finest—

CRASHHHH!

"Found it!"

Hanging over the railing, Teddy stood at the top of the staircase, waving her plane ticket high above her head like she had just won the lottery, and Cleo snapped out of her head, suddenly feeling nauseous.

You know, maybe I should have discouraged her from calling him? Or at least pulled the damn plug on the phone line!

Laughing, Teddy skipped down the stairs.

"Come on, Cleo, stop dragging your feet."

She kissed her on the cheek.

"We can't be late."

3

Let's Go

It was almost noon, and I-95 was bumper-to-bumper. They were already dragging twenty minutes behind schedule, and to make matters worse, Cleo was a horrible driver. Several horns blared as she swerved in and out of traffic, and Teddy frowned.

"I bet you have drive-a-phobia."

"Is there even such a thing?" Cleo doubted, her knuckles white from gripping the steering wheel hard.

"You drive like an old lady."

"Jesus, Teddy, taking you to the airport is the last thing I want to do today."

"Well, at least do the speed limit. You don't want to get pulled over for being a slowpoke, do ya?"

With the sun beaming on her face and the wind in her hair, Teddy felt alive. There was something about her adventure days that just seemed to fill her cup.

"Oooh, I *LOVE* this song!"

She cranked the radio and sang along, and boy, could she sing.

Her timbre was that of an old blues singer, the kind that could stop a crowd with just a few notes.

"Slowpoke, my ass," Cleo huffed. "We're here." She turned into the airport and headed up the ramp. "Do you have everything you need?"

"Hmm, I think so." Teddy flipped down the visor and stared at her reflection. She traced a faint line on her forehead and grimaced. "I'm getting old."

"Old? Don't be silly. You haven't aged one bit."

"Well, I feel old." Teddy closed the visor and looked out the window. "Life is just passing me by, and before you know it, I'll be decrepit and living alone in a tiny apartment filled with cats."

"So, that's what this is about?"

"No, I'm just saying…"

"Honestly, I don't know why you're leaving."

"I have to… If I don't, I'll always wonder what if."

"But why? Why now? You haven't seen this guy in ten years. There must be a good reason why the two of you broke up?"

"Pfft, there are plenty of reasons why we broke up, but one thing is for sure, we did have fun. Cole is good. Mm-mmm, too good if you ask me, and boy, did he know how to rock me."

"Eww, Teddy, that's gross!"

Cleo shook her head, trying to rid herself of the pervy images invading her thoughts, and Teddy laughed.

"You're such a prude."

"You know, he's probably fat and bald—or better yet, he could be one of those creepy stalker types. You know, the ones you see on the telly, who murder their exes and stash them away in the fridge as a memento."

"Don't be silly… he's not a stalker or a murderer—but he *better* not be fat," she frowned. "Or ew, bald…"

"So, do you really think that you can go back and pick up right where you left off, just like that?" Cleo snapped her fingers.

"I do, and *YES,* just like that," Teddy huffed, annoyed.

"Well, good luck, Missy, because life doesn't work that way. It never works out."

"Maybe it doesn't, but I've gotta try. Cole is the only man I've ever really loved."

"Loved? Ha—you left him! You didn't even wait for the flowers to die."

"That's so unfair! You know I can't sit in one place too long. Maybe, just maybe, this time will be different, and I'll stay. I could get married, have kids, and get a house of my own. Did you ever think of that?"

"Oh, come off it! You're just looking for a getaway."

Cleo pulled up to the baggage drop-off zone, and Teddy jumped out. She yelled to the baggage handler, waving a fistful of ones, and he rushed over to take her suitcase. Then she spun back to Cleo, furious. "And besides, what the *HELL* do you know? You've never taken a chance in your whole goddamn *BORING* safe life!"

Wounded, Cleo stepped back, cupping her mouth, her eyes filled with tears.

She's right, I haven't, but still, I don't want her to go! I have a bad feeling about this trip, and if I tell her, she'll say I'm overreacting—which I probably am. One thing's for sure if I don't support her, she'll never forgive me… I'll never forgive me.

Her soggy face scrunched into a loving, pathetic smile, and she sighed, "I'm so sorry. I didn't mean to upset you. You know I want the best for you, don't you?"

"Damn you, Cleo-*O!*" Teddy choked up. "Of course I do, but sometimes you can be such a *PAIN* in my ass!"

"Only sometimes?" she teased, knowing her sister was being too kind. "And just for the record, I can't wait for you to get married." Cleo caressed her face. "Oh, what a beautiful day that will be—*AND,* I want to be an auntie too, so you better hurry."

"Okay, okay, one step at a time," Teddy chuckled, wiping Cleo's tears away and then her own. "Now, please stop crying. You're ruining my makeup. And besides, for all we know, he could be a murderer."

"Wha-*what?*" Cleo slapped her on the arm. "Don't scare me like that, Theodora. That's not funny."

The baggage handler returned with her ticket, and Teddy sighed. "Well, it's time for me to go. I'll miss you."

"I'll miss you more, and you know I will." Cleo gave her a big hug and then quickly pulled back. "Does Cole know what time to pick you up?"

"Yes, Miss Worrywart, he'll be there and on time too, so don't you worry."

"Well, go on then. I don't want you to be late." She pushed Teddy towards the entranceway and watched as she headed in, then shouted, "Wait, where's your jacket? I heard it's going to snow up there!"

"Only light flurries. It's no big deal. I'll be fine."

"Okay, good… promise you'll call when you land?"

"I promise." Teddy crossed her heart.

"I love you."

"Love you, too." She blew her a kiss and entered.

The airport's concourse was packed. Teddy stood second in line at the ticket counter waiting to check in when a tall woman dressed all in black, wearing a formal sheath dress and pillbox hat, pushed her way to the front of the line.

"Where are the taxis to Hollywood?" she snapped at the male boarding agent.

"Over there," he said, pointing to a large taxi sign near the exit, and the woman abruptly turned, bumping into Teddy.

"Well, excuse me," the woman said, looking Teddy up and down, then huffed off.

"Looks like someone's in a hurry," Teddy laughed and handed the agent her ticket.

"Yes, and rude too." He stamped the boarding pass and gave it back. "You're all set to go, Ms. Hayes. Gate C7. Have a good trip."

"Thank you."

Teddy passed through security, then walked down the long breezeway to her boarding gate. The doors of the plane opened, and she let out a happy sigh.

And so it begins…

4

The Hayeses

Rows of white trailer park homes occupied a small but secluded area about half a mile from the Dania Beach pier. Like dominoes, they all lined up one right after the other with twenty feet of distance between them as they wrapped around a tiny makeshift church. A little ways down the road and off the path sat an old white cracker-style home with a metal roof and fenced-in yard. Butterflies flew figure eights around the potted wildflowers that lined the front porch. A black sedan was parked out front.

Special Agent Walters leaned up against the car. He was reading the morning paper. There was a military way about him with his dark crew cut, spit-shined shoes, and perfectly pressed suit. He frowned at his partner, who was fast asleep snoring inside the car, then checked his watch.

"Where the hell are they?"

POP! POP!

An exhaust pipe backfired, and an old 70s woodie station wagon chugged down the graveled dirt road. Walters tapped on the windshield.

"Wake up, they're here."

With a big yawn, Special Agent Stewart stretched his arms and scooted out of the car. He was definitely not military, and his suit could have used a good ironing.

"Fix yourself. You're a mess."

Stewart straightened his tie, then his jacket, and with a wink, ran his fingers through his greasy blonde crop. Then the agents put on their sunglasses and stood at attention, waiting for the elderly couple to exit the car.

"Mr. and Mrs. Hayes?" Walters flashed his badge.

"Yes," the Hayeses replied in unison.

"We're from the FBI. I'm Agent Walters, and this is Agent Stewart. We're looking for your daughter, Theodora. Do you know where she is?"

"Oh, good grief! What did she do now?" Mr. Hayes said, dreading the answer, and Mrs. Hayes clutched her bag.

"Henry, don't you say a word—that badge looks fake to me!"

"Now, now, Abby, settle down. Don't ya get all bent outta shape. It's probably nothing. Let's just see what these nice men have to say." He swallowed hard. "So, fellas, what has our little girl done this time?"

"Sir, there's been a—"

"Abby!" Mr. Hayes gasped as his wife's face went pale, and she swayed down to the floor. He caught her just before she landed.

"Jesus Christ, Missus!"

He smacked her lightly on the face. "Wake up, Abby. Wake *UP!*" She was out cold. His hand rose again, but this time, her eyes shot wide open.

"Henry Hayes, you hit me again, and you'll regret the day you were born. Now get me up, you old fool." Walters reached out a hand, but she shooed him away with an evil eye.

"You know folks, maybe this isn't such a good time," Stewart said, nodding to Walters. "We can come back later if you'd like?"

"Nah, that's all right, fellas. Just gimme a second here." Henry lifted his wife up and led her to a wooden rocking chair on the side of the stoop.

The Hayeses were simple folk who sometimes read too much and got into trouble with their lofty ideals. Henry Hayes was a kind man with a kind old face. He was very tall and too thin, wearing a neatly pressed white shirt and tan khaki trousers held up by suspenders—which he often played with when pondering things. His wife, Abby, on the other hand, was a pistol. Dressed in a floral muumuu, she was about thirty pounds too heavy for her five-foot-two frame, but that didn't slow the tough old broad down.

Slowly, she rocked back and forth with one hand pressed to her heart and the other resting on her forehead... and she swooned, "Oh Lord Jesus, why us? Have we not been good Christians?"

"Amen," Mr. Hayes chimed, nodding.

"Why couldn't she be more like her sister? Cynthia was always the good one."

"Ain't that the truth."

"Henry, get me my pills."

"Yes, dear." He checked his front pocket for the key to the house, then the back, and smiled when he found it.

"Now! Before I *die*," she barked.

"Yeah, okay, okay, I'm going."

He struggled to unlock the front door.

"Sweet Jesus, Henry, can you move *any* slower?"

"Dammit, woman, you know it sticks." With a heave from his shoulder, the door swung open, and he almost fell in.

Ignoring him, Abby stared out into the woods and continued rocking. "That girl's *ALWAYS* been trouble." She fanned her face. "Why me, Lord, why me? What did I do wrong? I gave her a home, fed her, bought her clothes, and even a bicycle for her birthday. Why am I the one being punished?" She looked at Stewart and shrugged. "She never did like us, you know? She never listened, and she was always in trouble—*ALWAYS* the troublemaker."

She let out a belly laugh.

"Yup, that Theodora gets her kicks out of driving me mad, *AND* she does it all the time. Lord knows you can't find a moment's peace with that one."

BAM!

Mr. Hayes rushed out of the house with the pills clutched in one hand and a glass of water spilling everywhere in the other. "Here you go, Missus. Now take 'em slow and easy."

"Henry, remember that time she took off all her clothes and ran up and down the street screaming and then dancing on old Joe's front lawn?"

"Yup, sure do," he laughed.

"It embarrassed the hell out of us." She popped a pill in her mouth and took a sip of the water. "They still talk about it to this day in church, calling it the craziest thing they ever did see."

Grinning, Mr. Hayes dragged on his suspenders with his thumbs and nodded.

"And Henry, remember that time she ran away?" Abby glanced at Walters. "She was only ten years old. We couldn't find her for two whole days."

"Two *whole* days," Mr. Hayes echoed.

"Where was she?" Abby slapped her knee. "Hell, she had been sleeping on the neighbor's roof."

"On the *neighbor's* roof."

"Can you guess why?" Abby said with a grin, and the agents shrugged. "She wanted to see if we were going to rent out her room." Mr. Hayes lightly kicked the side post and snickered, "We almost did too."

"Am I right, Henry?"

"Yes, Missus. When you're right, you're right."

Walters tried to interject, but Mr. Hayes stopped him with a wave of the hand. "Hang on, fellas." He reached for his wife and lifted her up. "Come on, Missus, it's time for you to go inside. Lemme take care of this." He escorted her in, then returned a moment later. "So, fellas, what's this all about? Our Teddy hasn't done anything to get herself into trouble, has she?"

"No, sir, not at all," Walters replied, trying to ease the look of panic on the old man's face. "A situation has come up, and we need to speak with her. Do you know where we can find her?"

"Sorry, fellas, I don't. That one there is a bit of a free spirit—if you know what I mean." He moved in closer, fearing Abby might overhear them. "She's always been a little odd. She's not like the other one… nope, not at all." He laughed. "Teddy is… hmm, how should I say?" He thought for a bit, then grinned. "Well, ya see… she's sorta like a fish you wish you had thrown back."

A chuckle dropped from Stewart's lips, and Walters glared

at him, incredulous. Then he reached into his pocket. "Sir, here's my card. If you do hear from Theodora, could you please tell her to contact us? We need to speak with her."

"Sure thing, fellas," Mr. Hayes said as he headed in, then turned back. "I'll do that, but you might be waiting a while. Teddy forgets to call sometimes… she's like that."

And with a snicker, he shut the door.

5

Stormy Weather

"Flurries... they said light flurries! I know I don't know much about snow, but these are definitely not *FLURRIES!*"

Freezing and alone, Teddy waited outside by the curb, looking similar to one of those snow-globe snowmen in a winter wonderland of swirling glitter. Her hair blew wildly from the movement of the blizzard's winds, which was in stark contrast to her body, which stood rigid and shivering as she donned only a thin scarf, neither hat nor glove, high heel boots, and a not-so-warm black leather jacket.

"Any minute now, Cole," she stuttered through chattering teeth. A gust of snow smacked her in the face, and she fell over. "Oooooh—I hate you," she shrieked, punching the snow. She climbed to her feet and was knocked down again.

"Oh, screw this—I'm going in!"

She dashed in through the sliding glass doors, and her eyes went wide. The place was a madhouse. Stranded travelers were scurrying everywhere, from ticket booths to service counters, trying to find a way to get home.

The intercom system clicked on, and a woman's voice rang out, "Ladies and gentlemen, can we have your attention, please? All flights have been canceled due to the weather. We apologize for any inconvenience. Please see a flight representative for further details." Confused as to where to go, Teddy stared at the sign hanging above her head.

↑ GATES ↑
→ TICKETING →
← TRANSPORTATION ←
↓ BAGGAGE CLAIM ↓

Then she gawked at the crowded maze of people before her, zigzagging all the way down for as far as she could see.

Ugh, I hate lines!

Instantly, she spun around, remembering there was a row of phone booths in a secluded area towards the back, and headed over.

Now where did I put Cole's telephone number?

She plopped down at the first booth and searched her bag and then her suitcase. And, to her dismay, she found it in her back pocket, drenched from snow.

"Ew, it's all soggy."

She stared at the blotched ink.

"Hmph, is that a seven or a *nine?* Let's try seven."

Picking up the handset, she listened for a tone, then dropped a quarter in the slot and dialed. It rang twice and clicked over.

"Hello, Cole... where are you? I'm here—"

"We're sorry, but the number you've dialed has been disconnected and is no longer in service. If you feel that you've reached this recording in error—"

Pfft, it must be a nine...

She hung up and tried again, but this time crossed her fingers as it clicked over.

"Hi, Cole... it's me, Teddy."

"We're sorry, but the number you've dialed has been disconnected—"

"Oh, wait, Cleo has his number." Quickly, she threw in more quarters and dialed, chanting to herself like she was praying to the phone gods. "Come on, pick up, pretty please, pick up... I swear I'll be good, Cleo, just pick up—"

"Hi, we're not home. Leave a message, and we'll call you back later. Bye—"

BEEP!

"Dammit, Cleo-*O,* where are you when I need you? Shit, shit, *SHIT!*" She slammed the phone down. "Now *what?*" Teddy stared at the massive amount of people standing in line.

"Oh, dread, it's gotten longer!"

Sulking, she dragged her stuff over.

Ugh, somebody shoot me!

6
Cleo's House

Back in Hollywood...

The mudroom door swung open, and Cleo entered the kitchen with her arms full of groceries that were about to drop to the floor. Quickly, she heaved them onto the countertop just in time to save the eggs.

Whew, that was close.

She looked up as the answering machine sounded.

"Can someone get that?"

BEEP!

"I told her if she didn't settle down, she was going to get into trouble, and sure enough, I was right! You know they came here looking for her today?" an exasperated Abby Hayes barked. *Who?* Cleo wondered as she placed some items in the freezer.

"Cynthia, are you there? This is your mother speaking. Is your finger broken? I haven't heard from you in days. Sally's daughter calls her twice a day, every day."

Cleo reached for the phone, "Hello Ma—*BEEEEP*," and shrugged as it buzzed in her ear. *Oh well, I'll call her later.*

"Hey, I'm home?" she called out whimsically.

Usually, the house was packed with kids this time of day, but oddly enough, it was empty with no signs of life except that every light was on, and the TV in the living room was blaring. She flicked off a few switches on her way to the stairs.

"Anybody up there?"

She waited a moment but then returned to the living room when she heard an urgent alert coming from the television.

"In today's news, a powerful nor'easter storm is expected to bring more than twenty inches of snow to New York City," said the male anchor.

"Wha—*what?*"

Alarm swept over Cleo as she stared at the montage of snowy images filling the screen. The caption read:

THE STORM OF THE CENTURY
HITS THE NORTHEAST

Oh, no...

"All flights have been canceled, leaving thousands of passengers stranded."

No fucking way...

"Electricity is out to more than one million people, with more expected, and all forms of transportation going in and out of the city have been halted."

Holy shit, Teddy!

The front door flew open, and Anna, Cleo's nine-year-old

daughter, charged in. She was a bit of a tomboy with beautiful green eyes like her mom's and had curly dirty blonde hair that always seemed to need untangling.

"Ma, Aunt Teddy called," she yelled, opening the fridge. The bells of an ice cream truck rang from down the block, and her head tilted like a dog. "Ooh, can I have money for a Creamsicle?"

"No—what did she say?"

"Er," Anna thought for a moment. "Um, she was mad, and… oh yeah, she said she'd call you later."

"Later? What time later?"

"Dunno." Anna grabbed her mom's purse off the counter and handed it to her with a big grin. "Now can I get ice cream?"

"I said no," Cleo scowled, holding her purse behind her back. "Think, Anna, what did she say?"

"Um," Anna bubbled her lips. "Well, she cussed a lot… and said the F-word about a gazillion times." The bells rang louder, and her eyes darted to the front door. "Oh, come on, Ma, please? He's almost here!"

"Oh, all right." Cleo pulled a couple of ones from her wallet and held them over Anna's head, which she knew was a form of bribery—*AND probably child abuse,* but she didn't care.

"Focus, Anna… what exactly did your aunt say?" Anna scrunched her face into a chubby little ball, thinking hard, then smiled. "Oh yeah, now I remember. Aunt Teddy said she was stuck in the snow and wants you to come get her."

"Wha—*what?* I can't get her. Is she crazy?" Anna jumped up, grabbed the money, and charged out the door. "Thanks, Ma!"

I'm such a sucker.

"And, in other news," the anchor continued. "Senator Blake Prescott and his wife were laid to rest today." Images of the funeral service flashed on the screen of all the mourners and dignitaries. Cleo motioned the sign of the cross as the camera slowly zoomed in on a lone woman seated up front. She was dressed all in black with her face hidden behind a funeral veil, and the chyron read:

Bridget Prescott
Daughter of Mr. & Mrs. Prescott

"Authorities still have not released the cause of death." A video clip of the medics wheeling the bodies from the mansion played, and Bridget could be seen in the background crying as her parents' bodies were taken away. "Aw, the poor thing..."

RING—BBBRRING!

"Ooh, that must be Teddy." Cleo muted the sound and rushed to answer, then shouted into the phone, "Where *ARE* you?"

"Theodora Hayes, please," inquired a soft but stern female voice. "Oh, I'm sorry, I thought you were somebody else. Teddy, I mean Theodora, is not here right now. Who's calling?"

"I'm an old friend. I was hoping to speak with her this evening. Do you know where I might reach her?"

"No, I don't—*um,* she is... well, to be honest, I don't know where she is at the moment." Flustered, Cleo grabbed a pen. "You can leave me your number, and I'll have her call you."

"No, that's okay. It's sort of a surprise. I'll call back in the morning. Thank you."

"But, wait, I didn't get your—"

BUZZZZ

"Name."

7

Woman In Black

The pale woman hung up the phone and gazed at her reflection in the hotel mirror. It had only been a few days since her parents' death, yet Bridget Prescott didn't recognize herself anymore. At thirty-two, her usual spirited hazel eyes now appeared flat and emotionless, sunken deep into her cameo-shaped face. She tugged at the pillbox hat pinned to her dark brown hair and winced.

Beauty is pain...

She tossed the headpiece onto the bed and sat down behind a small writing desk covered in documents. She sifted through the papers until she found the one that she was looking for—a life insurance policy.

"Now, why would Mother leave this for her?" Bridget reviewed it, then tucked it away in an envelope labeled THEODORA HAYES and pushed it aside, frowning. "I guess I'll have to wait until tomorrow to find out," she murmured.

Her eyes softened on an old thick leather-bound book with the initials ABP on its cover. She lifted the journal to her nose, closed her eyes, and inhaled deeply. Then slowly exhaled as she opened it.

Father...

An inscription on the inside read:

Property of
Andrew Blake Prescott
January 5, 1956

Slowly, she turned the pages of her father's diary, glancing over his scribbled notes that covered the entirety of each page. Tiny passages were squeezed along the spines, as were text-filled clusters that sat in the corners. She stopped on a page held by a bookmark, but it wasn't any ordinary bookmark. Instead, it was an old Confederate relic that looked like a key. It had been a treasured heirloom in the Prescott Family since the Civil War and handed down from generation to generation, then finally given to her father, the last of the Prescott men.

A folded handwritten ledger also sat wedged in the crevice of the page. She carefully released it from the book's hold and examined it. On one side was a list, and on the other, a hand-drawn diagram.

The list was full of names, dates, and in the last column, some form of symbol hierarchy that she didn't quite understand. Yet, Bridget did recognize some of the names. Some were living, and some were dead.

Curious, she flipped over the ledger and stared at the drawing. A set of numbers were scribbled on top. Bridget guessed it to be a passcode of sorts, but for what? She hadn't a clue, so she put it down and pulled another list from her purse—*her list.*

A slight smile came to her face, and she picked up her father's favorite pen. It was a beautiful 18-karat gold Italian Omas, and she rolled it between her thumb and forefinger. Then once again lifted it to her nose and inhaled deeply, sealing his memory in her senses.

I know you're here with me—

A breaking news alert sounded, and a woman's voice interrupted her thoughts. Bridget looked over at the TV. Her eyes pained as images of her mother and father floated across the screen.

"Authorities have now confirmed that Senator Andrew Blake Prescott and his wife Sarah died in an apparent murder-suicide. Our lead reporter Michael Brenner is onsite with more details."

"Jane, a suicide letter was found on a table near where the bodies were discovered. The police have not yet released the contents of the note, nor the name of the person who wrote it, but said they expect to release more information once all family members have been notified."

With a flick of the remote, Bridget turned off the TV and returned her attention to her list. She put a question mark next to Theodora Hayes's name, then picked up the phone and dialed. It rang a few times until an out-of-breath elderly woman answered, "Cynthia, is that you?"

"Abigail Hayes?"

8

Raging Tempest

Damn, it's freezing...

Shivering, Teddy woke in the darkness under a stairwell. "Where am I? Disoriented, she looked around and recognized several passengers from her flight sleeping nearby.

"Oh, God, the airport..."

Her words rose up into vapors and then disappeared. It was late, the clock on the wall read four in the morning, and she was exhausted. All planes were grounded. There were no hotels, no taxis, no trains, and definitely, no Cole to whisk her away to comfort. Instead, she was curled up on the floor in a bed made of clothes with her handbag as a pillow. It was neither comfy nor warm, but it was better than nothing. She pulled a long sweater over her legs and tried to settle in, but a rattling sound by the front entranceway startled her.

A janitor wearing a Yankees ski cap and an orange workman's vest rounded the corner. He was pushing a large garbage bin and seemed oblivious to his surroundings as he crossed over the threshold that activated the glass sliding doors. A blast of frigid air burst into the concourse, dropping the temperature by at least ten degrees, and he jumped back laughing.

"Holy crap, that's cold—"

AAAAAHHHHHH!

Teddy shot upright.

"Are you *KIDDING* me?!"

"Oops. Sorry, my bad," he said with a chuckle, then pushed into the darkness.

"What a *freaking* idiot! Oh, my God, what a nightmare!" She dragged the long sweater up to her chin and laid down.

FUCK! It's COLD!

Tossing and turning, she tried to get warm but couldn't. The cold air rising up from the concrete made it impossible.

"I-I can't get comfortable," she stuttered, then Cleo's voice screeched in her head, "Theodora Hayes, you get your bony ass up and get moving—*NOW!*"

Instantly, Teddy jumped to her feet, almost tumbling forward in the process. Her bones felt brittle, and she winced in pain.

Even my little toes hurt!

She could see lights way down on the other side of the corridor, and within seconds, she packed her things and headed over.

Ooooh, hot tea...

Aside from a few workers and bodies scattered about, the airport appeared deserted. The concourse's stark silhouette design had windows that ran from the base of the floors all the way up to the top of the high ceilings. And outside the glass, everything was blanketed in a white haze of snow, with the blizzard winds whip lashing the buildings along with an icy fleet of stranded planes.

Heh, so much for flurries.

Her face brightened at the flashing SUB sign down at the end of the row, and she quickened her pace but to no avail. It was closed.

This totally sucks.

Disheartened, she tried of few more places, but each light of hope turned grim. They were all closed. She started to head back, but something swaying outside the window caught her eye, and she walked over.

"Look at those giant snowflakes—wait, what is this?" She looked down. "Is that a foot *heater?*"

Her face lit up in disbelief, and she quickly bent over the radiator to warm her hands. But the good feeling was short-lived when a massive gust of snow crashed into the glass, and she jumped back, scared.

"Damn you, Cleo—you jinxed me!" She stared out into the abyss. The sky was falling. "Oh, this does not look good. I'll be stuck here for days with no bed, no phone, no Cole!" Her head dropped, and a single tear fell. Quickly, she wiped it away. "Don't cry, please don't... it's going to be okay."

She closed her eyes, refusing to let the tears fall. Her emotions were raw, and Teddy knew that if she let go, that was it—she was done for.

Just breathe...

With her lips inches away from the window, she slowly exhaled, and the warmth of her breath made a canvas out of the condensation. Then her fingertip pressed against the glass, and in one stroke, she drew a large heart and wrote Cole's name in the center, followed by hers. A silly grin appeared, and with an "I've got this" laugh, Teddy added an arrow.

Softly, she hummed...

Dreamiest eyes
of the bluest seas

Your beautiful smile
calls to me

A simple touch
and the heart unwinds

Oh, how I've ached
just hoping to find

So, as I breathe
I will go

For a love
pure as the snow

9

Bloody Bones

A huge hickory tree sat on top of an old ancient mound located near the mouth of the river in the newly acquired Florida Territory. The Tocobaga Indians placed it there centuries before. And in 1824, Colonel George M. Brooke, the outpost's first commander, felt it a fitting location and ordered his men to clear the area, and Fort Brooke was constructed.

In his early days, Jubal E. Prescott was considered Fort Brooke's most influential and accomplished soldier. Every evening, he would declare, "The morality of my fellow man is at stake." And then leave to patrol the area looking for troublemakers, thieves, and runaways.

He was a highly moral man with a strict set of rules that he, his family, and those around him lived by, which made him a force to be reckoned with. However, many years after the Civil War, at the ripe old age of eighty-two, his favorite pastime was sitting around the campfire telling stories to his grandchildren.

"Grandfather, please tell us again the story of how you lost your arm," said the young Charles Prescott, age ten, as he sat with his sister, Susan, age seven, and younger brother, William, age eight.

"Yes, Grandpapa, please tell us," Susan said.

"Well, children, with the fear of God leading the way, I left for my patrol. There had been a thief stealing from our provisions, and it was my job to bring him in. It was late and dark. It had rained all day, so everything was wet and quiet—almost too quiet for my liking."

Jubal stabbed at the fire with a long wooden stick. "I must have been ten minutes out, and I heard a sudden noise that stopped me in my tracks. 'Who goes there?' I shouted into the darkness. Suddenly, the bushes parted, and I saw this ghost of a man with the largest set of eyes that I ever did see. He was black as night, and I figured he was a runaway."

The fire's embers grew bright, and Jubal's eyes darkened.

"'Come on out,' I demanded. 'You got nowhere to go,' but the young man refused. He said he wasn't gonna harm no one, but I didn't trust him. So, I told him I was gonna count to three."

Jubal pointed the fiery stick at the children, and they cowered in their seats.

"So, I readied my gun, and I started counting…

One…

Two…

Three—"

CRACK!

The children jumped at the whipping of the stick.

"Well, if he didn't just lunge straight out at me, flying through the air from about ten feet away, swinging that hatchet like he was splitting wood."

"Oh, no, Grandpapa," Susan squealed, covering her mouth.

"Yes, my dear, it was indeed scary, and this is what he did to me."

He pulled back his sleeve, and the children gasped in horror at the evil-looking contraption that was now his arm. It was made of wood and leather and had a sharp iron hook on its cap. Jubal let out a hearty laugh and poked at the glowing embers.

"Thank goodness I had my pistol ready to go because the son of a bitch chopped off my arm just as I squeezed the trigger. Heh, I shot him dead square between the eyes. He was an evil one, the devil himself, I figure, and I sent him straight to hell where he belonged."

"Evil like the boogeyman?" William gasped.

"A real-life Tommy Rawhead?" Charles shouted.

"Yes, that's him, alright." Jubal leaned forward and threw more wood on the fire. "He was sneaky, hiding silently in the woods, watching me. Just like folks use to say ol' Tommy had been known to do." Jubal shuddered, remembering.

"After I killed him, I found the sack he had planned to use on the little ones. It was all bloody, filled with knives and ropes."

The children went silent.

"Y'all better steer clear of them folks, you hear me? They're evil." Jubal turned to his granddaughter. "And you, my sweet princess, promise me that you'll run fast and far if you ever do come across one?"

"Oh, yes, Grandpapa, I promise, but who is this Tommy what's-his-name?"

Jubal laughed.

"You never heard of ol' Tommy Rawhead, my dear?"

She shook her head, no.

"Well, honey, he was an evil man who lived in the woods—Bloody Bones, I think that's what they called him. Folks said he would kidnap children and carry them away in an old leathery sack and eat 'em whole." Susan shuddered, and with a husky drawl, Jubal recited the old nursery rhyme:

Rawhead & Bloody Bones

Steals naughty children
from their homes

Takes them to his dirty den

And they are never
seen again

• • •

A hundred years later...

Wednesday, 9:45 am
Tampa, Florida

Just blocks from where the old Fort once stood, Agents Stewart and Walters entered the Tampa FBI field office. It was a small building with stock windows, narrow glass entranceways, and no personality. They headed down the hallway and straight into the conference room.

"You're late," Stephens shouted. "The briefing is about to begin." He was seated at the end of a long table, having his makeup done by a female assistant. He gestured for the agents to sit across from him, then ripped off his makeup bib and shooed the girl out the door. Agitated, he stood, hovering over them.

"Did you find the girl?"

"No, sir, she wasn't there," Walters said. "But we're flying back later today. I'm sure we'll find her then, sir."

"What about the other one?"

"No word from her either," Stewart interjected. "We last saw her at the funeral, sir. But she left in a hurry, and we haven't been able to reach her since."

"There's word she might be unstable. I want you to keep an eye on her, okay?"

"Yes, sir," they replied.

Special Agent-in-Charge Paul Stephens was an attractive man with salty peppered hair. Most considered him to be a man's man. He graduated best in his class, top at the academy, and knew how to play the game, especially with those who pulled the strings of power. But lately, he was on edge. This whole business with the Senator was really getting under his skin. It didn't make sense to him. He personally knew the Prescotts and respected them—*hell, he even liked them.* And that was saying a lot when you dealt with the type of politicians he did.

"Gentlemen, the Prescotts were good people. Something in them must have just snapped." He walked to the window and stared out. "We're not going to let this get out of hand and ruin their good name, are we?"

"No, sir," they said.

"Hell, he could've been our next president. Now I want this handled the right way with no leaks and put to rest quickly, do you hear me—"

BAM!

The door swung open, and Agent Jones rushed in.

"Sir, we have a problem," he said, pushing his horn-rimmed glasses straight. He was a nerdy sort of guy in a suit that looked too big.

"What's the problem, Agent?"

"Saturday night, we found a dead body in the alleyway behind the Biltmore."

"And?"

"A single bullet to the head from a .38, sir."

"And, what's the problem?" the commander's voice grew more agitated.

"Well, sir, it seems the markings on the bullet match the Senator's gun."

"What do you mean? I thought we had the weapon." He shot a confused look at Walters, then Stewart.

"Um… no, sir—that's the problem. I just came back from ballistics, and the gun and Mrs. Prescott's letter are missing."

"How is that even possible?"

"I don't know, sir."

"Oh hell, Jones, are you incompetent?"

"Sir, there were only two of us on scene, Grady and myself. We tagged the items and sent them to the lab. We didn't learn they were gone until a few minutes ago when the report connected the Biltmore murder to the weapon."

"That's great, just fucking great, and I've got a bunch of reporters outside my door waiting to be briefed." Stephens ran his fingers through his hair, then his eyes went wide. "The press hasn't picked up on this yet, have they?"

"No, sir, nobody knows—oh, and sir, there's more. The man killed was Joseph Garcia, the head of security at the hotel. We think he was the one responsible for releasing the video of the Senator and his secretary to the media."

"Who identified him?"

"The maid, sir. She said she stumbled upon the body on her cigarette break."

KNOCK! KNOCK!

"Agent Stephens, it's time, sir," the assistant called.

"All right, one second." He turned to the agents. "Remember, not a word to anyone, follow my cues… and, Stewart, fix your tie!"

"Sixty seconds, sir—"

Goddammit, just hold your horses. I'm coming… I'm coming!

10

YOU!

IT'S DEAD!

She slammed the receiver into the phone's cradle.

I can't believe the lines are still down—FUCK!

Seated in the last phone booth at the end of the row, Teddy adjusted a stack of quarters, lining them up perfectly on the ledge just below the return slot.

It was after three. The day was dragging on slowly. She had just eaten lunch and was bored out of her mind. Outside, the weather conditions had calmed, but life was at a standstill. Everything was blanketed in heaps of snow. Grabbing the handle once more, she listened for a dial tone.

Dammit! How long could it POSSIBLY take to remove snow from the lines?

She cradled the handle again.

"Oh, happy times… pfft, I could just scream!"

BA—BAAMMM!

A loud crashing sound echoed off the walls, and the door in the corner swung open. A burst of brisk air rushed in, and much to her surprise, there he was. In from a flurry of snow, the janitor in the orange vest and Yankees ski cap appeared.

Hey, it's that idiot from last night! Because of him, I froze my ass off and couldn't sleep a wink. Well, screw him!

"Hey, you—*BUDDY*—Wait up!"

Teddy rushed after him, but he kept walking.

"I said, *WAIT!*"

Running full throttle, she caught up to him, grabbed him by the sleeve, and spun him around.

"Hey, *YOOUUU!*"

Kenneth O'Connor turned a startled look at her. His hair, dark and wavy, curled up at the edges of his hat. He had piercing blue eyes, a slight dent in his chin, and a beautiful smile that made her stop in her tracks. She let out a sharp breath and quickly released his shirt.

"Who me?" he said, surprised, pointing to himself.

"Yeah, you, buddy—*YOU!*" Winded, Teddy bent over to catch her breath.

"Take your time," he said with a curious smile.

"Did you have fun last night?" she sneered, staring him down with an evil eye.

"Fun? Um... what do you mean?"

"Did you think it was funny what you did to me—I mean, what you did to us? Huh, did *YOU?*"

"What I did to you?" He searched his memory. "Honey, do I know you?"

"You don't remember?" Teddy pulled back, crossing her arms. "Really?"

"Hmm, let me see…" He scratched his head. "Ah, nope, can't say that I do." He tried hard not to laugh, but his rugged grin kept pushing its way up.

"You think this is funny, don't you?" Incensed by the bewildered look on his face and the fact he wasn't taking her seriously, Teddy grew angrier by the second.

"I must admit, I am amused."

"Is everything a joke to you?"

"Trust me, princess, I would know if I'd ever met you, but I'm drawing a blank."

"Princess—*PRINCESS!* Who are you calling princess? It was you last night! You opened the door and laughed while we all froze!"

"Oh, that…" He winced at the memory.

"Yeah, that."

 He looked down, embarrassed. "I'm sorry."

"Is that *ALL* you have to say?"

"Yeah, my bad. I didn't mean to."

"You *LAUGHED* at *us!*"

"Well, it was kind of funny." Kenneth laughed again, but his smile faded as soon as he saw the incredulous look on her face.

"You're such an asshole! I can't believe you did that. I bet you get off on bullying little children too!"

"What? Wait. Where's that coming from? It was only an accident. You're blowing it way out of proportion."

"You didn't freeze your ass off, mister. I did! I spent the whole night shivering because of your so-called accident. Do you know how long it takes to shake off the chills when you're sleeping on concrete? Do you, *HUH?"* She poked him in the chest, and humored, he caught it. Teddy gasped in outrage, and he smirked.

"Now settle down, princess. It wasn't that bad." She tried to break free, but he tightened his grip. "Yes, I thought it was funny at the time, but I didn't mean to do it. Come on, let me buy you a hot cup of coffee."

"I *DON'T* think so." She tugged harder, and he released, which sent her wobbling back, about to fall over. Quickly, he reached out and caught her in his arms. "I gotcha… you're safe."

Teddy shuddered, startled by their closeness, then she growled.

"Oooh, *you!"*

"Oh, come on, princess… I said I was sorry," he playfully pleaded. "Let me make it up to you."

"Never," she grunted, pushing out of his arms. "I don't need anything from a man like you."

"Whoa, a man like me… what's that supposed to mean? How do you know what kind of man I am?"

"I know your type."

"And what would that be?"

"A guy who gets his kicks off by opening a glass sliding door during a blizzard and laughs when people are freezing—that kind."

"Oh, come on, don't be like that, don't be mad. It was only an accident, and I said I was sorry. My name's K. What's yours?"

"My name is none of your business. Besides, K isn't a name. It's a letter."

"K stands for Kenneth. That's what my friends call me, and you can call me K too if you like."

"Well, being that I'm not your friend, I won't."

The intercom clicked on, "Paging, Kenneth O'Connor... paging, Kenneth O'Connor... you're needed right away in Terminal B."

"Okay, Ms. None-Of-Your-Business, that's me, and I've got to go. This is your last chance for that make-up cup of coffee... what do you say, yes or no?"

"That'll be a no, Kenneth."

He smiled at the sound of his name ringing from her lips. "Well, then, princess, until we meet again. You take care." He winked a charming smile and left.

All flustered, Teddy watched until he disappeared into the crowd, and then she spun around in a huff.

Cole, I'm going to kill you!

11

The Swing

Back in Hollywood…

The name Hector Gonzalez was printed in red on the driver's license posted on the dashboard of the taxicab. The youthful photo didn't look at all like the old man seated behind the wheel with his weathered face and graying hair. Bridget pulled a hundred-dollar bill from her purse and handed it to him.

"Hector, I'll need you all day. Wait here for me, okay? I won't be long." Staring straight ahead, afraid to make eye contact, he uttered, "Yes, ma'am."

The quiet neighborhood was built in the late forties, and it had that old Florida charm to it with its cute little homes, gardens filled with colorful flowers, and lots of mango trees. A little park with a playground sat in the middle of the block.

Bridget stepped out of the car. The late afternoon sun washed over her, and she checked her look in the side view mirror—her appearance had changed. Her dark hair was gone and replaced with an angled platinum blonde bob cut. A strand of hair fell upon her face, and she neatly tucked it behind her ear.

Perfect.

Dressed in a black turtleneck and gorgeous pearl-colored pencil skirt, Bridget headed for the payphone at the park's edge.

"Anna, come inside and do your homework," Cleo hollered as she walked to the mailbox that stood by the curb, and Bridget looked over.

"But Mom, I told Mandy that I'd meet her by the swings."

"Okay, but promise me you'll do it later?"

"Yuppers!"

Bridget watched as the child shot across the street and climbed onto the swing next to a pudgy little redhead. A black sedan pulled up to the front of the house, and two men dressed in dark suits stepped out.

Hm, that looks like the FBI... why are they here?

She leaned back so that the agents wouldn't see her. Cleo gestured for the men to come inside, and she frowned, then looked over at the child.

WHEEEEEE!

Soaring up high, Anna squealed with joy, and Bridget smiled.

I guess I'll have to speak to the little one instead, but first, I have a call to make.

She inserted a coin into the payphone and dialed.

"Hello," a cheery woman's voice answered.

"Mrs. Kelly?"

"Yes, who's calling?"

"Bridget Prescott."

Dead silence filled the air, and then the woman said in a wilting voice, "Oh, Bridget, I still can't believe your father is gone. I'm devastated—"

"I'm sure you are. Listen, I don't have time for this. I have what you asked for, but more importantly, do you have what I want?"

"I do, but how do I know you aren't making this stuff up? What proof do you have that it was me?"

"Oh, how quaint, the cheater wants proof." Bridget rolled her eyes. "Well, Mrs. Kelly, does a certain red dress with a gold clasp in the back ring a bell? But most notably, you have a lovely tattoo on your backside that I think, aside from your husband, few know about."

"Jesus," Mrs. Kelly gasped.

"A single red rose, if I'm not mistaken, right?"

"Okay, okay, enough! I'll get you the money. When and where?"

"I figured you would. I don't think your husband will be so forgiving this time. The elevator scene was nothing compared to this video."

"I said I'll get you the money," her voice shook. "Now, promise you won't do anything rash?" Disgusted, Bridget turned and watched as the pudgy girl jumped off the swing and ran home. "Come on, for God's sake, don't do this to me. You know I loved your father. This will ruin my family."

The panic in the woman's voice irritated her, and Bridget sneered, "I guess you should have thought twice about stepping into that elevator with my father, Mrs. Kelly. It is you who ruined my family."

"But—but," the woman stuttered.

"But nothing… meet me on Thursday evening at nine at the Old Tampa Theatre on Franklin. Be on time and come alone. Don't forget to bring the money." Bridget struggled to contain her anger. "After all, you wouldn't want me to do anything rash, now would you?" She slammed the phone into the cradle and headed for the swings.

Rash? I never act rash… I plan. I get even.

Anna sailed up high, her feet floating towards the sun, then swoosh, down to earth she went.

"Again," she hollered, "Up, up, up, and *ZOOM!*"

At the top of her swing, Anna's body arched, her head tilted back, and she caught a glimpse of Bridget's shiny black heels and screeched, "Yikes!" Then in one motion, she swooshed down and jumped off, skidding to a stop just before her.

"My, that was impressive." Bridget clapped.

"Thanks—hey, you're pretty. Are you famous?"

"No, I am not, and whom might you be?"

"My name is Anna."

"Hello… and what a lovely name you have."

Anna giggled, then the ice cream truck's bells rang around the corner, and her eyes lit up.

"Do you like ice cream?"

"Ooh, yes, I *LOVE* it, yummy," she shimmied.

"What's your favorite?"

"Creamsicles! I can eat a million, nom, *nom,* nom." Anna made a goofy face, smiling joyfully.

"How would you like it if I treat you to one?"

"Really? Oh, yes, goodie-goodie!" Anna jumped up and down but then stopped, and her smile faded. "Oh poo, I can't." She kicked the grass. "I have to ask my mom first, and she'll say no. I'm not supposed to talk to strangers."

"Well, I'm not exactly a stranger. I'm friends with your Aunt Theodora. Besides, what your mother doesn't know won't kill her." Bridget winked, and Anna looked at her, curious.

"You know my Aunt Teddy?"

"Yes, I do, and I was hoping to talk to her today. Is she around?"

"No, she's stuck in the snow."

"The snow?" Bridget said, confused.

"Yeah, at the airport."

"Which one?"

"Um, dunno." Anna's face scrunched. "New-*art* or something."

"Newark?"

"Yeah, it's in the bliz*zart?*"

"Oh right, the blizzard." Bridget mulled it over, then waved the ice cream truck over. "Well, Anna, you've been a very helpful young lady, and for that, I am going to reward you." She pulled a five-dollar bill from her purse. "Here you go, and promise not to tell anyone, okay? This is our little secret."

"I promise!" Anna grabbed the money and ran.

Bridget watched in amusement, and then a darkness crept over her, and her mother's voice whispered in her memory, "Darling, there are certain things in life one must do to achieve goals. Your father depends on you. Don't let him down."

Her brows furrowed.

Daddy's li'l girl...

12

In Your Dreams

"The *NERVE* of that, that, that—argh! Blue-eyed *SCAMP!*" Steaming mad from her encounter with the janitor, Teddy stormed into the resting area and threw her bags on the floor. "Call me, K—pfft, as if! Like that's *even* a name?" she scowled, wriggling out of her leather jacket. Then she struggled with her scarf, and with each tug, she roared.

"IN ~ *YOUR* ~ DREAMS ~ *BUDDY!*"

Startled, the old woman seated nearby clutched her bag, but Teddy was too much in her head to notice. Exhausted, she plopped down on the nearest seat, threw her long legs up and over the back of the chair, and shouted at the ceiling.

"Princess… how *dare* he call me *PRINCESS!*"

It was ten degrees outside and about forty degrees inside, yet Teddy's face flushed red in bewilderment at how a man like *him* could get under her skin.

"And those eyes!"

She scrunched her jacket into a pillow, punched it a few times, then plopped her head down.

"I bet that's how he gets all the girls in bed!"

She kicked a leg into the air, tucking the other one under, and gazed at the ceiling. "And that cocky, *'Hey, babe, I'll make all your dreams come true'* smile." She punched the pillow again. "I know that look too well, and I've fallen for it way too many times, that's for sure." Teddy laughed, realizing how pathetic she sounded, and then with a swirl of her hand, she drew his name in the air.

Kenneth O'Connor

"Hmph, buddy... what's your deal?" she frowned. "Shit, I bet he's one of those love 'em and leave 'em types. You know, Mister Wonderful on the first date, gets you in bed on the second, *AND* then poof, you never hear from him again!"

She drew a large X over his name.

"He's probably not even a ten-minute man. He's likely just a fiver and only takes care of himself. Yup, I know the type." Shifting, she kicked the other leg up, then tucked it under. "Pfft, a *real* catch," she muttered, then exhaled. Fascinated, the old woman scooted in closer to listen.

Teddy reached into her suitcase, pulled out her long sweater, draped it over her knees, and cradled in.

"He's so not my type—Ha, well, the one-nighter part is, but the rest, no." She shook her head. "He's one of those muscle guys with no brains—well, maybe some brains, but no passion! Hmph, I need passion. That's my thing."

A squeal fell from her lips, and her eyes rolled.

"And all those muscles flexing every time he laughed at me—He laughed at me! Pfft, that *FUCKER!*" She slammed her fist on the seat, and the older woman jumped. Teddy took a double take, then shot up. "Oh, geez, ma'am, I'm so sorry. I didn't see you sitting there. I didn't mean to scare you... I was just having a moment. I'm not crazy or anything."

"Oh, dear, don't you worry about me," the woman gushed

and sent her a kind smile. "It's quite all right. We're all under a bit of stress here. You just go on having your moment. It's very amusing to watch."

Teddy's face softened, and she laid back down. She stared out the window at the white snow and pulled the sweater up to her chin.

Hm. I can't remember the last time a guy laughed at me. What an asshole. And yet, I can tell that he likes me—OWNED!

Slaphappy from the lack of sleep, she giggled.

Oh, my God, he grabbed MY FINGER! I swear my heart stopped. I felt it down there—YIKES!

She covered her mouth to mute the squealing.

And what's so odd is that I felt safe in his arms. Teddy cradled the pillow like it was her woobie. *And I never feel safe.*

Slowly, she began to drift.

And those dreamy blues...

13

Tempers Rising

Back in Hollywood...

Walters and Stewart followed Cleo into the house. Tchotchkes and knick-knacks filled the shelves before them, followed by dozens of pictures of Cleo and the kids. It had been two months since the divorce was finalized, and all memories of her ex-husband, Frank Bowen, had been tossed in a box and stowed in the attic.

The two-story house was old and funky, almost void of style, yet it had an essence of design that exuded creativity. Thick lath and plaster walls muted the sounds of the nearby trains that dragged on their horns every two to four hours. The floors were dark hardwood except for the kitchen—a multi-colored terrazzo, and the upstairs, which had ultra-heavy-duty plush carpeting, a luxury in a household that was always packed with kids.

Cleo's two boys Cory, thirteen, and Stevie, eleven, were in the midst of battle, seated on the couch in the living room, playing video games.

"Boys, go upstairs. I need to talk to these men."

"But Ma, I'm beating him. It's my best score ever," Stevie yelled, excited.

"No, he's not—you cheated!" Cory clamored.

"No, I didn't!"

"Yes, you did!"

"Boys! Boys, please quiet down and go upstairs."

Cory swatted at Stevie's head, missing by inches, and Stevie yelled, "Ouch, he hit me!"

"No, I didn't." Laughing, he swatted again.

"Stop it!" Stevie ducked and threw a punch.

"Ha-ha! You missed." Cory stuck out his tongue, then pulled back and let one fly.

POP!

The two brothers froze for a split second, then Cory's face lit up, and he yelled, "Ah-ha, *GOTCHA!*"

"Ooh, you," Stevie hissed, his arms and legs thrashing wildly as he tried with all his might to land a blow that would knock the silly grin off his older brother's face.

"ENOUGH!" Cleo screamed, planting herself between the two. She grabbed Stevie by the hands and dragged him away. "The both of you just quit it before I give you something to cry about. No more games! Now go upstairs and do your homework!"

"But, Mom," they cried.

"I said *NOW!*"

The boys raced to the stairs with Stevie in the lead, followed by Cory swatting from behind. "Ouch, quit it!" Stewart snorted in amusement, and Walters checked his watch, perturbed.

Visibly shaken, Cleo rushed to the stairs and stomped her foot down. "I'm warning you! Don't you make me come up there!" Laughing, the boys slammed the door shut, and she let out an exhausted breath, then adjusted her shirt and turned back to the men with a smile.

"Sorry about that, officers. Can I get you something to drink?"

"Agents," Walters corrected her. "As I told you on the phone, ma'am, we're from the Federal Bureau of Investigation. I am Agent Walters, and this is Agent Stewart."

"Yes, agents, that's right. Well, I can make you some tea or coffee if you'd like?"

Stewart smiled, "No, thank you, we're good."

"So, please tell me what this is all about." Cleo's pulse began to rise. "Why do you want to speak to my sister?"

"There is a matter that has come up," Walters replied as he looked around, assessing the place.

"Did she do something illegal?"

"No, we just want to talk to her." He gave her a clinical smile and then walked over to the wall of photos and inspected them.

Cleo followed, contemplating his words. "So, tell me, why would you, the FBI, need to speak with my sister if she wasn't in any trouble?"

"There are elements from her past that we need to discuss with her."

"Such as? I know everything about her—"

"Is Theodora here?"

"I told you on the phone she wasn't," she snapped, and he stepped closer. "Well, do you know where she is?" Cleo's eyes went wide, and she turned to a photo of Teddy and straightened it. "I do know where my sister is—well, at least for the moment, but I'm not sure how much longer she'll be there." Then defiantly, she crossed her arms and turned back. "And I am not going to tell you a thing unless you tell me why you want to speak with her—"

BAM!

The kitchen door swung open, and Abby Hayes entered, followed by Henry, who made a beeline to the men. "We heard you fellas were here—"

"Young man!" Abby charged, wagging a feisty finger at Walters. "I want to have a word with you! We've had her ever since she was a tiny boo, and yes, she's gotten into trouble, but it's never been anything more than a…" A blank expression appeared on her face, and she scratched her head.

"Well, *err…*"

She turned to Mr. Hayes for help, but his face drew a blank too. Then her lips bubbled up, and she blurted, "Oh, hell, who am I fooling? I reckon Teddy only gets into trouble just to piss us off!"

Stewart snickered, and Mr. Hayes glared at him. "Now you listen here, fella, our sweet Teddy might be a handful, but she's our handful, and we love her very much."

"Sorry, sir. I didn't mean to be disrespectful. I realize this might be a touchy subject, but can you tell us if Theodora knew anything about her biological parents?"

"What would she want to know about those people?" Abby huffed. "They left her behind with nothing more than a note and a

64

name. Just dropped her off on the front porch like you see in the movies and never came back to collect her."

Cleo turned to Walters.

"Does this have something to do with Teddy's birth parents?"

"We're not at liberty to say."

"Not at *liberty!?* How dare you?" she said, incredulous. "Who do you people think you are coming here and worrying us like this without any explanation?"

"Relax, your sister isn't in any trouble."

Henry looked at him, confused. "Well, if she ain't in no trouble, then what's this fuss all about, fellas? You nearly scared me and the Missus half to death the other day, and Cleo hasn't slept a wink."

"Now, now, folks, let's just calm down," Stewart said with a smile as he stepped between Cleo and Walters to lessen the tension. "Something has come up, and we need to speak with Theodora—not because she's in any trouble, mind you. We just want to make sure she's okay and not in any danger."

"Danger? What kind of *danger?*" Cleo shrieked. Walters shot him a silencing glare.

"Theodora is NOT in any danger. Agent Stewart misspoke."

"I don't believe you," she fumed. "All this hush-hush business certainly feels like danger." Her eyes narrowed on him suspiciously. "This is your last chance to be straight with us, detective—"

"Agent," Walters snapped.

"Agent!" Cleo shrieked. "You know I don't care who you are—officers, detectives, *AGENTS*, whatever. Either you come clean and tell us the truth or get the hell out of my house—*ARGH!*"

Flustered, she rushed to the front door and opened it so hard that it knocked into the back wall.

"Forget it. Just leave!"

With her foot tapping furiously, she clutched the handle, just waiting to slam the door shut the moment they exited. "And from now on, anything you have to ask me, you can ask my lawyer!"

Blowing out a frustrated sigh, Walters started forward, then stopped. "Look, what Agent Stewart meant to say is that we want to speak with Theodora because she might be able to shed some light on a case that we are working on."

"What case would that be?" Cleo glared at him.

"It's a high-profile case that we do not have permission to discuss with anyone but your sister." He picked up a photo of Teddy and examined it. "Yes, there are aspects of the case that have elements of danger, but we do not feel that they pertain to her at this time. However, as a precaution, we need to make Theodora aware of the situation."

Walters returned the photo to the shelf, and Cleo cocked her head, gauging his words. "So, Teddy is in danger?"

"No, that's not what I said. You got it all wrong."

"Oh, did I? Well then, explain it to me, Mister FBI." The Hayeses stepped in closer to hear, and Cleo crossed her arms. "This better be good, Agent." Her eyes bore into his, and he dropped his head in defeat.

"Look, Ms. Hayes, I didn't mean to upset you or your parents. We've been under a lot of pressure lately, and the truth is this may or may not have anything to do with your sister. We don't know yet. At the moment, we're just looking for answers. And, for the record, Stewart and I could lose our jobs over what we've told you already.

So please, don't mention this to anyone."

Cleo pursed her lips, nodding as she studied his face, then she grabbed a piece of paper off the counter and scribbled on it. "Come on, I'll walk you out." She gestured for her parents to stay put.

Stewart opened the front door, and Anna pushed her way in. "Whoa, hey there, little one."

"Hello to you," she roared. Smudges of ice cream dripped down her chin as she ran up the stairs and into the bathroom.

"Ms. Hayes, you have a lively bunch here. I bet there's never a dull moment in this house."

"Never, Agent."

Stewart climbed into the front seat of the car and waved goodbye. Walters walked straight to the edge of the driveway, and Cleo followed. "So, I'm guessing he's the good cop, then?" Her eyebrow rose, and she handed him the paper.

"Yeah, I guess," he said, frowning, then looked at her confused. "Who's Cole?"

"Teddy's boyfriend. She flew up north to be with him. He lives in the Village, but I don't think she made it there yet due to the storm. I think she's stranded at the airport. That's her flight information."

"Well, this is unfortunate…"

With a sigh, he tucked it in his pocket and met her gaze. "Hey, I'm sorry for being the bad cop. That's usually not my thing." The corners of his mouth lifted into a smile, and his pensive dark eyes softened. "I hope you can forgive me?"

"I'll tell you what, Agent. If you find my sister, not only will I forgive you, but I'll make you dinner—*uh*, never mind." Cleo caught herself and laughed, "I better not go there." Then with a wave, she headed in.

"Take care, Agent. Please call me as soon as you find my sister."

"Will do, Ms. Hayes."

A smile rose on his face.

Mmmm, Dinner...

14

The Cleaner

My Dearest Uncle Paddy,

I'm devastated. My heart is broken, and I feel so alone. Yet, your kind words have helped me get through it all. Meet me at Olustees on Thursday at seven.

Love always, Bridget

Wednesday, 4:45 pm
Tampa, Florida

Lost in a trance from the drizzling rain tapping on the limo's glass, Paddy Mills folded the beautifully written cursive note and placed it in his inner chest pocket. He was on his way to the newly built B&B headquarters in downtown Tampa.

Aside from feeling crushed by grief and sorrow, Mills was pissed. It had only been a few days since the Senator's death, and the Council of Elders had already called for an emergency meeting to elect a new leader to the Blood & Bones Society. Yet, as mad as he was, he knew he had to play along to secure a place for himself within the organization now that Blake was no longer around.

Patrick "Paddy" Mills was an imposing figure in the Tampa political scene, standing just shy of six foot five and weighing two hundred and forty pounds of intimidating muscle. He fancied bespoke suits from Savile Row just like his hero, James Bond, and his good looks attracted many women. Yet, he always stayed true to his first love—his wife, Jenny.

He kept secrets safe, and his clients paid a high price for that trusted service. Mills was the best in the business. If he couldn't hush someone up with cash, a single .22 to the head would do the job. To scare folks, he'd often brag that he liked how the bullet would just rattle around inside the brain for a bit before killing its victim. This form of killing became a calling card that few wanted to receive, and most took the offer without sputtering a word of discontent.

The Mills family owned one of the oldest dry-cleaning chains in the South. For him, it was the perfect front for his services. If someone had a dirty job to do, they knew where to find him. He was known as the Cleaner. He didn't have many friends, few uttered his given name, and only a handful of his closest confidants called him Paddy. Blake was one of the few.

Mills had known the Senator since grade school. A gang of eight neighboring kids tried to jump Blake in the playground, and Mills came running to his rescue. He was flinging a two-by-four as if it were a bat, and in the end, six of the eight had welts on their heads, and the other two were knocked out. From that moment on, the two were inseparable and made a powerful duo, with Prescott being the brains and Mills the brawn.

Paddy Mills prided himself on being fast, efficient, and trustworthy. To him, life was simple. Things were either good or bad, black or white, right or wrong, and there were no in-betweens. In-betweens confused him, and he didn't like to be confused. Most of all, he never questioned Blake. If the Senator said something needed to be done, he did it. He was the closest thing to a brother that Blake had ever known. And aside from being his best friend and best man, Blake chose him to be his only daughter's guardian, a role that meant the world to him.

My poor sweet Bridget...

He pressed a hand to his pocket and held her note to his heart.

I can't even imagine what you are going through. First, you lost your fiancé and now your parents. If only I could have prevented it.

A knot lodged in his throat—he swallowed hard, and a single tear fell down his cheek. He wiped it away, then laughed.

My friend, you were just itching for trouble.

He reached into his pocket, took out his flip phone, and then scrolled through the messages until he found Blake's last call and hit play.

"Paddy, it's an emergency. I have a big mess that needs to be handled right away. No loose ends!" Slurring his words, he laughed, then hung up.

At the time of the Senator's death, Mills and his wife, Jenny, were away in the Bahamas celebrating their 35th anniversary. It was their first vacation alone since they were married—no kids, no dogs, and definitely no Blake Prescott.

They had told everyone they were turning off their phones, so don't bother calling, but Blake wasn't having any of it. As soon as the plane took off, he left a series of phone messages saying that he wanted Mills to return immediately. It was a stunt he often did to test Paddy's loyalty, but this time Jenny put her foot down. For her, this was her second honeymoon, and no one, not even the Senator, was going to ruin it. So, she took Paddy's cell phone and locked it away in the hotel safe.

Why couldn't you have just waited for me?

The Senator had become sloppy. Over the last few months, Mills had spent a great deal of time cleaning up after his mishaps, and there were many. Blake was very popular. Women loved him, men wanted to be him, and he took advantage of both. Even those that hated his policies couldn't resist his charismatic charm.

On the surface, the Senator had it all, a beautiful wife, a loving daughter, strong Christian values, and money—old money, which bought him respect. In truth, most of Blake's power came from being at the head of the Blood & Bones Society. His third great-grandfather, Jubal, founded it in 1865 at the end of the Civil War as a beacon of light to guide the local townsfolk through the challenging times. They called him the Judge.

In its early days, it was a small place of worship that helped keep the peace and cleanse the sick. But as time went by, it quickly grew in numbers due to the popularity of the Judge's blessings that members received for good behavior.

Blessings came in the form of food, clothing, livestock, and sometimes money. When it came to determining who was worthy, Jubal used his strict Christian morals as a guide to decide who was pure at heart and who wasn't.

Questionable souls were offered a second chance by confessing their sins. These confessionals were performed by Jubal's personal task force, a group called the Testa Men, who were sworn to secrecy. They kept logs on everyone and everything. Townsfolk would make monthly visits to the 'listeners' as they liked to call them, telling of their woes or needs with the hope that their grievances would make their way up to the Judge's ear and he would help them out. The more secrets you told, the more blessings you received.

Through the years, the leadership of the Blood & Bones Society was passed down to the eldest son of each generation of Prescott, with all keeping in strict guidance with Jubal's vision of giving to those in need—all, that is, except Blake.

On the morning of his father's death, the lure of the secrets became too much for the newly elected B&B leader to ignore. And with Mills by his side, Andrew Blake Prescott wielded its power by blackmailing friends and foes alike. He was ruthless, but most of all, he enjoyed watching the great and powerful fall from grace. It empowered him, corrupted him, and with such power, the Senator became reckless.

So reckless...

Mills stared out the window.

I should've tried to stop him. I should've said something.

The rain fell harder.

Who am I kidding? Nobody tells Blake what to do.

Mills closed his eyes and leaned back. He had seen death many times but never had it hit so close to home. He couldn't get the images out of his head—the flashing lights, the yellow tape, the creamy saffron walls splattered over with dried blood and skull fragments. And then there was the smell... the putrid smell of death that he was all too familiar with, but this time, it was different. This time it was his best friend. He shuddered.

I need air.

He rolled down the window and inhaled deeply, but the humidity was too thick, and he choked. Quickly, he gulped in a second breath, and the damp smell of the rain brought his memories back to the little musty bar in the Bahamas.

It was a quaint little dive with a maiden's figurehead at the doorway and a sign above it that read, "Enter at your own risk." Painted in faded blues and gold, the rustic place was decorated with nautical objects that covered most of the wall space in anchors, buoys, and fishing nets.

About ten or so happy drunks sat at the bar, drinking, singing, and laughing cheerfully. Jenny stood at its edge, signaling the bartender for another round. She was dressed in a halter top and a long denim skirt. Her beautiful red hair flowed down her back, and her face glowed pink from the day's sun. It made her look twenty years younger, he thought.

He sat alone at a small table in the back, anxiously waiting for her to return. He knew he needed this vacation but struggled to unwind. Business had been crazy, and with Blake's presidential aspirations, Mills knew that things would only get crazier. Plus, it didn't help that the Senator had left him with an annoying job to do when he returned.

He wants him out. How the hell am I going to convince Peters to walk away? The guy lives for the Order. Shit, this could get ugly.

Furious, Blake called Paddy the day before he left. He had heard that Jeffrey Peters, one of the Council of Elders, wanted to take over as the head of the B&B Society when the Senator put in his bid for the presidency.

What was Peters thinking? Shit, Blake would rather see the place burn to the ground than hand it over to anyone, especially him.

Jen saw the dark expression growing on her husband's face. She scowled, then put two fingers in her mouth and blew a loud piercing whistle. The entire bar went silent and turned in her direction.

"Oops! Sorry, fellas, that was for my husband," she laughed and pointed at him.

"Lucky fellow," quipped the bartender, then he grabbed a bottle of tequila and raised it up. "Who's up for another?"

The drunks cheered.

Smiling, Jen looked over at Paddy and instantly knew the spell had been broken.

He blew her a kiss. She was the love of his life, and the love she felt for him twinkled in her eyes. He knew that he was indeed the luckiest guy on Earth.

She grabbed the drinks and headed back to the table, but out of the corner of her eye, she recognized the Senator's face on the television set hanging on the back wall. With a shriek, Jenny dropped the drinks and cupped her mouth.

ANDREW BLAKE PRESCOTT
DEAD AT 58

CRACK!

A bolt of lightning flashed outside the limo, and Mills snapped out of his thoughts. He looked down at the cell phone in his hand and pressed play.

"Paddy, it's an emergency. I have a big mess—"

With a click, he deleted the message.

"It's cleaning time."

He pressed Bridget's note against his heart.

And you, my sweet angel... you're not alone. I'm here and will forever be 'til my last dying breath.

15

The Vaults

The rain had stopped by the time the limo pulled up in front of the B&B complex. The beautiful glass structure was built on the remnants of Fort Brooke, where the Tocobaga mound once stood, and was styled in black Italian marble, rare coral fountains, gold-plated fixtures, and a pair of exquisite ornamental glass elevators that floated up and down in the atrium.

Mills marched into the grand entranceway, straight past security, and into a private elevator hidden from the public. There were no floor buttons for navigation. Instead, the doors closed, and a keypad slid out. Mills typed in his passcode, and the elevator began a downward descent.

Moments later, the doors opened, revealing a dark narrow passageway that Mills likened to stepping back in time. The walls were carved out of limestone and fortified with brick and mud, emitting a cold, damp, musky smell. Old metal gas lanterns lit the path before him. Winding and weaving, he followed them around to an underground tunnel. The Order had used it to smuggle goods in and out of the city during prohibition in the early twenties.

Blake Prescott delighted in its shady past and had it drained, sealed, and repurposed as a gateway. He wanted new recruits and the brotherhood to journey through the claustrophobic walls, feel the bending of the wooden planks under their feet, and hear the sounds from a time that had long since passed.

At the end of the tunnel stood a large wooden door. On its face was an iron crucifix with a sword for its body and a bone for its cross, the Blood & Bones emblem. Mills pulled a skeleton key from his pocket and unlocked it.

Slowly, the heavy door slid open, and he stepped inside. A bright flicker of flame guided his way further into the den. Jubal's original war maps were displayed perfectly on the tables throughout, and wall after wall exhibited vintage Civil War weaponry of knives, swords, and bayonets.

The chamber was primitive, made of earth, wood, and stone, and showed no signs of the twentieth century. At its center stood a large brick fireplace that burned eternally in memory, and just above it hung a wooden plaque:

BLOOD & BONES SOCIETY

Founded in 1865 by Jubal E. Prescott

Grand Seeker of the Way

|

The Council of Elders

|

Enforcers | Testa Men | Messengers

Mills walked over, kneeled, and bowed his head in respect. He could hear voices bickering down at the end of the hallway. "And who left you in charge?" a raspy older man's voice yelled.

"I am the one—the *ONLY* one!"

Peters, you snake...

A hazy cloud of smoke escaped from the ritual room as he entered. Eight men dressed in black robes sat around an old war table engulfed in a heated debate. The room was dimly lit, the walls shrouded in black, a life-sized portrait of Jubal hung on the back wall, and a lone stool sat in the center.

"Enough. He's here," Williams thundered, and all the Elders went silent. Their faces brimming with angst as they watched Mills cross the room. They were uneasy. He was not one of them. He was Blake's boy, and they didn't care much for him. Mills had the goods on each of them, and they knew it. For all had hired him to do their dirty work. They owed him, feared him, but most of all, they needed him.

"Did you get the files?" Peters asked, jumping out of his seat. "Of course I did," Mills said with a smug laugh. "One day, that grin of yours is going to get you killed, my friend." Mills brushed past him and sat on the stool. "Well, at least I'll go out smiling."

Jeffrey Peters was in his late fifties and didn't take kindly to being made fun of. Yet, Mills had a habit of doing just that. It didn't help that he was unnaturally tall with dark brown eyes, graying hair, a pencil-thin mustache, and a long, slim nose that gave the impression he was looking down at you. Still, his lust for power made up for his awkwardness, and like the Senator, he had the brains and a sizable ego to back it up.

"Did anyone see you?" he paced behind Mills.

"I was able to get in and out without notice."

"What about the key?"

"No."

"Did you find the vaults?" Elder Johnson said.

"No, sir."

The chattering from the Elders grew louder, and Williams, the oldest member, called to the others, "Does anyone know if these things really do exist?"

"I don't," Stevens said.

"Not me," Thompson added.

"I asked him about it once, but he just brushed me off," Stuart laughed. "Yeah, me too," echoed Carter.

"Well, I've heard that it's not even a key at all," Johnson blurted, and then Marks jumped in. "Once, I saw Prescott fidgeting with this shiny thing in his hand, and I asked him about it. He joked and said it was one of his father's hand-me-downs. Now, when I think of it, I bet it was the key."

Elder Williams silenced him with a wave and turned to Mills. "Son, would you be able to recognize the key if you saw it?"

"I don't know, sir. I might—"

"You've seen it, haven't you?" Peters scowled.

"Probably," Mills snapped back. "He collected that kind of stuff all the time, but if it's the key to the vaults, then I'd say it's with his journal."

"His what?" Peters gasped.

"Well, it's more like a diary. Blake has had it ever since high school, and boy did he love to write in that thing—"

"Jesus!" Peters threw up his hands, furious. "No wonder we're all being blackmailed. Who knows what that fuck wrote about us!" He spun to the portrait of Jubal. "And this freak of a grandfather! For over a century, the Prescotts have been dragging us into their dark, twisted family past—and you!" He turned to Mills. "You propped him up and killed all that got in his way."

"Why, you arrogant prick!" Mills lunged from the stool and, in a beat, had the barrel of his gun pressed against Peters' temple. "How dare you speak of my friend that way. I should kill you right here in his honor, you fucking traitor—"

"Calm down, Mr. Mills… just take it easy," Elder Williams sputtered nervously. "Please, son, put the gun away and have a seat." He quietly gestured, and Mills obeyed. "Now let me just say, on behalf of the Elders and myself, I would like to apologize if we have offended you in any way. That was not our intention. We all have been on edge since the Senator's death—"

"Don't apologize for me," Peters snarled.

"You just hold your horses there. You knew what you were getting into." Williams turned to the others. "We all knew… but you, Peters, were the first one in line with your hand out, grabbing the cash and lining your pockets. The Senator was a good man, and we should treat him as such."

"Amen," the Elders replied.

Flustered, Williams returned his attention to Mills. "Son, I trust you will take care of this mess that we find ourselves in for the good of the Order, but most importantly, to protect the Senator's good name and his legacy."

"Yes, sir, you have my word."

"Ha!" Peters huffed. "You're such an obedient warrior. Tell me… now that the pissing contest is over, who do you think has the diary?"

Mills shrugged.

"Could it be your sweet little Bridget?" A crooked smile lifted on his face. "Ooh, did I hit a nerve?"

Mills stared him down, the vein in his forehead pulsing. "If

I didn't know better, I'd say you were trying to push my buttons."
He cracked his neck and then stood up to leave.

"Gentlemen, I must go—"

Peters blocked his path. "If you don't bring me that diary by
Friday, I'm going to pay our little Bridget a visit, and trust me, I
won't leave without it."

"Is that so?" Seething with anger, Mills scoffed, "Have you
ever wondered what it's like to have a .22 rattling around inside
that wimp-ass skull of yours?"

"Oh, fuck off!"

With a laugh, Paddy Mills aimed his thumb and forefinger at
Peters' head and kicked it back.

BOOM!

He winked at the Elders.

"Good day, gentlemen."

16

Robbed

The day was turning dark fast. The rest area emptied out as the stranded passengers headed towards the dining area for supper. The old lady tucked away her romance novel and glanced over at Teddy. She was fast asleep with her legs stretched over the top of the chairs.

Oh, the poor thing... bless her heart. She looks so peaceful. Maybe it's best not to wake her. She'll eat when she's ready. Besides, some rest will do her good. It'll take away some of that craziness she was feeling earlier.

Grabbing her bags, she let out a hearty laugh and left. A moment later, the side entrance door flung open, and in from the cold came two boys wearing army green parka jackets with fur hoods and carrying backpacks.

"Brrr, it's cold out there," shivered Jojo as he pushed back his hood and pulled off his gloves with his teeth. He was young, probably in his late teens, with dark curly hair and a happy-go-lucky smile.

"Hey, check this out!" He pointed to a divider wall that housed the airport's directory map. "We can do it here."

Frankie frowned as he removed his ski mask. "Yuk, it's not the best canvas." He was just as young as Jojo, a bit taller, and had a patch of facial hair sprouting from his chin. "We gotta be quick. I don't want to get caught again. I can't do another thirty days in juvie. My mom will kill me."

"Yeah, I hear ya, but no one is around, and we can do what we want." Jojo opened his backpack and pulled out a can of red spray paint. He shook it until he heard the pea rattle and then paused. "Are we going freestyle or sketch?"

"Free, it's gonna be a throw-up anyways." Frankie grabbed his Polaroid camera from his satchel and placed it on the ground, then took out a can of spray paint and shook it vigorously. A rustling sound came from behind him, and he looked over.

"Hey, Jo—stop!" He hushed and pointed. "Someone's here."

Teddy shifted in her sleep.

Curious, Jojo threw his stuff back in his bag and tiptoed over. "Oh, lookie-lookie here," he whispered, hovering over her. "She's a pretty thing, ain't she—and totally out of it, too," he laughed. Frankie scowled, "Yup, she is, and you know she's gonna wake as soon as we start."

Jojo nodded, bubbling his lips, then grinned as he eyed her stuff. "Hmph, well, maybe it's not a total bust." He grabbed her suitcase and gestured for Frankie to take the handbag cradled in her arms.

"Uh-uh, no effing way." He shook his head.

"Come on, I got the last one. I betcha she won't wake." Jojo nudged him.

"Oh, all right—*fuck juvie…*" Carefully, Frankie lifted Teddy's hand up by the pinky and tugged on the handbag.

"Easy now—"

"They *said* light flurries," Teddy moaned, and the boys froze.

Without breathing, Frankie slid the bag out and lowered her pinky back to her chest. And in a blink, the boys dashed for the exit.

BAMMMM!

The door slammed shut, and Teddy woke.

"Ma—*what?* Who's there… *Cleo?"* Disoriented, she sat up, slowly pulsing awake. "Hmm… where is everyone?" She stretched her long arms high above her head, looking around the room, and then curled her hands inward. "Ouch, every bit of me hurts. I need aspirins."

She reached under the seat, feeling around.

Hmm…

She bent her head down to have a better look.

Confused, she looked at the empty seats before her, and then she stood and did a slow three-sixty.

Huh, where is it?

Her brows knitted together. "I put it right here." She pointed to an empty spot on the floor. "With my *stuff—*"

NOOOOOO!

Frantically, she scrambled around the room, searching under the seats, behind the counters, and in the trash containers.

"No, no, noooo—oh, God, no!" She stomped her foot down. "Please tell me my stuff's not stolen!"

Teddy ran into the main drag. "Help, I've been robbed," she

yelled, but her voice just dispersed into the hum of the lights. No one was around. Way, way down at the end of the corridor, she saw a security guard reading a paper.

"Help!" she screamed, running full throttle at him with her heels clicking loudly on the polished floors. As she neared, he looked up from his paper, and the stout little man with the shiny badge snapped to attention. "Sir, I've been robbed!"

"You *what?* Are you alright?" His stubby fingers clutched his nightstick.

"No, they took everything!"

Worry grew on his face as he comprehended what she was saying.

"Who *did?*"

"I don't know," she cried.

"Just calm down and tell me what happened."

"I was sleeping in the rest area, and when I woke, *POOF!* Everything was gone, my luggage, my bag, my—*oh, my GOD, my MONEY!*"

Teddy let out a high-pitched wail that made the hair on the back of his neck stand, and then she crumpled into a gasping sob.

"Whoa, sweetheart, take it easy."

He could see she was seconds away from having a complete mental breakdown.

"Now, now, it's going to be alright. No more crying, okay? Come here." He cupped Teddy's chin and patted her face dry with the cuff of his sleeve. "Aw, that's much better. Everything is going to work out, I promise."

His eyebrows shot up.

"Hey, I got an idea. Let's go down to security and see Max. Maybe we'll get lucky, and someone turned your stuff in."

"Really, do you think so?" she gulped, her teary eyes searching his.

"Yeah, come on, let's go." He took her by the hand. "Hey, what's your name?"

"Theodora," she sniffled as the heaving in her chest slowed.

"Well, Theodora, don't you worry. I'm going to take good care of you. My name is Harvey, Harvey Lebowski from the Singing Lebowski Brothers. Have you heard of us?" Teddy shook her head. "Heh, not many have, but one day they will." His eyes twinkled. "I just do this gig to pay the bills. I'm a crooner like Frank. Wanna hear?" Her swollen lips crinkled into a smile, and he let out a jolly laugh.

"That a girl."

And with his jet-black Elvis-style pompadour pushing up, Harvey led the way singing Sinatra tunes. Every now and again, he'd let go of her hand just long enough to make a grand musical gesture, then pull her back in with a wink and a sway. It was a sight to see, Teddy thought as she quietly followed.

They strolled past the baggage area, skipped down a flight of stairs, and then stopped in front of an office with a windowed view. Behind the glass, a man was asleep, slumped over his desk with his head resting on a pile of papers.

"That's our guy…"

17

Airport Security

Max Felling's wife told him, "Don't *EVER* bother coming home again," when she found out that he had planned to stay at work during the blizzard instead of being home safe and sound with her and the kids. Twenty-four hours later, and chilled to the bone, regret set in.

I just need a little bit of sleep, that's all… just a little bit—

"Hey, Max… wake up," Harvey called as he barged into the office. "This woman was robbed."

Max's eyes jerked open, and he swung back in his chair, glaring at the two of them. His middle-aged face had a billing receipt stuck to it, and with a flick of his finger, it was gone. He was bundled in a black puffer jacket, and the few hairs he had left on his head were combed over to cover his bald spot.

"Sorry, but did you say she was robbed?" he asked, befuddled.

"Yup, she sure was." Harvey clutched his nightstick and rocked back on his heels. "They took all her stuff. I betcha it was those damn kids."

"All right, Harvey, thank you. I'll take it from here. You get back to your beat and keep an eye out for anything suspicious, okay?"

"Sure thing." Harvey squeezed Teddy's hand. "Now, sweetheart, you take it easy, and if you need anything, you know where to find me, okay?"

Grateful, Teddy thanked him, and he left.

"Ma'am, did you see who did this?" Max asked.

"No, I was sleeping."

"Did you hear anything?"

Teddy shook her head.

"Was anyone else around?"

"At first, there were, you know, when I fell asleep." Her voice broke, "But when I woke, everybody was gone. The rest area was empty."

"I see." He opened a drawer, pulled out a set of forms, and handed them to her. "Please fill these out."

"What? I don't have time for this." Her heart fluttered; she was on the verge of tears. "Sir, the robbers are getting away."

"Sorry, ma'am, but it's the rules. Forms first, and then we'll get someone on it."

"You've got to be kidding me!" she squealed and collapsed into the chair by the door. "I'm never going to see my stuff again, am I?" Her eyes welled up. "And I'm stuck here all alone—"

BAM!

The door kicked open, and Kenneth entered. "Hey, Max, look what I found in the men's room." He was carrying a tweed suitcase.

"YOU?"

Teddy jumped to her feet.

"That's mine!"

"Yours?" He did a double take.

"Yes, *MINE!* Did you steal it?"

"Of course not."

"Then who did?"

"How do I know—wait, so this is yours?" Concern grew in his eyes.

"Yes, I just told you it was mine. I was robbed."

"By who? How?"

"I don't know! And like *YOU* care." Her eyes burned into his.

"Are you hurt?"

"Um, no," she uttered, confused by his concern.

"So, where did you last leave it?"

"I didn't leave it anywhere. It was stolen—*AND* it's all your fault!"

"Mine?" he said, outraged. "What'd I do?"

"Your little stunt—"

"Oh, give me a break, princess. I told you it was just an accident." Max's face pinged back and forth, trying to follow the conversation. "K, do you know this woman?"

"Yes, sir. I mean no… but yes, sort of," Kenneth said, exasperated.

"Well, which is it?"

"He knows me, all right. He made me freeze last night." Teddy crossed her arms and glared at him. "I didn't make you freeze," he pleaded. "I walked in front of the glass sliding doors, and they opened."

"And he laughed at me!"

"You laughed?" Max said, incredulous.

"I didn't laugh at her. Well, I guess I kind of did, but ONLY because I was embarrassed—NOT because I thought it was funny, even though it kinda was—Hey, princess, I told you I was sorry!"

"Who are you calling princess? And I don't need *YOUR* lame-ass apology. What I need is my stuff. So would you mind taking your grubby hands off my suitcase?"

"You'd be lucky to have my grubby hands—"

"Enough!" Max shouted. "Both of you, just settle down. Especially you," he pointed to Kenneth. "Now, Miss… uh, I didn't get your name."

"It's Teddy, I mean Theodora Hayes," she said, flustered. Kenneth smiled and mouthed, "Theodora?" And she shot back with a biting glare. She wasn't ready to end the war. Instead, she held out her hand. "My suitcase, please."

Amused by her feistiness, he laid the case on Max's desk. The zippers and locks were busted. Teddy pursed her lips, bracing for the worst, and then flipped it open.

"Jesus," she bellowed, rummaging through what was left of her stuff. "Those assholes took everything, my clothing, my jewelry… oh, and of course, they left behind Cleo's ugly furry boots—dammit!" Distraught, she flipped the lid shut and sighed. "Kenneth, please tell me this isn't all you found?"

"I, ah…" he stammered, his piercing blue eyes pained. The fragile sound of her voice hit him like a lightning bolt to the heart, and just at that moment, he knew he needed to make things right. He looked out the window at his garbage bin and almost cheered. "Wait, I did see something!" He rushed out the door, then returned a few minutes later with a small plastic bag and handed it to her.

"Are these yours?"

Apprehensively, she peered in and grimaced. Everything was drenched in a pink substance that smelled like tainted lemonade.

"Eww, gross," she moaned and picked through the sticky items. Her wallet wasn't there, nor anything of importance. Most of it was garbage. Then her eyes softened, and she let out a long sigh, "Oh, thank God." She pulled out her birth control pills and stuck to it was Cole's address and number. Max gave her a warm smile and patted her on the back.

"Well, Ms. Hayes, at least it wasn't a total loss. And you don't have to worry because we'll take good care of you while you stay here." He gestured to Kenneth. "Go into Judy's office and grab some food vouchers and anything else you think she can use. Oh, and find her something to put her stuff in."

"Sure thing, sir," Kenneth said almost joyfully as he charged out of the office.

"Now, Ms. Hayes, I still need you to complete the paperwork." He handed her the documents and a pen. "I have to go down the hall and check in on a few things, but K will be back shortly. He'll take care of anything you need, okay?"

Teddy nodded, and he left.

Twenty minutes later, all paperwork was finished, and a dull headache sat in the middle of her forehead. Teddy couldn't sit still a second longer *or* even think straight, for that matter.

She was starving, and her stomach growling.

BAM!

Kenneth kicked the door open.

"Hey, look what I found!" he said, flashing a big grin, then held up a handful of vouchers and a large glittery backpack. "It's a bit tattered, but it should do, don't you think?" Teddy took hold of it with just two fingers like it was a dirty sock.

"Yeah, I guess," she uttered, figuring it must have been lost since the seventies. Then begrudgingly, she transferred her stuff into it.

"Oh, and here." He reached into his pocket and pulled out a small wad of cash. "Everyone chipped in. It's not much, mostly ones, but it should help. I tried to get more, but the ATMs are still down."

"No, thank you. I'm good."

"But I thought you said they took everything?"

"They did, but I found thirty-five dollars in my back pocket. That should be enough to get me where I need to go."

"Are you crazy? That's nothing. Stop being a brat and take it." He shoved the cash at her, and she pushed his hand away.

"No, Kenneth, you stop—you're the one being a complete brat."

"Me?" he looked perplexed, his eyes searching hers. "Ms. Hayes, are you always this difficult?"

"Who me?" she said, mocking him, and his rugged grin went wide. "We'll talk about this later. Come on, let's go and see Ms. Mae before she closes." He grabbed the backpack and opened the door. "You'll love her. She makes the best mashers on the planet."

18

Auras

Ms. Mae's cafe was the secret craze of the concourse that few knew about because it wasn't listed on any of the airport's directories. It catered mostly to airline club members and had the best soups, subs, and goodies by far.

It was just after ten when they arrived. The sign on the door read closed, and Kenneth peered in through the glass.

"Ms. Mae... are you around?"

A middle-aged woman wriggled from the back room wearing a burly coat and knickers. A bright red trapper hat sat crooked on her head with its extra-long ear protectors flapping down.

"Well, hello darlin'," she said in her whimsical Tennessean voice as she unlocked the front door. "Have you been keeping warm, my dear?"

"I'm doing better than expected," he smiled. "How about you?"

"I'm just peachy. This cold weather has been dandy for my hot flashes." She let out a hearty laugh and welcomed them in.

The cafe had a French bistro vibe to it with its quaint patio, rattan chairs, beautiful displays of pastries, and black-lettered walls that just popped. It smelled like freshly baked bread, and Teddy's stomach rumbled as she entered.

"Ms. Mae, I'd like you to meet Theodora Hayes. She was robbed earlier today, and I'm looking out for her. Any chance we can get a bite to eat?"

"You poor thing, you must've been so scared?"

"I was." Teddy's eyes grew large. "They took everything while I slept. Just the thought of it makes me tremble inside."

"Oh, that's horrible, dear."

Kenneth's face darkened. He hated that she blamed him.

"Well, don't you worry. The grill is still hot, and I'll get you something warm to eat. You'll be right as rain in no time. Plus, I know K will take real good care of you, won't you, dear?" She sent him an adoring smile, and he nodded. Her southern way just seemed to make everything better, he thought, then quickly changed the subject.

"Hey, can I get my usual?"

"Sure thing, darling."

"Oh, and give Teddy whatever she wants." He grinned and waved a handful of vouchers. "Compliments of Security." He placed them on the counter and headed to the self-serve bar. "Theodora, would you like something hot to drink?"

"Yes, a small tea, please, with honey and lemon."

"One hot tea coming up," he hollered, and Ms. Mae laughed.

"Oh, the joy of being young." She turned to Teddy. "Now, darling, what can I get you? You probably haven't had a good meal in days."

"I haven't. It's been a nightmare, and I'm afraid it's only going to get worse."

"Oh, bless your sweet soul… you just mark my words. It'll get better." She pulled a hand full of meat from the fridge and threw it on the grill. "I can see it in your aura." She circled a hand over Teddy's essence. "A rebirth of energies is coming your way."

"A what?"

"Your aura is green, darling."

"It is?"

"Balance, growth, change. I know it doesn't feel like it, but you're on the right path to finding whatever it is you're looking for."

"I am?"

"Yes. And he likes you." She glanced over at Kenneth, and Teddy's eyes followed.

"Who—*him?*"

"Yes, darling, it's written all over his face. Plus, his aura is red, which means passion." She fanned herself. "Damn, these hot flashes."

Teddy chuckled, instantly smitten with the older woman, and she continued watching Kenneth fix her tea. Then, without warning, he looked up. It was an unexpected jolt that made her stomach flutter.

Huh…

He gave her a warm smile, and she almost smiled back but then remembered that she was still angry at him and scowled.

"Yeah, *no*… he's not my type."

"What? Are you crazy? Any woman in her right mind would

fall madly in love with a guy like K."

"Hm, I guess…"

"He's the whole package and then some, darling."

Teddy chewed it over for a split second, then wagged her head. "Nah, he's a bit muscle-*ly* for me."

"Ha," Ms. Mae hooted as she flipped the meat on the grill. "Let me guess, you go for the brooders?"

"The who?" Teddy said, confused, then smiled when she realized Ms. Mae was right. "Heh, I guess I do like the complex ones."

"Well, if you ask me, a man like K would do you some good. Those brooders carry a lot of dark energy. Now hush, here he comes."

"One steaming cup of hot tea with honey and lemon coming atcha," he said, cautiously handing Teddy the mug. Then he eyed Ms. Mae suspiciously. "You didn't tell her all my secrets, did you?"

"Who me, darling? I wouldn't dream of it." She shot him a devilish grin. "So, tell me, my sweet K, do you want your usual with or without my famous mashers?"

"With, of course. I was just telling Teddy how delicious they are, but I have to say that they're making me fat." He patted his belly, and Ms. Mae let out a grand ole Tennessean chuckle.

"Well, darling, you could use a little cushion on those bones. Some women prefer a man that's soft and cuddly." She winked at Teddy. "Now, Theodora, what can I get you? I've got a spicy hot chicken sandwich with your name on it. Wanna try?"

"Oh, yes, that sounds delish, and can I get fries with it too?"

"What?" Disbelief shot across Kenneth's face.

"Sorry, I'm just craving them, that's all."

"Darling, I make the best fries too, so don't you worry. Now the two of you go and have a seat. I'll bring it out when it's ready."

Thirty minutes later, they sat alone on the outside patio. Teddy popped a fry in her mouth and moaned, "Mmm, these *are* good."

"I still can't believe you didn't try the mashers." Kenneth finished his meal and pushed aside his plate.

"I imagine there are a lot of things I do, O'Connor, that you wouldn't approve of." She eyed him with a glint of humor and popped another fry.

"I'm sure there are, Ms. Hayes." He smiled, charmed by her defiance. "So, are you visiting New Jersey, or do you live here?"

"Just passing through on my way to the City."

"Oh, the Big Apple. Is it for work or pleasure?"

"Well, it's definitely not for work," she sighed. "And at the moment, it doesn't feel like pleasure."

"I see." He grinned. "So, I take it you don't like to talk much about yourself, do you?" He reached over and grabbed her last fry, and her eyes went wide as he popped it into his beautiful *kissable* mouth—*NO!*

"Kenneth," a shudder ran through her. "I was going to eat that!" His guilty face beamed with joy. "Oops, sorry, my bad."

"You could have asked."

"Would you have given?"

"*NO*… but still."

"So, you don't like to share your fries either?"

"I *SHARE* fine," she huffed. "Just not with you." Amused,

97

he winked. "You mean a man like me, right?" Teddy rolled her eyes. "Ha, you're cute."

"I'm *cute?*"

"Yeah, come on, let's go."

He grabbed her backpack and led her into a roped-off section. Within seconds, her mood lifted as she felt the heat on her face and the plush carpeting under her boots. "Ooh, it's nice and warm in here," she cooed, almost orgasmically, and he smiled. They continued past the executive lounges and then turned into a secluded area that housed a ritzy salon. He stopped out front and handed her a day pass.

Teddy looked at him, confused.

"What's this for?"

"A hot shower." His eyebrows rose. "It's a spa."

"No," she gasped. "Really?" She could've wept.

"Hand it to the girl at the desk, and she'll take care of you."

Teddy took a step, then hesitated.

"Problem, Ms. Hayes?" He tilted his head, enjoying her process.

"Um, no, but I would like to say that I…" she locked eyes with him. "Well, if I wasn't still mad at you, I'd give you a big kiss."

"You *what?*" His breath quit. She smirked, knowing her point hit home and brushed past him.

"That's all, Kenneth."

"Huh, I guess I should've asked for that fry?"

"Most definitely."

"A makeup kiss would do?"

"Don't push it, O'Connor."

She headed in, and his eyes followed until she disappeared, and then he grinned.

Makeup sex is even better…

An hour later, Teddy strolled out all flush and relaxed, and Kenneth called to her from the back corner, "Over here!" He was putting the finishing touches on her bed that he made out of airline blankets.

"Is that for me?" she said with a laugh, eying the multi-colored lump on the floor.

"Wow, you look refreshed." He gave her a warm smile. "Do you feel better?"

"Yes, thank you."

"I know it's not much, but it's better than what you had last night. Here, give it a try." He patted the bed, and she sat down.

Almost immediately, she clutched her backpack tight, and he could see the fear grow in her eyes.

A pang of guilt shot to his heart. "Don't worry, you're safe here." Kenneth dragged a blanket over her knees and handed her a pillow. "If you need me, I'll be right over there by the bathrooms." He pointed to a set of chairs along the wall and smiled. "Now get some rest." And with her eyes as round as a frightened child's, she laid her head down.

"Sweet dreams, Theodora."

19

The Diary

January 23, 1961

Today I found Grandpa's Zippo in the car. He's had it since the war, and it's a real beauty. Solid brass with a BIG Prescott "P" carved on its face. And O' boy, do I love the way it smells... it's intoxicating.

Later on, Paddy and I stopped off at Biffs for burgers, and there she was talking to HIM again—Jesus, my blood boiled! I wanted to rip his head off, but Paddy told me to chill. He promised we'd teach him a lesson. So, we waited out back and followed him to a rundown shack by the river. It was a real scumhole. Paddy joked that it would be better off burnt to the ground, and I agreed. So, I took out Grandpa's lighter... and wow, did those flames fly high! I've never felt so alive. It was beautiful.

—HA!

Back in Hollywood...

It was late. Bridget sat at the tiny desk in the hotel room with her chin propped up on her hand, staring at an old newspaper clipping taped next to the entry. It showed a house razed to the ground by fire. The headline read:

GAS EXPLOSION KILLS FAMILY
Late Monday night, a family of five was killed in a house fire. Nearby residents say they heard a loud explosion. Local authorities suspect a gas leak. Story on page 3.

That's interesting... January 23rd is the same day Mother killed Father. Hm, I wonder if there's a connection...

She flipped through the diary looking for more information. A dark fascination swept over her as she devoured the pages. Her father, a different man than the one she knew, revealed himself to her like never before. With each entry, his inner voice screamed, cried, laughed, and loved, but mostly sought revenge.

Oh, here we go...

TWO BODIES MISSING
The search continues today at the ruins of the small house destroyed by fire. Only three bodies were found in the wreckage. Officials have ruled out a gas leak. Story on page 15.

—I'll find you!

"Who?" Bridget wondered as she removed the clipping from the diary and turned it over with hopes of finding a name.

Heh, nothing...

She searched a bit longer, then a pleasant, exhausted smile appeared. She loved how her father jotted down the bits and pieces of his life. His thoughts were colorful. He liked to boast about how wonderful he was, how brilliant, and how many women were madly in love with him. Yet, what surprised her the most was her father's obsession with her mother.

Sarah Julia Jenkins was unique—an individual with an independent spirit. Bridget could tell from her father's earliest writings that her mother was just a mystery to him. She was beautiful, elusive, and the only woman he couldn't control.

I bet that drove him nuts.

Notation after notation of 'wonder whys' were scribbled everywhere in tiny, almost unreadable print.

Why doesn't Sarah call? Why won't she listen? Why is she always hanging out with those freaks at the coffee shop?

Bridget laughed at how pathetic her father sounded, and then her eyes narrowed on a passage crammed in the corner.

It's already May 10th, and I still haven't heard from Sarah. Where the hell could she be? Her father said she was down south visiting family—I don't believe him. Something is suspicious. If I don't hear from her soon, I'm gonna go find her!

Bridget closed the diary and pushed it aside.

Hmm, I wonder if this has something to do with Theodora. I'd better go see her mother tomorrow. Maybe she can answer a few things. This unfinished business must be taken care of before I leave.

She kissed her fingertip and gently touched the top of the diary.

Goodnight, Father.

20

Kenneth

His watch read three. He let out a long sigh and leaned his head back against the wall. He was exhausted—*she exhausted him.* Never before had he met someone so defiant, so reckless, and yes, so beautiful. But still, it didn't make sense.

I've had plenty of beautiful women.

He looked over at Teddy. She was sound asleep under the blankets.

But this one is special…

The thought pulsed in the pit of his stomach. *Women are too easy,* he laughed. *You give them that look, and they melt—but not Teddy…* He closed his eyes, and a sweet smile appeared.

Nope, she's different.

Things just weren't the same since he stopped playing ball. Kenneth was an outfielder for the New York Yankees when the baseball strike happened. It had lasted two hundred and thirty-two days—the longest in Major League history. Even the World Series had been canceled, which hadn't happened since 1904.

The Yankees had been hit hard. They were the best in their

division, and most considered them the favorite to win everything. But players refused to cross the picket line, and replacement players were brought in.

Game after game, K would scream in anger at the TV as the inferior players took the field. "That's my team—my field! My job! This is such bullshit!"

He was only thirty-three at the time and planned to retire in two years in a blaze of glory, surrounded by women, covered in champagne, and with the press begging for quotes... but that didn't happen.

Instead, in an unexpected move, the Yankees dropped him. No celebrations, no interviews, nothing but a pink slip. His world stopped.

At first, he just partied until the wee hours of the night. He decided that if he couldn't play ball, he'd explore his next two favorite pastimes—women and booze. After all, he was rich, desired, and totally self-indulgent.

Days of drinking turned to weeks, which flew into months, and finally ended in a high-speed car chase with the entire Catskill Police force on his tail as he plowed into a huge snowdrift. Judge Malcolm Stevens, a Yankees fan, sentenced him to six months of rehab, a year of house arrest, and three years of probation.

Rehab was cake, but house arrest... well, he just went stir-crazy and fell off the wagon and into a binge that lasted weeks. His probation officer stepped in before it got out of hand and found him a job working the night shift at the airport.

Being a janitor was a bit of a blow to his ego, and it didn't pay much, but then again, he didn't need the money. K just needed a place to escape and keep out of trouble. On the plus side, no one was around, and he could do as he pleased. It also gave him time to think about what he wanted to do with his life, which, on most nights, was a good thing, but not tonight.

"O'*Connor!*"

Teddy sat upright.

"What?" he jumped, startled.

"Are you going to stay up all night just hovering in that corner?"

"I told you I'd watch over you to keep you safe. I can't do that if I'm sleeping, now can I?"

"That's just silly." She grabbed a blanket and a pillow, then laid them on the floor next to her. "Come, sleep here."

Somewhat perplexed, he collected his stuff and headed over. "Goodnight, Kenneth," she whispered and turned to her side as he lay down. "G'night, Theodora."

Resting his hands behind his head, he stared up at the ceiling.

She thinks I'm a janitor.

The thought made him smile. Teddy didn't know who he was, and he guessed that even if she had, she wouldn't give two hoots.

A girl like Teddy doesn't watch baseball.

He loved that she challenged every ounce of what he knew a woman to be, and all Kenneth could think of was how much he wanted to make love to her. The feeling swept over him, and he closed his eyes.

I'd give you a big kiss…

Her words lingered as he drifted off to sleep.

21

It's Him

The morning came fast, and Teddy woke with a smile. She looked over at Kenneth, who was out cold, all crumpled up, sleeping next to her. Wow, that was the best night's sleep I've had in a long time, she thought as she quietly got up and grabbed her backpack.

"Thank you," she whispered, tiptoeing off to Ms. Mae's place.

Breakfast was amazing, the cinnamon buns were out of this world, and for some unknown reason, Teddy felt like she had a little bit more of a bounce in her step. The day seemed just as cold and isolated as the day before, but something was different.

It feels almost magical…

At least that's what she thought when she strolled over to the front window, near the booking agents, and bent over to warm her hands on the foot heater. Outside, the golden sun glistened in the periwinkle sky. Everything was covered in drifts of snow, with no human movement anywhere for as far as she could see.

"I have the sensation that I'm the magpie in Monet's painting," she said with a happy sigh, remembering the tiny bird sitting on a crooked fence in the vast French countryside of Étretat, surrounded by pale luminous colors and lots of snow.

Suddenly, a red jeep with big black tires swerved onto the airport's entranceway. It plowed its way up the departure ramp, then skidded to a stop at the first drop-off zone. A man jumped out of the driver's side. He wore an army green field jacket, a black knitted beanie pulled down over his ears, and laced-up black combat boots. His white cargo pants looked dirty as if covered in paint stains. Teddy couldn't see his face, but his gait was familiar, and her heart leaped into her throat.

Is that... no, it can't be!

Her eyes blinked rapidly as she watched him step up to the curb, then they grew large, and she pounded on the glass, screaming.

"Cole! Cole!"

Her urgent cries echoed loud, but he was out of ear range.

She grabbed her backpack and rushed after him. He looked a bit hurried as he dodged in and out of the lines of people, eyeing them down.

Is he looking for me?

Picking up the pace, Teddy ran faster and faster. A maintenance man came in from the cold, pushing a luggage cart covered in icicles. She swerved to the right to avoid slamming into him, oblivious to the melted ice dripping on the floor.

WHOA!

Her heel slipped, and her boot gave out. She contorted her body just enough to keep from falling, but her ankle twisted. She bellowed out in pain and halted to a stop. Frantically, her eyes searched through the congestion of the bodies, but—*POOF*, he was gone. She lost him. At least that's what she feared until the path cleared, and his black beanie popped back into view.

"Oo-oo-*ooh*, there he is," she hooted and charged forward.

It had been the third day since the storm hit, and the computers and phones were just coming back online. The place was packed. Crowds of stranded travelers stood in lines, zig-zagging all the way from the ticket counters to the front entranceways.

"*COLE!* Wait up! I'm *HERE,*" she called out, wobbling through the lines, but he kept going.

That's definitely him... um, I think? Well, it does look MOSTLY like him, but eww... what's with the drab military look? I thought he was a pacifist. Heh, maybe I'm thinking of Pablo? It has been over ten years. Anyways, I'm just grateful that he's finally here. Ugh, but I'll just die if he's bald under that hat!

He stepped up to the ticket counter, and a rush of relief swept over her as the female booking agent motioned for him to wait. Teddy was just two airlines away, and she slowed to a moderate walk.

Now take a deep breath and relax. There's no need to yell because he's right there. Be cool, give him that smile he loves, and don't be needy!

The pain in her foot throbbed, but her heart sang for joy.

Soon this nightmare will be over, and I'll be in the arms of the man I love. Cause he's my ONE true—NOOOOOO! Where's he going?

He darted from the ticket agent and headed towards the exit.

"Wait! Don't go—*STOP!*" she hollered, hurrying after him, but he kept moving. She hobbled faster, pushing through the wall of people. "Get out of my way, please. *Just MOVE!*" With just a few strides, he crossed over the threshold and was out the door. "Stop him," she shrieked, and everyone gunned their attention to her. "Grab him, please!" Out the window, Teddy could see the heel of his boot climbing in.

NOOOOOO!

She quickened her pace, but she was too late. The jeep left.

"Cole! *COLE,"* she yelled, waving her arms over her head, hoping he would see her in the rearview mirror, but he didn't. Instead, the car skidded to the left, then drifted to the right, and corrected itself on the snowy ramp as it chugged past the last terminal and headed for the highway.

Crushed, Teddy dropped to her knees, her head collapsed in her hands, and softly she cried, "Please don't leave me, Cole."

A small crowd gathered around her, and Kenneth rushed out of the building.

"Teddy," he stammered. A sudden burst of panic washed over him as he saw the tears streaming down her face. "Are you alright? What happened?"

"Nothing, Kenneth." She looked up, embarrassed. "I'm good." She wiped her face with her sleeve. "I just slipped, that's all."

Teddy didn't want him to see her like *this*. She didn't want his *pity*. But most of all, she didn't need *ANOTHER* man acting as if he cared only to let her down.

"Did you get hurt?"

He reached out to help her up, but she pushed his hand away.

"No, Kenneth, really, I'm fine. I can get up on my own." She tried to stand but slipped, landing hard on her ass with a thump, and snow dusted up all over her.

"Here, let me help you," he said with a grin, reaching out.

"You're such an asshole, Kenneth!" She punched the ground. "Dammit, I need to get the hell out of this place!" She struggled to stand and shot him a '*don't you even think about it*' look.

"Are you crazy, Theodora? Where are you going to go? You're stuck in the middle of a blizzard. Everything is down."

"Crazy... how dare you call me *CRAZY!*" She shook with rage.

"Whoa, relax." His palms shot up. "Teddy, I'm just saying."

"What are you just saying?"

"It's just that... in a couple of days, all the snow will be gone—"

"*AND?*" Pissed, she swatted at her jeans, trying to remove the snow.

"Everything will be fine, so stop freaking out."

"Really, is *THAT* what I'm doing, Kenneth—freaking out? You don't think this has anything to do with me being *FROZEN* to the bone, *ROBBED* while I slept, *AND* stuck in this *GOD*-forsaken *PLACE?*"

SWAT ~ SWAT!

A chuck of slush flew off her sleeve and hit him in the eye.

"Ouch," he winced, staring at her in disbelief. "Thanks a lot."

"My pleasure," she said, somewhat satisfied, and crossed her arms, sneering.

"Oh, and one more thing, Hayes." His eyes narrowed. "You're acting like a complete brat."

"Who are *you* calling a *BRAT?*"

"You, princess. Got a problem with that?" He stepped closer.

"Don't try me, O'Connor." Her finger pointed to his face.

"I'm not in the mood—"

SNATCH!

"Ha! I gotcha," he gloated.

"Oooh, yooouuu!" she grunted, trying to pry her finger loose with her other hand, but he caught that one too. "Damn you, O'Connor!"

"Settle down, princess, settle down." He tugged her hands inward, and she crashed into his chest. Their lips were a breath apart.

"What's the matter, Hayes... cat got your tongue?" He grinned. *She fits perfectly in my arms, and in just a few seconds, she'll be mine—*

"Kenneth, let go of me," she said through clenched teeth.

"Say pretty please."

"Never!" she hissed. "When I get free—"

"Whadda ya gonna do?" he laughed, amused.

Oooooh, this overconfident HEDONIST fucker!

Her face flushed red, and she jerked so hard that his ski cap fell off, revealing his dark wavy hair. Teddy's breath skipped.

Holy shit, he's GORGEOUS!

"Come on, Hayes, you can do better than that—"

STOMP!

The heel of her boot landed square on his foot, and he yelped out in pain. Then her finger shot up to his face, but this time, he didn't dare touch it.

"*FIRST* of all, you don't *OWN* me, *SO* you don't get to tell me what I *CAN* and *CAN NOT* do! Do you hear me, O'Connor?"

"I, ah…" he swallowed hard, staring at her bloodshot eyes. They were on the verge of tears. "Teddy," his voice broke as regret swept in. "I'm so sorry. I was just being playful. I didn't mean to upset you. I thought I could cheer you up."

He wanted so badly to hold her, to kiss her, to make things better, but he realized he was only making things worse.

"I came here to help."

"I don't need your help, nor any other man's, that's for damn sure." Angrily, she wiped at the single tear that managed to escape down her cheek. "I can take care of myself just fine."

"You're impossible, Hayes." He shook his head in frustration, unable to understand what went wrong. *Why the mood change? Things were going great last night, and now she hates me—what gives?*

Teddy turned to the crowd.

"Does anyone know how I can get the hell out of this place?"

A few muttered no, but a familiar voice rang out in the back, "Yeah, I do!" Her eyes searched through the faces, then softened when she saw Harvey's jolly smile beaming at her. "Hey, kid, they cleared the tracks to Penn Station this morning."

"Really, Harvey?" A rush of hope swept over her. "How do I get there?"

"All you gotta do is just follow the bend around and wait for the shuttle. It'll take you to the transit station." His eyes twinkled. "There's a train coming and going every hour until six."

"That's great, Harvey. Thank you. You're my angel." She blew him a kiss, then turned an evil eye to Kenneth. "And just so you know, O'Connor, this is the kind of help I needed."

"Oh, gimme a break... I didn't even know," he said, exasperated.

"Whatever—*pfft,*" she scowled and checked her watch. "It's almost eleven. The next train will be coming soon."

"Wait," Kenneth pleaded, his voice sounding needier than he wanted it to. "I can take you later when I get off of work."

"No, thank you. I'd rather take the train." She picked up her backpack and threw it over her shoulder. "Hey, Harvey," she called out whimsically. "Maybe someday, I'll catch that show of yours."

"That'll be great, kid. I'll put your name on the list."

"You do that."

She waved goodbye, then turned to Kenneth.

"And you..." Teddy stared into his intense eyes. It was obvious that he didn't want her to go, which surprisingly made her happy, and her lips lifted into the most beautiful *'you drive me crazy'* smile. "Thanks for last night. It was really sweet."

"Anytime, Theodora," he sighed.

"Well, I'd better go then. I'll see ya in the funny papers." She let out a waggish laugh and waved, then headed for the bend.

The game's over, and I lost...

Kenneth stood rigid, watching her slush through the snow, knowing he'd probably never see her again. Defeated, he looked down, trying to remember the last time a woman left him feeling so helpless.

"She's a hot pistol, that one," Harvey said, siding up to him. He hadn't known K long, but he could tell that the anguished look on his face wasn't because he had lost the pennant. He clutched his nightstick and rocked back on his heels. "Yeah, and I bet she knows how to keep the sheets warm at night too." He let out a hearty laugh and slapped K on the back. "Hey, Slugger, if it were me, I'd go after her."

"You heard her. She hates me."

"What I heard was foreplay."

"Huh, ya think?"

Harvey grinned. "I know."

Kenneth's face lit up, and he pulled out his wallet and counted what little cash he had left. "Hey, Harv, you got any money on you?"

"Sorry, Slugger, I'm down to my last dollar."

"Shit, well, give me your pen then." He grabbed it from Harvey's pocket and took off running, his lungs burning from the crisp air as he barreled through the snow.

"Hey, Theodora—wait up!"

Teddy was nearing the shuttle stop, and without turning, she waved a backward hand above her head, dismissing him.

"Stop!" He leaped in front of her with his hands out. "Hold on a second, please."

"Not now, Kenneth. I can't do this," her voice broke. "I don't want to miss the next train."

"Do you even know where you are going?"

"To the Village."

"Where in the Village?"

"I don't know, but I'll know it when I get there."

"What?"

"I've seen it in a photo."

"Are you kidding me?" he stammered in disbelief. "You don't have an address?"

"I *HAD* an address, but it disintegrated!

"But why can't you wait?"

"Because I have to go now." She threw up her hands in frustration. "I have to find him. He was just here, looking for me—"

"Who?"

"Cole."

Kenneth struggled to follow.

"My boy-*FRIEND*, okay?"

The incomprehensible words left her mouth and exploded in his brain.

"Ouch, the boyfriend," he uttered.

"Yeah, that guy."

"I see. Well, um… I can help you find him when I get off work."

"That's very kind of you," she said awkwardly and adjusted her backpack. "But I need to do this on my own—"

"Are you crazy? You have no money and don't know where you're going."

"There you go calling me crazy again. Why do you even care?"

"Because I do."

"But—*WHY?*"

"I don't know… I just do."

"You should be happy that I'm leaving—"

"Well, I'm not!"

His eyes burned into hers. The need, the passion, the cry in his voice caught Teddy by surprise, and her insides tightened—her cheeks blushed pink.

"Huh…" he uttered as his piercing blues danced at the notion that maybe, just maybe, Harvey was right and that she did like him.

"Enjoying the show, O'Connor?"

"Always, Ms. Hayes." His rugged grin beamed, and her eyes rolled. "That's the look you gave me the first time I met you."

"Is it?" he said sheepishly.

"Indeed, it is—"

DING… DING…

The sound of the shuttle rang in the distance, and they both grew anxious. Teddy looked down, suddenly feeling guilty.

"Kenneth, I know this doesn't make sense to you, but I have to go. I have to find Cole. If I don't… well, it's just that I'm afraid that if I don't go now, I never will. And I don't want to be that *GIRL*, you know, the one that's always full of regrets?" She turned a kind eye his way. "Do you know what I mean?"

"Unfortunately, I do," he sighed, watching the approaching shuttle with dread, knowing he only had seconds left.

"Hey, give me your hand."

"Why?"

"Come on, just give it."

"Hmm, I don't know—" Kenneth grabbed her arm and pulled up her sleeve. "Hey… what *ARE* you doing?"

"Steady now," he warned as he wrote down his number.

"Are you crazy?"

"Who are you calling crazy?" he said with a wink, mocking her. "Now, if you need anything, call me day or night. Oh, and promise me you won't wash it off until you're safe and sound, okay?"

"Um, we'll see," Teddy frowned, conflicted. She didn't like to commit to such things, and agreeing to such a contract always left her feeling bad because she almost never called.

"Hayes, I'm not asking you to marry me," his eyes skewed.

"Okay, fine. I promise."

"Oh, and here." He pulled the cash from his pocket.

"No, thank you. I'm good."

"Please don't fight me on this, Theodora—just take it." He put the money in her hand and cupped it closed. "It's not much, but it'll help. You can pay me back later." He smirked, "We can go for fries or something."

"Okay, Mister Sarcastic, but it's just a loan then."

"Deal—Oh, and it would be nice if you checked in with me later on tonight or tomorrow. You know, so you can pay me back?" His grin went wide, knowing he was pushing his luck.

"Hm, I guess." She eyed him suspiciously then, despite herself, smiled. "There's something oddly familiar about you, O'Connor."

DING!

The final shuttle bell rang out, and she looked over with a sigh.

"Well, that's me…"

"Please be safe, and don't forget to call, okay?" He shot her a pleading look, and she laughed. Then, without warning, Teddy reached up and kissed him. "I'll see ya later," she said with a naughty smile and dashed to the shuttle.

Kenneth waved goodbye and wondered if she ever would… then he touched his lips, the warmth of her kiss still lingered, and he grinned.

First base?

22

The Fiancé

Back in Tampa...

Agent Stewart bit into his baloney sandwich and scowled at the pile of bank statements scattered across his desk. He popped a peanut in his mouth, then typed a few numbers into the computer. The noisy machine whizzed as the hard drive calculated the results, and then he frowned.

Something's not right—

"Hey, Stewart, they found another body," Walters said, barging into the small, cluttered office.

"Same gun?"

"Nope, a .22 caliber."

"Any connection?"

"It's too early to tell." Walters pushed aside a stack of papers and sat on the edge of the desk. "Man, this place is a mess. How do you find anything in here?"

"I like it this way. It's organized." Stewart spread out the papers a bit more. "Everything's within my reach. It makes for easy findings."

"They say a cluttered desk is the sign of a disturbed mind."

"So that's my problem?"

Walters' lip curved into a grin.

"Huh, well, don't tell my shrink. I'd hate to give her another reason to keep me in therapy." Stewart held up a brown bag. "Boiled peanut?"

"Oh, I love these." Walters dipped a hand in and took a handful. "I haven't had them since I was a kid. Where'd you get them?"

"The new vendor on Hickory. You know, something doesn't feel right with this Prescott case. I've been going over the books, and I found several large sums of money that were deposited into his account just days before his death. I can't tell who they're from."

"Ooh, was the Senator on the take?" Walters crushed the soft-shell casing with his thumb and popped the nut into his mouth.

"Possibly."

"Blackmail?"

"Maybe? You know, that bodyguard of his seems pretty curious to me. I've been sniffing around, trying to find out more about him, but no one's talking."

"I'm hitting that same wall with his daughter, Bridget, too." He threw the shell casings into the trash. "However, I did some digging and learned that her fiancé died two months ago in a car accident."

"No kidding... huh, first, her boyfriend and then her parents." Stewart leaned back in his chair.

"Supposedly, Bridget was head over heels in love with the guy and asked Daddy to make it happen."

"How so?"

"The engagement was arranged by the Senator himself."

"Wow, I didn't know they still did that sort of thing anymore."

"Yup, and out of all the nice guys in the world that she could have chosen, she picked Russell Channing, the playboy son of Victor Channing of Channing Enterprises, over in Ybor." His brows rose. "Have you heard of them?"

"Yes, of course... they're big-time importers, right?"

"Indeed, they are, and it seems our boy Russ was dealing in illegals from Mexico... drugs, I figure."

"Do you think Prescott knew?"

"I imagine so." Walters shrugged. "Supposedly, the Senator pushed a few buttons and gave him free rein to do whatever he wanted over at the ports. He was bringing in around four million a year."

Stewart let out a long whistle. "Wow, that's a lot of dough."

"Yup... and word on the street was that the Senator wanted him to reel it in before he put in his bid for the presidency, but Channing refused. Also, there were rumors that he was cheating on Bridget with some young model from Brazil." Walters grinned. "And then next thing you know, his car was found in a ditch off the side of the road with its tailpipe sticking out of the water."

"Coincidence?"

"Maybe… but the official cause of death was ruled an accident. The coroner's office said there was no foul play involved."

"And what's your gut say?"

"It's suspicious—and guess who did the autopsy?"

"Who?"

"Williams, one of the Elders at Blood & Bones. He was brought in at the last minute—their usual guy fell ill with a stomach virus."

"No shit." Stewart's mouth went slack. "You know, for such a goody two-shoes organization, they have a whole lot of dead bodies showing up. Hmph… something doesn't smell right." He popped a nut and held out the bag to Walters.

"Any update on the Hayes girl?" he smirked, grabbing a handful.

"Nothing. Everything's still down last I checked this morning."

"So, what's your take on those Hayeses? That Cleo's got a temper."

"My take? Ha, Jesus… my take is that they're a bunch of—"

SCREEECH!

"Walters, Stewart, to the media room—*NOW!*" Agent Stephens' voice roared into the intercom.

They raced down the hall and into a room filled with TV monitors. The words REVENGE MURDERS were plastered on the screens.

"Deputies found businessman Richard Schilling's body floating in the Hillsborough River early this morning. He was shot once in the head," the male anchor said as video footage of the body being retrieved from the water played, then the onscreen image cut to an official FBI document.

"And just moments ago, an internal memo was leaked to the press, suggesting that the recent string of homicides in the Tampa Bay area may be related to the death of Senator Andrew Blake Prescott. The FBI has not confirmed nor denied the authenticity of the memo. However, tax records confirm that Schilling had business dealings with the late Senator."

Fuuuuuuuuuck—Stephens let out a long hiss, then threw the remote at the screen.

"A GODDAMN LEAK!"

He turned to Walters, madder than hell. "What part of 'We're not going to let this get out of hand and ruin the Senator's good name' didn't you understand?"

"But, sir—"

"But NOTHING! There's a gang of reporters outside my door demanding answers!" He rubbed his temples. "I want this wrapped up by the weekend. Do you hear me?"

"Yes, sir."

"And watch your step—NOW get the fuck out!"

23

Mrs. Hayes

Back in Hollywood...

"Damn that weatherman, he promised me a cold front! Jesus, it's like ninety degrees in here." Cleo wiped the sweat off her chin as she sat waiting in the minivan for Anna to be released early from school for a doctor's appointment.

BEEP!

To say she was irritable was putting it lightly. She hadn't slept a wink. The thought of her sister being stranded and alone at the airport left her on edge, and to make matters worse, her mother was torture-phoning her all night. Abby had become obsessed with the FBI agents. She was paranoid that they were going to steal her car because it was a classic.

Cleo cranked the A/C and pushed up the vents so that the cool air hit her directly in the face, but it didn't help much. The air was thick, and the humidity was high.

BEEP! BEEEEP!

Dammit, Anna, where are you?

She checked her watch.

I'm late. Mom's gonna kill me!

The thought made her entire body tense up. Oh, how she hated the wrath of Abby Hayes. Her mother's tangents were notorious. Yet, as crazy as her adoptive mother was, Cleo was grateful to have her. Her adoption wasn't the same as Teddy's. Cleo's birth parents, Bill and Betsy Clapsaddle, were so overjoyed when they learned that they were going to have a baby girl that they immediately converted their guest room into a nursery and filled it with hand-knitted flowers, porcelain dolls, and more stuffed animals than any one child could possibly play with.

"Anything for my beautiful baby girl," Betsy would often say as she patted her growing belly.

A week before Cynthia Marie Clapsaddle was due to arrive, Betsy sat on the couch in her living room, talking on the phone with her best friend, Abigail Higgins.

"Well, whaddya know, that Henry Hayes finally asked you to marry him, and it's about time too! He'd be lucky to have a woman like you for his bride."

"From your mouth to God's sweet ears, Betsy. Now if I can only get him to stop comparing me to some great fish he caught. Ha-ha, good Lord, that man associates everything in life with fishing."

Betsy let out a hoot, then grabbed at her sides.

"Ouch, what was that… oww, there it is again!"

"What is it?"

"Huh, I think it was a contraction."

"Oh, don't be silly. You're not due for another week. It's

probably just gas."

"Ouch, there's another one. Oh no, my water just broke. I'm going into labor."

"Where's Bill?" Abby shrieked.

"Downstairs."

"Tell him to take you to the hospital now, and I'll meet you there." Moments later, Bill threw her overnight suitcase in the trunk, buckled Betsy into the passenger seat, and pulled out of the driveway. The contractions were coming fast and steady.

"Hurry, Bill," she gasped, clutching her sides. "Our little girl is on her way!"

"Sweet Jesus," he said, stepping on the gas. The streets were empty as he sped down the hilly road that led to the hospital.

Outside the emergency room, Abby nervously waited. She heard the sirens before she saw them. The ambulance's lights flashed bright as it turned onto the street. Bill's eyes went wide as he tried to swerve out of the way, pressing down hard with both feet on the brake, but it was too late. The two vehicles collided head-on in a fiery crash. He was killed instantly, but Betsy survived. She was in critical condition but conscious. The doctors rushed her into the emergency room and performed a C-section to save the baby. Abby stood by her side, refusing to leave, and held her hand while she gave birth.

"It's a girl," the doctor called, and bittersweet tears streamed down Betsy's face as she cried for joy. She knew she didn't have long.

"Abby, listen to me. I need you to be strong. I need you to take care of my sweet baby girl. I know you're not ready, and I know it will be a burden on you." She kissed Abby's hand. "I am so sorry to ask so much of you."

"Of course, I will love her as if she were my own. You know I will," Abby started to ramble in a crying frenzy, not realizing time was limited.

"Now, Abigail Higgins, stop crying this instance and listen to me. You have to promise me that every day of her life, you will remind her how much her father and I loved her and how sorry we are that we can't be there for her."

"I will. Of course, I will, Betsy. I promise with all my heart."

"Abby… please don't ever let her forget us."

"I won't." Abby crossed her heart. The two women sealed the promise with a pinky swear like they used to do when they were young. Abby kissed her forehead, and she passed away.

In all of her forty years on this earth, there hadn't been a day that went by without Cleo wondering what her life would have been like if her parents had lived, and days like today really amplified the missing.

RING!

"Cynthia, are you there? It's your mother."

"Hi, Ma—"

"Did they turn off your phone?" Abby huffed as she stood in the middle of her vegetable garden with the cordless phone in one hand and the hose in the other, waving it around like a conductor as she watered her plants.

"What do you mean?"

"It's been two whole days since you last called me. I could be dead, and you don't care."

"Ma, I spoke to you last night, don't you remember? Besides, you know I'm busy with the kids. Have you heard from Teddy?"

"You know that one doesn't call unless she's in trouble."

"Mom, she is in trouble. Geez, I can't believe you forgot!"

"Oh, don't get all bent out of shape. She'll be fine. She always is. You know, Cynthia Marie, I think she plays you for a fool."

"Just stop! First, you know how much I hate it when you call me Cynthia, and throwing in Marie is just overkill. And secondly, she doesn't play me for a fool."

"Well, it's your God-given name. Who knows where you came up with a crazy name like Cleo? It's beyond me. I'm sure that troublemaker sister of yours had something to do with it."

Cleo rolled her eyes. "Anyways, I hope you didn't forget about your doctor's appointment today."

"Of course, I didn't. I'm not senile."

KNOCK! KNOCK!

"Oh—there's someone at the door." Abby peered over the fence. "Ooh, she's pretty… huh, I bet she's from the FBI."

"Who*?"*

"Cynthia, I gotta go—"

SLAM!

Cleo snapped out of her head as Anna climbed into the car.

"How many times have I told you not to slam the door shut like that? You scared the hell out of me. Now put your seatbelt on."

"Ma, I forgot to bring my paper to school today."

"But you said you had it with you this morning."

"I thought I did, but I didn't."

"You know Anna, sometimes I wonder if you just yes me to death." The nine-year-old bubbled her lips and looked at her, bewildered. "Dunno, but my teacher said I have to bring it today, or else I'll get an F, and if I get an F, then I'll have to stay after school every day until five for a whole month."

"Geez, that's pretty harsh." Cleo dismissed it with a shrug. "Well, first, I need to take you and grandma to the doctor. We're late, and you know how Nana gets. I'm going to pull up to the house, and you run in and get her, okay?"

"Okey-dokey."

A stack of utility trucks lined the graveled road. Cleo never quite understood why her parents moved to such an isolated area, but in the back of her mind, she figured it had something to do with Teddy.

SCREEECH!

A yellow taxi fish-tailed around them, nearly sideswiping the minivan. Cleo jammed on the brakes just in time, and the cab took off down the street.

"Hey, Ma, that's Aunt Teddy's friend," Anna said, pointing to the blonde in the back seat.

"Who?"

"That lady."

"Don't be silly. Aunt Teddy doesn't have any friends like that." Cleo pulled into the driveway and beeped the horn. "Go get your grandmother and tell her to hurry."

Anna skipped to the front door, tried the handle, peered in through the glass, then knocked. "Nana, you in there?" She shrugged. "Ma, I don't think she's home."

"Go around back. She's probably still working in the garden." Anna ran into the backyard and then let out a blood-curdling scream.

Oh, dear God!

Frantically, Cleo rushed out of the car and through the gate. Abby lay motionless, face down in a pool of blood. A broken flowerpot sat nearby. She quickly turned her over. Blood gushed from a large wound on the top of her head.

"Is she dead?" Anna cried. The look of horror was etched on the child's face. "No," Cleo said, checking her pulse. "She's alive. Quick, go get me a towel." Anna rushed into the house and came back within seconds. Cleo pressed it to her head. Instantly it was drenched. "She's losing a lot of blood. Hold this for me."

"No!" Anna stepped away from the body.

"Look, we don't have time. I have to call an ambulance. Now hold it, dammit!"

"No, I won't! You can't make me!"

"Aww, honey, Grandma needs you. Please don't be frightened. It's going to be all right," Cleo said softly. "I just need you to stop the bleeding while I call for help."

"But what if she dies?" Anna's lip quivered.

"She won't die if you help her."

"O-*kay*." Anna inched closer.

Cleo guided her hand to Abby's head. "Hold it just like this, and I'll be right back." She kissed her forehead and rushed inside.

"9-1-1, what is your emergency?" said the female operator.

"I need an ambulance. My mother's bleeding."

"What's the address?"

"2230 Serenity Lane in Dania."

"Ma'am, can you tell me what happened?"

"I don't know. She's unconscious. I think she fell and hit her head. She's losing a lot of blood. How long before they arrive?"

"They're on their way—"

"MAAAAAAH!"

Abby's body convulsed, and she started to foam at the mouth.

Cleo rushed out.

"Make her stop, Mom!" Sirens roared down the street. "Hurry, Anna, go and tell them we're back here!" And just as the words left Cleo's mouth, her mother's body rose up, and she gasped, then went still. "Get back," the male paramedic said, pushing Cleo aside. "She's going into cardiac arrest. You need to stand back!" He dropped to his knees and started working on Abby's chest. A second male paramedic brought additional equipment.

"Mommy," Anna cried, reaching for her mother's hand, but Cleo pushed her towards the gate. "Anna, wait in the car—*NOW!*"

"CLEAR," the medic shouted.

Abby's body lurched as the defibrillator sent a bolt through her body. Anna ran out, screaming.

"CLEAR!"

The lifeless body jolted.

"I can't watch this!"

Cleo ran into the house.

I'm gonna be sick.

She rushed to the sink and heaved, vomiting in waves. Over and over, her body retched until the churning stopped. She covered her mouth, trying to hold back the tears but couldn't. The emptiness, the loneliness, the hollowed feeling that lurked inside her whole life caused by the death of her parents, the breakup of her marriage, and now, Abby, the only mother she had ever known, lay dying on the verge of death. Cleo felt helpless. There was nothing she could do to stop it. She sank down to the floor.

"CLEAR!"

In a surge of anger, Cleo slammed her head back against the cabinet door. The physical pain felt good. It went in tandem with the doom that sat in the pit of her stomach.

Why is this all happening?

She didn't understand how her life could fall apart so easily.

Dammit, this is so unfair!

She slammed her head against the door again, but this time harder, and a brown cardboard box fell on top of her head. Shocked, then pissed, she kicked it.

"What the fuck!"

And all of its contents of rare coins, photos, and papers flew everywhere.

Cleo froze. Her eyes, swollen in her sockets, glared at the mess, and that's when it dawned on her—all was quiet.

Oh shit, they left. I've got to get to the hospital!

She jumped to her feet and—

CRUNCH!

F-U-C-K, what did I do? Mom's going to kill me!

Quickly, she dropped to her knees and scooped the items into a pile. *I don't have time for this shit.* She grabbed at the loose pages and put them back into their folders. *What the hell is this stuff doing here anyways? I thought she kept it in her safe deposit box.* She plucked up the coins one by one and placed them in the little section of the box that Abby had designated for them. Then she paused when she saw a young photo of Abby and her mother at a dance. She kissed it.

What am I doing? I need to go...

Cleo knew she was stalling.

What if she's dead? Oh, God, no... I can't handle that. It's just too much loss!

She sat back against the cabinet and slammed her head a third time, but this time, a sharp sense of clarity came to her, and determined, she said, "I have to be there for her the way she was there for Mommy." She pressed the photo to her chest, dried her eyes, and then looked down at the pile.

"Let me clean this up before I go. Folders first, nice and neat the way Nana likes it." She grabbed the stack of folders and banged them on the floor, hoping to straighten the edges, but some of the folders were overstuffed and wouldn't behave.

"Let me do them one at a time."

She pulled the box in a bit closer.

"First one in, MORTGAGE, and then, INSURANCE, and now the overstuffed INVESTMENTS—I'll die if they're rich.

Next, eww... LIVING WILLS—oh, shit, I need to tell Dad! Jesus, he's gonna freak out. He can't live without her. This is gonna wreck him, and I can't handle it when he cries! Wait, he's out fishing... maybe I'll get lucky, and this will all blow over by the time he comes home?"

She blew out a long exhale and leaned back against the cabinet.

"It's all going to work out. I know it will. Mom's tough," Cleo sighed, knowing it was just wishful thinking. "Okay, just two more folders—mine and Teddy's."

What the hell?

Hers was full, but Teddy's was empty. She shook it upside down in disbelief.

Nothing, heh... that doesn't make sense. I know Mom bought Teddy bonds because she's always threatening to sell them. So where are they?

Cleo glanced around. She didn't know what she was looking for, but any stack of papers with Teddy's name on it would do.

Hmm, they must be lying around here somewhere.

She looked inside the box again, confused.

Maybe the FBI needed them—

SLAM!

"Ma! They took Nana!" Sobbing, Anna ran into her mother's arms, her worried little face streaked with dirt-stained tears.

"Oh, my beautiful little one. It's going to be all right." The warmth of her daughter's embrace made her realize how lucky she was, and she kissed her.

"I love you so much."

"Ma, is she going to be okay?"

"I don't know, honey, but we better go. She'll kill me if she wakes up and I'm not there." Cleo took her by the hand and led her to the door, then she stopped.

"Anna..." her eyes darted over to Teddy's empty folder. "Tell me about that woman. You know, Aunt Teddy's friend, the one in the cab?"

24

Penn Station

Damn, those piercing eyes.

Teddy hated to admit it, but she liked him. And with only a moment to spare, she jumped over the yellow line at the platform's edge and rushed through the closing doors of the departing train. The noise from the outside world instantly sucked away as the silence of the empty compartment car enveloped her. She threw her backpack on the first seat of the front row, then plopped down by the window. The train slowly picked up speed.

I did the right thing by leaving. Who knows how long I would have been stuck at the airport? Plus, it makes no sense fussing around with a guy like Kenneth when Cole is the love of my life.

The train was warm and surprisingly comfy. Teddy melted into the cushioned seat. It amazed her how her entire body could be frozen stiff, but her face was on fire. She pulled out her lip gloss, dabbed some on with her pinkie, then smacked her lips with a pop.

"You never know… a girl just might get lucky." She let out a giddy laugh. "And a big *HELLO* kiss from Cole is just what I need right now. Heh… I probably shouldn't have kissed Kenneth—ha, but the look on his face made it worth it!"

She kicked up her legs onto the rear-facing seat.

"OUCH, my foot!"

With all the commotion, she forgot about it.

"My boot does feel a bit tight," she grimaced. "But the pain isn't that bad... well, compared to the rest of my body. It's probably best to leave it alone for now." She sat back and let out a sigh.

The ride was smooth. Teddy stared out the window, watching as the bland, colorless houses drifted in and out of the window frame. Every few minutes, a male voice would squeal from the harsh metal speaker on the wall and call out the upcoming stops. Her eyes shifted to the transit map near the exit, checking to see how much further she had to go when the speaker squealed again.

"Next stop Penn Station."

Oh, shit, that's me!

Panic set in, and she grabbed her backpack and held it tight to her chest. The interior lights flickered on and off as the train entered the tunnel. Teddy had never been to New York City before, and she began to have second thoughts.

I must be crazy! Who goes out in the middle of a storm to find a man?

She never thought of herself as a 'lonely hearts' kind of girl, but she had to admit, she was feeling a bit desperate. And with the little money she had left in her pocket and no game plan, things did look pretty grim. Yet, Teddy knew it would be an adventure, and oddly enough, that made her happy.

"Only me, I guess," she laughed and readied herself for the unknowing.

The loud drumbeat of the metal wheels on the steel tracks kept a steady rhythm, rocking her back and forth. Fluorescent lights strobed through the glass, and then, without warning, everything went black. Her heart pounded loud in the silence as the wheels slowed to a glide, and then the platform faded into view.

SCREEEEECH!

The train came to a stop, and she jumped out as the doors slid open.

"Welcome to New York," she said, beaming.

The damp, musky smell of the old station greeted her. And with eyes bright and nothing but hope tugging at her heartstrings, Teddy climbed up the long staircase to the first level, then jockeyed over to the second. With a few short turns, she made her way to the upper level, stood at the entrance, and soaked in the view. It was packed, more like overstuffed, with all sorts of people walking and talking fast.

The place had a grunge vibe, like one of those futuristic underground dystopian cities you see in cheap Sci-Fi movies with its ultra-low ceilings, dim lighting, and clusters of shops that cut in and out of sections of the station. Commuters bustled from newsstands to shoe shiners, hot dog vendors to coffee shops—*Oh, my God, COFFEE!*

"I have to splurge," she bellowed and ordered the largest, hottest, *MOST* delicious cup of java she had ever had. As she sipped, Teddy walked around, exploring the various street exits, and cussed out loud when she realized that finding Cole might not be as easy as she thought. None of the signage directed her to the Village. She frowned, but then her face lit up.

MADISON SQUARE
GARDEN →

Ooh, I've always dreamt about singing there. How exciting!

Following the arrows, Teddy stopped in front of a large escalator and looked up.

"Pfft, I guess there's no time for daydreaming today. Well, up we go, then. Let's see what this big city has to offer us." She finished off the last of her coffee, savoring every bit of it, then tossed the cup in the trash and glided up the escalator. At the top, a burst of fresh winter air smacked her in the face.

"EGAD, that's COLD!"

Her breath exhaled into frosty white puffs. The day's sun hid behind a wall of clouds, and the temperature had dropped since the morning. Similar to the airport, everything was covered in drifts of snow. Teddy tightened her scarf and pulled down the sides of her hat, shivering.

The streets were empty except for a single noisy snowplow and a few daring souls determined to prove that nothing stops Manhattanites. By the street's edge, a muddied wall of ice stood about six-foot high by two feet deep and extended to every block in all directions, blocking the sidewalks off like a fortress.

Now how do I get to the Village? Heh, should I go left or right? She looked for a street sign. Oh, wait, there's a police officer!

"Sir, excuse me, sir," she called out as she rushed over and instantly began sliding on a layer of ice hidden beneath the snow.

WHOAAAAH!

"Careful now, Missy," the tall officer bellowed as he held out his hands, waiting to catch her as she skidded over to him. He stood behind the ticket booth, shielding himself from the intermittent gusts of wind. He looked cold, all bundled up in his NYPD winter garb and fur trooper hat. His earflaps were strapped down so tight they scrunched his face. Still, Teddy could tell he was handsome.

"Can you tell me how to get to the Village?"

"Greenwich Village?" he said, perplexed. "It's a bit cold to be out sightseeing."

"Oh, no, sir… I'm not sightseeing. I'm staying with my boyfriend—I mean, not at the moment, but I will be in a bit," she sighed. "You see, I was stranded at the airport, and he came looking for me, but then my ankle twisted, and he left before I could reach him. So, I hopped on the first train, and here I am." She gave him her best smile, hoping to break through his stoic expression.

"I see," he frowned, unyielding. "Well, the temperature is supposed to drop another ten degrees, and it could be dangerous for you to be out in this weather. That jacket of yours doesn't look very warm… and where are your gloves?"

"Is the Village far from here?" Teddy said, dismissing his concerns. She bit down on her lip, trying to hide the chattering of her teeth, and he huffed in annoyance.

"Well, if you insist on going, then you should know that all of the subways are down, and there are no taxis or buses running. So, you're on your own. And if you get into trouble, nobody will be around to save you." Then he cracked his neck and gestured as if he was directing traffic. "The Village is about a mile that way. Oh, and it gets dark early around here, so if you don't want to freeze to death, make sure to be someplace warm, okay?"

"Good to know. Well, thank you for your time. I guess I should be going then."

He waved, dismissing her, and Teddy hurried off.

Wow, that was unnerving…

"Heh, maybe, he's right," she sighed, feeling somewhat defeated. "Maybe I should go back… but back to where? To

Florida—*no way.* To the airport—*that would never work.* Back to a life of being alone?" She abruptly stopped, and her brows furrowed. *Pfft, I think I'd rather freeze to death.* Then out of the corner of her eye, she saw it.

A PHONE BOOTH!

It was one of those old-fashion enclosed types with a seat. Teddy opened the door, grabbed the handset, and listened for a tone.

"Of course, it's dead."

She dropped the handle back into the cradle and noticed a phonebook dangling under the tray.

Ooh, that might help...

She closed the door and sat. She was still furious with herself for destroying the piece of paper with Cole's address on it. "I was tired. It was covered in lemonade. Who knew that soaking it in hot water would make it fall apart?" She pulled a pen from her backpack and frowned. "Besides, it's all Kenneth's fault anyways." A goofy smile appeared on her frozen face, and she shook her head with a laugh. She could almost see him standing there with his rugged grin, pleading his innocence—

"Concentrate, Theodora!"

Thumbing through the directory, her eyes grew large as she turned to a map of the city, and there it was in bright blue lettering, GREENWICH VILLAGE. She tore the page from the book's hold and stared out into the massive wall of snow, trying to recall where Cole said he lived.

"Babe, it's directly over the old Fat Black Pussy Cat Theatre in the Village. Dylan performed there in the sixties. Now it's a Mexican restaurant, but in its heyday, it was this great music venue. It's inspiring me. I've been painting nonstop—"

That shouldn't be hard to find.

She turned to the T's, looking for the theaters. *No pussycats here,* then switched to the R's, humming while she searched.

After all, how many Mexican restaurants can there be around here?

She scrolled down the page.

"Okay, so there's one, two, three in the Village." She circled them on the map. "Hm, two are close, but that third one seems a bit far. So, I had better hurry."

Treading the streets was easy enough as she navigated through the maze of compacted snow walls. Her long legs were warmed by the steam coming up through the grates from the subway tracks below. The bright sun peeped out from the clouds just long enough to thaw her face, but then without warning, a frosty breeze swept in from the Hudson River, and a deep groan howled from her lips.

"Son of a bitch—*BRRRRR!!!*"

Shivering, she quickened her pace. Most of the businesses were closed, but the few that were open were filled with locals.

The city's skyline left her in awe as she tried to absorb all of the beautiful architecture. She searched the tops of the buildings, looking for the gargoyles that Cole had told her about but didn't see any. The further she traveled from the station, the smaller the structures got.

There it is...

Crossing the street, Teddy stepped up to the first destination and caught her reflection in the window.

"Yikes, is that what I look like?" She shrieked, "I'm a mess!" Then in a heartbeat, she pulled off her hat, primped her hair, and dabbed her lips with gloss. "Aw, that's much better," she sighed and tugged on the restaurant's door handle.

"Oh darn, it's closed!"

She peered in through the glass and then stared at the menu taped on the door. "Well, it's definitely a Mexican restaurant." She stepped back to have a better look at the shiny black five-story building with its colorful flower boxes and shook her head.

"This can't be the place, it's too new, and besides, it looks nothing like a theater." Flustered, she pulled out the map and studied it.

Heh, I'm not going to let myself get discouraged. I'll find him—I have to. He's the love of my life, and no one has ever LOVED me like Kenneth—oops, I mean Cole. With a roll of her eyes, she tucked the map away and checked her watch. *Heh, it's already two o'clock. I'd better hurry.*

The blocks streamed by, and the constant pounding on the frozen pavement sent jolts up her leg. Teddy just ignored the pain and charged ahead, trekking through the mounds of snow.

Boy, I could use a hot bath right now. You know, one of those BIG steamy tubs with lots of yummy smelling bubbles.

Her memory flashed to Kenneth handing her the spa pass, and she felt a pang.

Jesus Christ, Theodora! What's wrong with you? Just push that janitor right out of your head—and don't think about him again!

ZOOOOM!

The noisy snowplow sped by her, kicking up slush everywhere.

"Ewwww, *GROSS!*"

It had splattered all over her. Frantically, she brushed it off, hoping the stains wouldn't set. When she was done, she looked up and realized the eatery across the street was her next destination.

Huh, fingers crossed...

The tiny one-story building was painted in bright pastels and had no windows. A flashing neon sign above the doorway read OPEN, and Teddy let out a sigh of relief. She put on her best face and entered.

Beautiful murals depicting Mexican sunsets were hand-painted on the walls. Various sombreros, shakers, and flamenco guitars hung throughout. The afternoon rush had just finished, the place was empty, and two young waitresses stood at the counter, counting their tips.

"Hola," said the younger of the two as Teddy approached.

"Hi," she said nervously. "Can you tell me if there's a Cole O'Keefe here?"

"Quien es Cole?" the girl replied, confused.

"You don't speak English?"

The girl shook her head, and Teddy turned to the second one and repeated his name, but louder and slower as if that would fix the language barrier.

"Oh, no. Si, si, si, no, Cole O'Keefe," she said with a slight head shake.

Teddy glanced around the room, checking for any signs of the old theater, then frowned at the two women. "Never mind, I must have the wrong place. Thank you for your time," she said and left.

"Shit, there's only one more place to go—*fuck, fuck, PHUUCCK!*"

She felt like screaming, but instead, she just put on her hat, adjusted her scarf, and headed for the next destination. The winds were picking up, and the melted ice was starting to harden.

Teddy took out the map and reviewed it again. Her fingers were achy, frozen stiff to the bone. She could have kicked herself for not buying gloves when she had the money, but it made no sense fussing about it now since she was broke.

"Okay, so I turn onto Bleecker, then make a left at MacDougal, but I don't ever recall Cole mentioning those names before. Yet, I do remember him saying something that started with an M, like Minnow or Minnie or Minta. Ugh, this totally sucks!" She threw up her hands, and her stomach growled.

"And I'm hungry!"

Daylight was sinking fast, so Teddy picked up the pace. As the buildings got smaller, the city became less dense. She reached Bleecker and turned left. About two hundred yards in, a street sign caught her eye. At first, she thought she was mistaken, and she quickly spun back for a second look, then her mouth dropped.

MINETTA STREET

"No way... that's it," she gasped, and her hands began to shake.

Tucked in between 6th and MacDougal sat a very narrow, crooked, old cobblestone road that had yet to be cleared of snow. And maybe in the swinging sixties, the place was bustling with artists and musicians, but on this cold day, there wasn't a soul around. A single path of footprints led the way, and Teddy followed.

The area was once a natural stream called Manette or Devil's Water by the native Lenape Indians. In the 1600s, when the Dutch settled there, they referred to it as Bestevaer's Killetje or Grandfather's Little Creek. And then, about two centuries later, New Yorkers paved over the waterway and erected buildings on top.

They called it Minetta Brook. However, it's most famously known as the home to one of the oldest black playhouses in America.

"The Fat Black Pussycat... wow, I don't believe I actually found it." She stared in awe at the faded black sign above the red Mexican restaurant. "No wonder Cole loves it here. It's absolutely magical."

Teddy heard the faint sounds of men's voices laughing inside and quickly removed her hat and ran her fingers through her hair. A small set of steps led to a big white door. She peered in through the windowpanes and saw two men talking in the back. She tried the door handle, but it was locked, and just as she went to knock, a husky female voice called out.

"You looking for somebody?"

Teddy turned to see this beautiful, tall brunette with dusky eyes coming from the white apartment building across the street. She wore a red halter top that pushed her boobs way up high, skin-tight jeans tucked into black thigh-high boots, and a black leather jacket. She gave Teddy a once over. "You're one of his girls, aren't you? I know your face."

"You do?" Teddy said, startled.

"Of course," she said, pursing her lips. "But sorry to say, he's not here." She reached out a long-fingered hand to Teddy's cheek and lightly touched it. "You're freezing." She had a hint of a German accent. "My name is Enilika, and you are?"

"I'm Teddy, Theodora Hayes."

"Eni, who's that?" a bitchy man's voice shouted from the window above on the second floor.

"One of Cole's girls."

"Bring her up," he huffed, then slammed the window shut.

146

"Come on, let's go in. It's warm upstairs, and you could use the heat." Eni opened the door and tugged at her sleeve. "After you," she said with a grin.

At the top of the staircase, the burly middle-aged man stood watching as they entered. He weighed around three hundred pounds and was dressed in an oversized red cashmere shawl that hung loosely over his bright floral tank and baggy white sweats, which were wadded up at his belly. With a swirl, he led them into the living room, then sat on a throne chair and kicked up his feet on a footstool.

"And whom might you be?" he demanded in a snide, authoritarian tone and hung a limp hand over the armrest. "I thought I knew all of Cole's girls."

"Her name is Teddy, and she's one of his models," Eni beamed.

"Mm-hmph, I see. Well, turn around and let me have a look at you." He waved a glittery, ring-filled hand. "I am Michael and don't even think about calling me Mike. I won't answer to it." He puckered his lips. He was impressed by the beauty before him. "So, you're looking for the mysterious Cole." He let out a puff of air. "Aren't we all, dear—"

"Michael, who's there?" a crotchety old lady's voice called from the bedroom.

"One of Cole's girls."

Teddy almost laughed out loud.

Pfft... of course, he lives with his mother!

She had guessed as much as soon as she had walked through the door. Aside from the stinky old lady smell that permeated every single air particle, the apartment was cluttered with handmade quilts, portraits of saints, and tons of wigs—

although she assumed those were his.

His eyes darkened as he caught her smile. "I'm glad I amuse you," he hissed, clutching his neck. "Oh, and I hate to break the news to you, dearie, but you came a long way for nothing. Our lovely Cole moved out last week. Hmph, and without paying his rent—*MOTHER!*"

Teddy jumped from the screech.

"Mother dearest, come out here now!" he demanded, stomping his foot down.

The bedroom door creaked open, and the old woman hung her head out. "Screw, O'Keefe," she squawked. "That loser owes us money… and *YOU*," she pointed at Teddy. "You go to hell too!" She flipped Teddy the bird, then retreated, slamming the door shut.

"Oh my," Michael snickered, fanning his face. "Heh, I guess Mother doesn't like you very much." He let out a boisterous laugh and batted his eyelashes.

"You know, it's getting late," Teddy uttered, slithering backward towards the stairs. "And I should be going." She had spent a lifetime around gay men and knew that when they got this bitchy, it was best to leave. "Goodnight," she said with a wave and headed down the steps.

"Dearie… you stay warm," he roared with laughter as he rushed to the banister and hung his head over the railing, tickled pink. "I wouldn't want you to freeze to death in this dreadfully cold weather—and come back soon. We'll play, okay?"

She stared at him, incredulous, then pushed out the door. Her whole body was shaking, and she felt sick to her stomach. Teddy wasn't sure if it was from the old lady smell, the bitchy fag, or from the disappointment of not finding Cole. All she knew was that she needed to get away as fast as possible.

"Jesus, what a freak show," she huffed, charging forward. It didn't take more than three steps before her heels kicked out from under her, and she flew up in the air.

WHOAAAAHHHHHH!

Thump.

"Ouch, my *ASS!*"

"Hals uber Kopf." Eni smiled, hovering over her.

"Excuse *ME?*"

"You're head over heels," she laughed and reached out a hand to help her up. "Thank you," Teddy said, rubbing her backside. "Was that German?"

"Ja, and *that* tail doesn't look broken to me," she said with the slightest hint of flirtation. "Darling, are you all right?"

"Yes, I'm just frustrated, that's all. This trip has been a complete disaster."

"You Americans give up too easily. Meet me here tomorrow at eleven, and I'll take you to Soho. I know of a few places where Cole likes to hang out. Maybe we'll get lucky." With a wink, Eni crossed the street. "Auf Wiedersehen."

Teddy waved goodbye, watching as she disappeared into the white building.

Until tomorrow…

25

The Olustee

01/23/98

That FUCKER leaked the video to the press. I'll rip his fuckin' head off! Where the FUCK is Mills?

Hm, Father wrote this the day he died... but who is he referring to?

DING!

"Ladies and gentlemen, this is your captain speaking. Welcome to Tampa. Local time is 6:15, and the temperature is 81 degrees. For your safety, please remain seated while the 'Fasten Seat Belt' sign is on."

Bridget checked her watch. "Perfect, I'm on time. First, Uncle Paddy, and then off to see Mrs. Kelly at the theater." She closed her father's diary, and the Confederate key fell onto her lap.

Hmm, and I wonder what you open?

● ● ●

For as long as Jeffrey Peters could remember, besting Andrew Blake Prescott was his single goal in life. Yet, he didn't always hate the Senator. There was a time when he called him his best friend, and he followed him wherever he went. The two had known each other since they were babies, being that they lived next door and their families were close.

However, that ended the day Blake was jumped in the schoolyard. Peters stood there shaking, too afraid to move, and he watched as Mills saved the day. From that moment on, he became invisible, a joke, and they never let him forget it.

Fucking assholes...

But his true hatred and jealousy of Prescott began the day he met Sarah—*It was love at first sight*, he thought as he sipped his cocktail. She was the most beautiful angel he ever did see, and he had spent a lifetime pining for her, but out of all the possibilities he had dreamt about, Peters never imagined she'd kill Blake and then take her own life.

"Why, Sarah? Why?"

Surrounded by dark woods and the finest leather furniture that one could buy, Peters stared down through the one-way mirrored glass in his office at the patrons below in his restaurant. He stroked his thin mustache, recalling his last conversation with Sarah the day of her death. He had never heard her so angry. She was furious with all the news coverage about her husband's affair. He tried to comfort her and pleaded with her to leave Blake. He promised to take her away and give her the life she deserved if only she'd give him a chance.

But now she's gone...

The Olustee Station was a steakhouse located in downtown Tampa. Frames of black and white photographs of stoic men cradling rifles equipped with bayonets and donned in Confederate military uniforms decorated the walls. The old business was a hand-me-down from his third great-grandfather, Willis Peters, who fought alongside Jubal E. Prescott for the Southern rebellion in The Battle of Olustee.

A familiar face walked into the restaurant, and he scowled, "What's he doing here?" Peters watched as the hostess walked Paddy Mills and a young blonde to a nearby table. "And who's that woman with him?" He inched closer to the glass for a better look. "That's not his wife!"

Mills pulled her into his arms for a long embrace.

Cheating bastard—

KNOCK! KNOCK!

"Who's there?" Peters barked, still watching the couple. "It's me," Agent Jones said as he entered—he was unrecognizable, dressed in a black hoodie, t-shirt, and worn-out jeans. He plopped down on the couch. "You're late, and what the hell are you wearing? I run a respectable place around here. No road rats allowed." Jones shrugged. "Sorry, my suits are at the cleaners. Besides, chicks dig the look."

"Not the women I know. You look like a bum, and what's with those boots? Jesus, did you spit-shine them—Christ, and don't you wear glasses?"

"I do, but I'm wearing contacts."

"Heh, I guess it's good that you don't look like an agent. No sense drawing attention to yourself." Peters walked over to his desk. "Did you find Bridget?"

"No, sir, all leads went flat. There were rumors she went down south to stay with family, but I couldn't find any."

"I don't ever recall Prescott mentioning he had family there.

Plus, he hated everything south of Tampa. What else did you find?"

"I stumbled onto these, sir." Jones pulled two old photos from his backpack and handed them to him. "Who is this?" Peters said, confused, staring at the little girl with dark curly hair.

"Sarah Prescott's kid."

"Her what?"

"Supposedly, this is her illegitimate child. Her name is Theo or something odd like that. I'm guessing she's probably in her late thirties by now. The notes on her were sketchy."

"You mean..." Peters scrutinized the photo more closely, "the rumors were true?" His face turned pale, and he swayed back. Jones caught him by the arm.

"Sir, you okay?"

"Get your hands off me!" Peters jerked away. "Dammit, Jones, I pay you a lot of money, and this is all you brought me?!"

"Uh, no, sir, I've got more." He reached into his satchel and pulled out a folder stamped FBI CONFIDENTIAL. "Is this what you're looking for?"

"Ah, yes... now we're talking." A dark expression grew on Peters' face as he inspected the documents. "This is exactly what I wanted."

With a cocky grin, Jones handed him a second folder. "Well, if you like those, sir, here's a little bit more candy for you."

Peters' long nose crinkled, and he snickered at the naked eight-by-tens of the Senator and sexy blonde. "Yes, yes, yes... now this should cause a stir in the press and show the world what a sleaze Prescott was." He tossed the photos on the desk and reached into his top drawer. "Good work, Jones. Here's a little something for your troubles." He threw a thick envelope at him, and the agent caught it and quickly tucked it away in his backpack.

"Thank you, sir. Is there anything else you need?"

"Yes, in fact, there is." He walked over to the glass and peered down. "We need to take out the Cleaner."

"Sir?"

 He pointed to Mills.

"Oh, gotcha, the bodyguard."

"Yes, and get the girl too."

"Which one?"

"Both of them. Now leave."

As the door shut, Jeffrey Peters picked up his drink and saluted the man he had hated his whole life.

One down, and one to go...

26

She's Back

"Thank you, Uncle Paddy, for such a lovely dinner." There was a slight smile on Bridget's face as the silver Aston Martin sped away from the restaurant. Hanging out with her uncle always made her feel special.

"My pleasure," he beamed, realizing that for the first time since her father's death, he felt a moment's peace.

"And thank you for the ride. I've been living in and out of cabs all week. It feels good to be home."

"Anytime, sweetheart. So, who are you meeting at the theater tonight?"

Bridget caressed the dashboard. "Ooh, I just love this car," she fawned, hoping to change the subject. "And you look so sexy driving it."

"Bridget, you know how to make an old man feel young again. I almost didn't recognize you with that stunning blonde hair. You look like a different woman."

"I feel like a different woman." A sad smile appeared on her face, and she stared out the window. "What a difference a week can make."

"And that haircut looks so amazing on you."

"Oh, you're too sweet, Uncle Paddy. Mother always said, 'Change your look, change your life.' I wonder if that's true?"

He contemplated her words for a moment, then nodded. "Yes, I imagine so."

"And at this time, I certainly could use a change."

"I couldn't agree more." He offered a kind smile and then shifted gears. "Listen, Bridget, I need to talk to you about a few things."

"Can't it wait?"

"No, I'm sorry, but it can't. The Elders have been hounding me—"

"The Elders?" she gasped. "I thought you hated those guys?"

"I do," he laughed, then sighed. "But with your father gone, there are many things that need to be tended to right away, and I need your help."

Bridget pursed her lips and gave him a guarded look. The thought of doing anything for those ungrateful bastards made her blood boil. Especially after everything she read in her father's diary.

"Alright, I'll make a deal with you, Uncle Paddy. First, you answer my question, and then I'll answer yours, okay?"

"That seems fair enough," he said wearily. "Go ahead, ask away."

She braced herself and then blurted, "Did my father have my Russell killed?"

"Wha—*WHAT?*"

The car swerved into the next lane, just barely missing a large truck, and he dragged on the horn.

BEEEP!

"Jesus, Bridget, of course not! Where the hell did you get that crazy idea from?" He punched the steering wheel in anger, and she froze in fear. She had never seen him lose his temper before.

"I don't know. It's just a gut feeling."

"Look, I know everything seems dark at the moment, but please, get those negative thoughts out of your head. Your father loved you very much. He'd never do anything to hurt you, especially that."

"Yeah, I guess…"

Bridget wasn't sure about anything, not even her father's love. Her instincts told her that her uncle was lying, but she knew better than to push the issue.

"So, what is it that you want to know?"

He frowned, still disturbed. Russell's death had always been a touchy subject for him. He had tried to prevent it because he knew how much Bridget loved him. But he also knew that when you crossed Andrew Blake Prescott, that was usually the last thing you did.

"Okay, so there are three things that the Elders asked me to find, and I was wondering if you knew where they were?"

"I doubt it, but for you, I'll try."

"Great, I was hoping you would say that." He smiled, trying to ease the tension. "As you know, your father never chose a successor for B&B nor trusted anyone with its secrets, and now that he's gone, the Elders are worried that certain items may fall into the wrong hands."

"I bet they are," she snickered.

"So, the first thing we need is the location of the Prescott Family vaults. Have you seen them?"

"No. What's in them?"

"We don't know." He shrugged. "The Elders think it's a storage facility that houses financial records, logs, and things like that. They said it dates all the way back to your great-grandfather Jubal's days, but no one really knows."

"Well, Father never spoke of such things in front of Mother or myself."

"Yes, I know. He was old fashion that way."

"What's the second item?"

"A key."

"For?"

"The vaults."

"Oh, that makes sense," she laughed. "What does it look like?"

"Once again, we don't really know. Some of the Elders said it was a skeleton key, others said it was jeweled, and one suggested that he saw your dad playing with an old Civil War item of sorts. Have you seen anything like that?"

Bridget's mind flashed to the relic wedged in her father's diary.

Huh, could it be?

"Bridget?"

"Oh, sorry. You know, Uncle Paddy, even if I had seen it, I wouldn't know what I was looking at. You know how Father loved to collect those things."

"Yes, he sure did." He squeezed her hand and smiled. "So, there is one last item, and I am hopeful that you may have seen it."

"And that is?"

"Your father's journal."

"His what?" she gasped.

"His diary. He's had it ever since we were kids. After his death, I looked for it but couldn't find it."

Bridget's hand rose to her neck.

"And did my father ever let you read his diary?"

"Oh, hell no! Ha, he'd turn over in his grave if he knew the Order wanted it."

"Yes, that was my thoughts exactly," she quipped, her voice a sharp, biting tone. "Uncle Paddy, knowing my father as well as you do, don't you think he would feel betrayed by this?"

"I-ah," he stuttered.

"These men want nothing more than to destroy Father's good name and to profit off his legacy."

"Jesus, I'm so sorry," he sighed, pulling up to the curb at the Old Tampa Theatre. "I guess with all the commotion over your father's death, I didn't think about it, but you're right. That bastard Peters has been causing us nothing but trouble."

"Listen to me, Uncle Paddy. No matter how dire the situation is, your first priority is to protect the memory of my father and our family's legacy. Only you can clean up the mess Father left behind. Isn't that what you do?" She sent him a knowing look, and he nodded, realizing she was giving him a direct order. "It has to be done discreetly. Nobody can know our family secrets. My father would have demanded as much from you."

"I understand."

She leaned over and kissed him on the cheek. "I have to go now. I can't be late but thank you for dinner and the ride."

"Sure thing. Hey Bridget, is it okay if I stop by this weekend?"

"I would love that. Call me." She grabbed her things and hopped out.

"Will do." He gave her a small wave and watched as she headed over to the ticket booth. Then with the sweetest smile, she turned back and blew him a kiss.

She's still my angel.

Paddy Mills put the car in gear and began to drive away when a tall blonde crossed in front of him. He hit the brakes.

"Is that... *Mrs. Kelly?*"

27

It's Getting Dark

Where to next, genius?

Clueless, Teddy stood on the corner of Minetta and Bleecker, staring at the maze of snowy streets before her. Daylight was dropping fast, as was the temperature.

Inside her thin leather boots, her feet felt like brittle twigs, and her swollen ankle throbbed. She shivered, and the cop's warning popped into her head, "If you don't want to freeze to death, make sure to be someplace warm—"

Ugh, I need to hurry.

The city appeared deserted with not a soul around. She pulled the sides of her hat down over her ears, tucked her hands deep into her pockets, and then schlepped across the street to 7th Avenue.

So, what are my options? Well, first off, I'm definitely NOT sleeping in a doorway, on a bench, or in the park. Heh, I guess I could get a hotel room, but I really can't afford it. Or I could sleep at the train station, but ugh, it's worse than the airport. And then there's Kenneth—

Abruptly, she stopped.

"No, he's *NOT* an option! And better *yet*—"

Teddy lifted her sleeve, licked her thumb, and wiped his number off her arm. "I need to focus. I have to see this through to the end, even if it kills me."

Determined, she weaved in and out of the dirge of the ice walls as she headed back to the station. Knowing that Eni was going to help her find Cole gave her hope, and she quickened her pace. Then a few blocks up, she noticed a line of people wrapped around an old, cobbled stone building.

"Ooh, is that a church?"

Teddy made a beeline for the entranceway.

"Hey, *YOU*, back of the line! Back of the line," a crusty woman yelled. She was covered in blankets and wearing bright yellow galoshes that screamed lunatic.

"I'm sorry," she said, embarrassed. "What's this line for?"

"A warm bed," the woman scowled. "There's not many of them. Yesterday, I had to sleep on the floor, and I froze my ass off. Hopefully, tonight I'll get one."

"Hopefully," Teddy repeated with a kind smile, then she hurried to the back of the line. An engraving on the wall caught her eye.

ANNO DOMINI 1856

"Heh, I never heard of him before," she muttered, contemplating the name. "It's a date, silly," the man in front of her corrected. He was bundled up from head to toe in a blue and white ski suit, with only his brown eyes showing. "It means in the year of our Lord."

"Oh, I must have missed that in Sunday school," Teddy laughed, and he shook his head as if she had just committed blasphemy.

She shrugged, feeling a bit stupid because she should've known what it meant, especially since Abby made her go to church all the time when she was younger. Yet, Teddy prided herself on blocking out just about everything the Hayeses ever taught her. Although she did have to admit that on rare occasions, some of it seeped in and, in her darker moments, brought her comfort.

Twenty minutes later, she crossed over the threshold and entered the old church. It wasn't one of those cathedrals with marble sculptures and beautiful stained-glass windows that made you feel like you were in the presence of a higher power. Nope, not at all. Instead, ugly plaques hung on scuffed-up walls, torn flyers were taped to rusty doors, and the faded carpeting was worn to the concrete flooring below.

Still, Teddy felt grateful to be there. The warmth of the sanctuary wrapped around her like a blanket, christening her with the smell of incense and lifting her spirits. She sat on the last available cot and blew a kiss up to the almighty.

I owe you one.

Her eyes floated around the room. There were homeless people, businessmen, and lots of bodies everywhere. The woman with the yellow galoshes had her arms out, staking claim to her territory, and numerous volunteers were handing out blankets and pillows. A little old lady dressed in a white uniform and wearing a WWII nurse's cap rolled the soup cart up to her bed. "Care for some soup, dear?" she said with a twinkle in her eye.

"Yes, I would love some."

"I think you'll enjoy it. I made it myself this morning and filled it with lots of love. Plus, it's plenty good for your soul too. So, make sure to drink it all up, okay?"

"Ooh, I will. It smells delicious." Teddy sensed something special about the woman and wondered aloud, "Are you an angel?"

"I sure am, dear," she said with a devilish grin. "But shhh, don't tell anyone. Let it be our little secret." Teddy pressed a hand to her heart, and a peaceful calm settled over her.

"Now eat up and get some rest. Tomorrow, you're going to find what you've been searching for."

"I will?"

"Yes, of course, dear, but you have to believe." She gave Teddy a knowing smile and then moved on to the next bed.

I DO believe!

Teddy took a sip.

Ooh, this is yummy.

A short time later, the bowl was empty, and all she could think of was sleep. Fearful of the worst, Teddy decided to leave her boot on and propped up her ankle on a pillow, then laid back on the cot and closed her eyes. Just then, a loud crying sound came from outside the vestibule, and a young woman stammered into the church. She was carrying a baby in her arms and was struggling to breathe. She clutched at her scarf, trying to remove it.

A male volunteer rushed over to help, and she fainted in his arms. He called to Teddy, "Ma'am, please take the child." Then he carried the woman to Teddy's cot. Quickly, he loosened her scarf, and in a breath, she woke and looked around, startled at all the people staring at her.

"Where's my baby?" she cried.

"Here you go. Your little girl is missing her momma," Teddy said with a heartfelt smile. She handed the baby to her and watched as the mother lovingly kissed the child over and over, promising never to let anything bad happen to her.

"Aw, I wish I had a mother like that," Teddy sighed, her heart swelling with emotion. Then in a split second, reality sank in.

Pfft, what am I thinking? This nut job had that poor child out in this freezing cold weather and almost got them both killed! Clearly, she's not all there.

Her lips pinched together. "Heh, maybe Abby and Henry weren't so bad?" But almost as soon as she said it, she laughed, remembering the insane things they put her through. "Nah, they were just as whacked."

Quietly, she grabbed her backpack and stepped away. The male volunteer approached her with a handful of blankets and pillows. "Bless your heart. That was very kind of you, and I'm sorry to say that there are no more cots available. However, you can sleep up front by the pews. It's very tranquil there." He handed her a cookie. "May the good Lord be with you."

Exhausted, Teddy made her way over and laid a blanket on the floor. It was nice and quiet, away from the others. She finished off the cookie and laughed.

"Well, at least it's not by a glass sliding door. Thanks, Kenneth!" A goofy grin rounded on her face, and she snuggled under the blankets.

I wonder if he misses me...

She smiled.

I bet he does—

BAM! BAM! BAM!

A group of noisy drunks stumbled into the church and

parked themselves right next to her.

Oh, COME ON! Really?

The stench of body odor, urine, and stale alcohol swirled in the air, and she held her breath.

Ewww, gross!

She hid her face under the blankets, trying to evade it, but it was useless. The smells were too strong, too pungent, and they permeated everything.

Ugh, I can't take it anymore!

Teddy grabbed her backpack and bolted for the exit with one objective in mind—*run, baby, run.* At first, she sprinted down 7th Avenue but then quickly slowed to a fast hobble as the sharp pains from her ankle shot up her leg. The wind slapped at her face, and her lungs burned from the frigid cold air.

Only twenty blocks to go!

The streets flew by, and her stomach growled as she fantasized about getting a long hot dog dripping with sauerkraut—OR maybe one of those toasty hot pretzels smothered in mustard! Her eyes honed in on the glowing lights of Madison Square Garden.

Just five more blocks…

Four…

Three…

Two…

OUCH!

Her ankle wobbled.

SNAP!

"What the *PPHHUCK?*"

The heel on her wounded foot broke off, and she steadied herself against a mailbox to keep from falling over. Teddy wanted to cry, but instead, she picked up the broken stump and hobbled down the escalator. Her ears perked up at the sound of the live music playing.

"Welcome to the blizzard party," a scruffy-bearded hippie yelled, and instantly, her heart lifted.

My people…

Musicians lined the walls of the underground station, waiting for their turn to perform. Travelers floated about with drinks in their hands, singing and dancing.

In the past, Teddy wouldn't have thought twice about joining in on the fun, but instead, she headed straight for the drugstore on the other side of the platform.

I need aspirins for my head, ice for my ankle, and hopefully, they have some type of glue to fix my boot.

Moments later, she found a quiet spot in the corner, away from the noisy crowd but close enough so that she could see the musicians. She dropped her stuff on the floor and sat. Her ankle was throbbing, and she carefully removed her boot.

"Yikes, it's huge!"

It was a deep shade of purplish blue, and her foot had lost all definition. "Ew, it looks like a blowfish." She filled a plastic bag with ice, wrapped it around her ankle, and popped two aspirins in her mouth. A soft melody played, and she leaned back against the wall, closed her eyes, and swayed.

This is my kind of shelter.

Forty minutes later, Teddy picked up the package of glue and read the directions. "So, it bonds to wood, rubber, plastic, and metal in sixty seconds. Hmph, that sounds too good to be true. I'd better wait a few minutes longer."

With a shrug, she dabbed the stickum to both sides, pressed the parts firmly together, and then watched as the clock on the wall ticked down five minutes.

"This looks pretty sturdy," she said, twirling the boot by the heel. "Okay, now for the real test." She slipped it on and stood, cautiously putting her weight down on it. "It seems to be holding."

She wiggled her ankle and smiled, then walked around.

"Ha! I fixed it."

An upbeat song played, and she began to dance, then—

WHOMP!

Flat on her butt again.

OUCH!

"Son of a bitch—hey, wait… what about those ugly Cleo boots?" She pulled the tan sheepskin waders from her backpack and cringed. "Eww, they're hideous. Geez, Cleo, you have no taste!" She put them on and took a few steps. "They do fit okay, except for this one." She wiggled her toes. "Something's pinching me." She took off the boot and pushed her hand deep inside.

"What's this?"

A wad of paper was stuck to the lining, and she unfolded it.

My Sweet Sister,

Don't you just love these things? Ha! They look like Eskimo boots. I figured they'd keep your feet nice and toasty in that cold place, so snuggle up! Oh, and here's some $$$ in case you find yourself in a pickle.

Love you, Cleo

PS... You better call
PSS... I mean it
PSSS... Seriously, don't make me come up there looking for you!

Teddy busted out laughing.

"Oh, you nudge!"

A flood of emotions swept over her, and she began to cry. "Cleo, I am in a pickle, and I don't know what to do." She wiped at her tears, and then her eyes went large.

"Wait, why am I crying?"

Without another thought, she threw everything in her backpack and ran up the escalator. When she reached the top, she cheered at the flashing hotel sign across the street and then gasped.

A steamy hot bath!

Quickly, she crisscrossed the ice walls, pushed through the revolving doors, and stepped up to the front desk. A male concierge at the other end of the counter flashed her the one-minute sign, and she smiled.

The lobby was a vast open space with extremely high ceilings and marble flooring. Multiple couches sat in the middle of the room, ticket booths lined the outer walls, and a tiny snack shop hid in the corner.

"Hello, my name is Arthur. How may I help you?" the older gentleman asked in a smooth, Midwestern accent.

"I'd like your cheapest room with a tub for the night, please."

"Great, that'll be sixty dollars, and I'll just need your driver's license and a credit card."

"My what?" Her smile faded. "Um, I don't have either. I was robbed, and they took everything."

"Oh dear, I hope you didn't get hurt?"

"No, thank God."

"Well, ma'am, I am so sorry to say this, but I can't give you a room without them. We have a strict policy here at the hotel."

"Oh, come on… can't you make an exception just this once?"

"No, I'm sorry, but I can't. I could lose my job."

"You don't understand!" Teddy snapped. "I've been stranded at the airport for days. The phones are down, the shelters are full—*AND* I spent the entire day slushing through this *FREEZING* cold city trying to find my boyfriend—who, as it turned out, has moved!"

The volume of her voice rose, and fear grew in his eyes that one of the other guests might hear. He waved a hand to quiet her down, but she continued on her rant.

"Smelly homeless drunks, *CRAZY* ladies in galoshes—*AND* my favorite boot broke on a pothole!" She threw up her hands at her wits' end. "And did I tell you that I twisted my ankle? It's all swollen and purple—wanna see?"

He shook his head.

"Arthur, I just need one night." A tear rolled down her cheek. "Please don't make me sleep on the floor at the train station."

"Oh, hell," he sighed. "I could never let you do that. Besides, there must be a blizzard exception in the rule book," he winked, and his expression softened. "Promise not to tell?"

Teddy crossed her heart and handed him the money.

"Okay, so let's see what we have available." Quickly, he typed into the terminal. "Ah yes, room 1511, a room with a tub."

He went to the end of the counter and returned with the key.

"Here you go, Ms. Hayes. If you need anything, just let me know. I'll be here all night, and I'll see you in the morning. Enjoy your bath."

"Thank you, I will. Goodnight, Arthur," she said with a grateful smile, then headed to the elevators. The area was quiet, and no one else was around.

While she waited, she learned about the hotel's history from the historical plaques that hung on the walls and guessed it hadn't changed much since it was first built in 1919 because everything from its brass mailboxes to elevators seemed way, way old.

Like from the Titanic old!

DING!

The doors slid open, and up she went. The ride was slow, and when she reached her floor, the smell of musty wallpaper almost knocked her over. Her suite was at the end of the hallway, and with a jiggle of the key, she entered.

To say the room was a bit small was an understatement. The queen-size bed took up most of it, leaving little space for the bulky wooden nightstand and dresser. She dropped her stuff on the bed and headed to the bathroom, undressing on the way. It too was very tiny, almost claustrophobic, with about a foot of space between the black and white tiled walls and the claw-foot tub. She put the stopper in the drain, then cranked the water temperature to hot and added a dash of cold.

While it filled, she walked over to the window and stared out at the city's neon lights. Her skin tingled from the mixture of the cold air seeping in through the glass and the hot air rising up from the heater. A rush of hope swept over her, and she glanced at the phone on the nightstand.

I wonder if it's working...

She picked up the receiver, hit 9, and it buzzed.

Mmm, that's promising...

With a grin, she pulled Cole's number from her backpack, grateful that she had saved it from the lemonade disaster, and dialed. It took a moment to ring, and she grumbled under her breath, "Please don't be the operator... pretty please—"

CLICK!

"Hi, I'm not home. You know what to do—"

BEEP!

"Hi Cole, it's me, Teddy... I made it to the Big Apple," she laughed. "I'm staying at the Hotel Pennsylvania across the street from the Garden on 7th Avenue. Come visit and let's have fun. I can't wait to see you, bye."

Teddy cupped her mouth in disbelief, then screamed for joy as she danced to the bathroom. "The angel lady was right!" She stepped into the tub and moaned. "Ooh, this is heaven. Thank you, my beautiful, sweet, pain in the ass, sister!"

Blissfully, she submerged.

28
Bridget

—They were screaming, and we couldn't shut them up! So, we dragged the darkies out of bed and into the woods. We even had them dig a hole just to scare the crap out of them! Ha-ha... that'll keep those bastards from ever looking at my girl again!

Back in Tampa...

It was after midnight when Bridget entered the old mansion. The lighting, the decor, the pictures, everything was the same, but it wasn't. She dropped her keys on the foyer table and headed up.

And oh, how she dreaded this moment. Her heart, gripped by panic, pounded loud in her ears. She could barely breathe, yet, she was determined to see it through.

"I must do this..." With each step, the grand staircase brought her closer and closer to the door—*their door*, and she gasped in trepidation. "The room of death."

Silent tears glided down her face. A splash of melancholy, so pensive, filled her psyche with memories of snuggling up in bed with her parents on her birthdays, holidays, and yes, even when she dreamt about the one-armed boogeyman who was the villain in all her nightmares.

Her hands trembled as she stepped up to the door and ripped off the yellow crime scene tape. Then with a quick turn of the handle, she pushed it open and entered. A mixture of decay and Pine-Sol smacked her in the face.

Bridget rushed to the window and opened it, gulping in the fresh air to keep from vomiting. She waited a moment for her stomach to settle, then slowly turned and took in the room for the very first time since her parents' death.

The walls had been bleached clean, but she could still see faint outlines from where the blood had splattered. She stared at the broken pieces of the lamp lying on the floor and tried to imagine what happened that dark night. Her eyes fixated on a smidgen of blood left behind from where her father's head had rested on the wall.

"Oh, how dreadful!" She burst into tears. "These gruesome mosaics will forever haunt me. I can't deal with this—Alpheus," she screamed into the dead silence. "Alpheus, where are you?"

"Yes, Madame," the old manservant said, entering the room. He was in his late seventies, meticulously groomed, and even though it was after midnight, still dressed in his butler's attire. His family had served the Jenkins family for generations. Yet, when Sarah and Blake married, her father, Frederick, insisted that Alpheus go with her to help manage the household—but mostly to keep a close eye on things.

"There you are, Alpheus," her lip quivered. "I was afraid that I was all alone." She caught her breath. "I am not strong enough to deal with this."

"My dear child, give it time." His worried eyes studied her carefully. "You've suffered a great loss."

"I am so grateful to have you here." She grabbed his hand and squeezed it. "Always, Madame. This is my life, and you are my family." His kind eyes eased her pain, and he guided her out of the room. "Shall I bring you something to eat?"

"Yes, please." Her face softened. "I'll be in Father's study."

"Very well, Madame."

Alpheus headed down the stairs, and her eyes followed, scrutinizing the place. It was as if she was seeing the mansion in its true form for the very first time. Priceless antebellum collectibles were displayed everywhere, making the house more like a museum than a home. The antique papered walls showed their age with curled seams and faded patterns, and behind them was the rarest mahogany woods that one could find, but to her, it was now her parents' burial tomb.

Lightly, she dragged her fingers over the thick wooden railing as she passed by her mother's study, then hesitated. A nervous intake of breath climbed into her lungs, and Bridget stared through the French glass doors expecting to see her mother seated behind the big white desk. Curious, she entered and slowly made her way around the room. Of course, it was beautifully decorated, covered in romantic florals, shimmering crystals, antique lace, and meticulously in order. She expected as much from her mother. Yet, there was a letter sticking out of the desk's top drawer.

She looked over her shoulder to ensure that Alpheus wasn't around and then nervously sat, which she was never allowed to do. And with a quick pull of the drawer handle, Bridget opened it. The handwritten letter stared at her.

01/22/98

My Love,

I don't know how much longer I can wait for you. My heart longs for the day we can be together—

Quickly, Bridget pushed the drawer shut. Shame swept over her as the last conversation that she had with her mother on the night of her death came to mind. It was raining. She had just come home from a party, and her mother was seated behind the desk reading the letter and looked up.

"Bridget don't hover by the door. If you've something to say, then say it." Dozens of letters lay open on top of the desk, which her mother quickly threw in a floral treasure box and tucked away deep in the back of the closet.

"Mother, you called saying you needed to see me."

"Oh, yes, ha—I guess I did. Darling, did you know that your father is a no-good cheating liar?" She let out a shrill laugh, grabbed her drink, and guzzled it down.

"Are you drunk?"

"None of your business—you're just like him. I should have never married that bastard. Without me, he'd be nothing."

"You know how I hate it when you talk ill of Father. He adores you and lives to make you happy."

"Naturally, you would say that." Her eyes narrowed. "You have no idea who your father really is." She cackled, "Lil, sweet innocent Bridget loves her daddy."

"Stop it!" Bridget stomped her foot. "Father worships the ground you walk on, as does everyone else. Besides, I don't believe any of those horrible rumors."

"Are you calling me a liar?"

"Of course not."

"How dare you take his side."

"I am not taking his side—"

"Yes, you are. Just as you always do!" The vein in her mother's neck bulged, and she shrieked, "Get out! Just get out! I can't stand to even look at you!"

"Mother, stop!"

"You make me sick! Now just leave!" She collapsed into her chair and started to cry. "Before him, I knew what real love was…"

Her mother's words hung in the air as if they were just spoken, and a tear rolled down her cheek. "Maybe if I had listened to her and given her the benefit of the doubt, they'd still be alive." The thought made her want to vomit.

I need air.

Bridget rushed down the hall and into her father's study. Instantly, she was greeted with the delicious scent of vanilla. His pipe sat cradled by the edge of the desk, filled to the brim with tobacco.

"Waiting for its master."

A sorrowful smile rose, and she ran her fingers down the back of his chair. A sense of calm washed over her. In some odd way, the dark woods, rich leather furniture, and wall-to-wall bookcases made her feel as if he was there with her.

It's your favorite…

She lifted his pipe to her nose and, for a brief moment, forgot about death and delighted in its aroma. Bridget idolized her father, and he spoiled her like no other man ever could.

"A pony for me?" she shouted on her sixth birthday.

"Of course, my sweet darling. How much do you love me?" he teased, cradling her in his arms and kissing her angelic face.

"More than everything!"

Bridget sank into her father's chair, still feeling his arms cradled around her. "Oh, how simple life was back then." She closed her eyes and softly cried. "Without you, I am lost. I need your guidance—"

"Madame?" A gentle knock tapped on the door. "I thought you might like a glass of your father's favorite brandy," Alpheus said as he entered and placed a tray of food and drinks on the desk.

"Yes, thank you."

It broke his heart to see the hopeless tears streaming down her face, knowing he couldn't make things better. "Now, now, my child, it's going to be all right, you'll see. You'd be surprised at how life has a way of working itself out, even in the darkest of times."

"But Alphy, this is too much for me to bear." Her lip trembled. "I want to be brave. I want to be strong, but I know nothing of Father's world. How could he leave me this way?"

"Your father was a very complex man," he sighed and poured the brandy into a snifter. "He left this world way too soon, and if I may say, with a great deal of unfinished business." He handed her the drink, then pulled a skeleton key from his pocket. "Unfortunately, time is of the essence, and there is much for you to learn. Come, follow me."

Confused, Bridget watched as he walked over to the bookshelf, pushed the light switch casing up, and inserted the key. With the twist, the wall became a turnstile to a rustic-looking stairway.

Apprehensively, she peered in and smiled. "Oh, Alpheus, Father did like his secret hiding places, didn't he?"

"Yes, Madame, he did." He gave her a knowing look. "I imagine you'll find the answers to the questions you seek in there."

"Like always, you know just what I need."

"Very well, Madame. Is there anything else I can get you?"

"No, thank you, that'll be all."

Fascination took over, and Bridget stepped into her father's secret world.

No judgment here, only love…

Down three flights of stairs she went, and then she paused at the last railing so that she could take in the cavernous room in its entirety.

Wow, look at all this… clearly, this is the darker side of Andrew Blake Prescott!

The chamber was laid out in sections of three, with clusters of exhibits here and there, almost like a carnival. It had black walls with colorful, provocative posters, low ceilings, and dark wooden floors.

Bridget glanced over most of the displays until she came upon a white hooded outfit on a mannequin. Instantly, she realized it was a shrine to the Ku Klux Klan.

We dragged the darkies—

Heh, so that's what he meant.

Mementos, photos, and keepsakes were showcased on the table before her. She stepped in closer to have a better look, and to her shock, there was her father dressed in his KKK robe, proudly holding a pointy hat under his arm and smiling along with his other fellow Klansmen. She knew the men and cringed a little.

I wonder if Mother knew ...

With a shrug, Bridget moved on. Occasionally, she would stop and peer into one of the many boxes scattered throughout the room and pull out a newspaper clipping on the death of one of her father's friends.

With each display, a growing sadness swept over her at the reality her father was no hero and that maybe her mother was right.

"So many lies and so much deception." She collapsed to the floor, crying. "I can't do this... I just can't. I'm not strong enough— but Father needs me! I can't forsake him now! He's the only one that ever truly loved me—I don't *CARE* what he's done!" Her lip quivered. "And I'm his only daughter."

She dried her eyes and stood.

"So, what's next..."

A table sat before her, covered in large books and multiple ledgers. She grabbed one of them, opened it, and laughed. "Oh, you got to be kidding me. It's Father's symbols from his diary." She frowned but wasn't surprised to learn that the red slash through a name meant death.

Bridget pulled up a chair and sat, then scanned through each ledger, scrutinizing the names of those who owed her father money, the type of blackmail he had on them, and whether or not they paid up.

Extortion, blackmail, murder, Uncle Paddy is the Cleaner. And yet, there is nothing about the vaults or Theodora Hayes. Heh, what am I missing here?

Pursing her lips, she looked around the room one last time.

Wait, what is that?

A small table sat in the back with only a tape recorder and microphone upon it. Curious, Bridget walked over and hit the play button.

"*CLICK*—Thursday, January 22nd, 1998. Today, I caught Sarah reading a bunch of old love letters, and in a fit of rage, I told her that I was the one who started the fire that killed her beloved poet."

He sipped his drink and sneered.

"At first, her anger, all fiery and combative, was brilliant to watch. Absolutely stunning. It reminded me of the girl I fell in love with so many years ago, but then all the blood drained from her face, and she stammered to the door. I thought she was having a heart attack—"

CRASH!

"Oh, shit, my drink fell over. Ugh, what a waste of good liquor. Where's that towel? Oh, here it is… ah, that's much better." He pushed the glass aside.

"Okay… so where was I? Oh, yeah, a heart attack—nope, ha! She was just pissed. That bitch turned to me with those damn cold eyes of hers and said she was going to make me pay for what I had done. Said she'd hate me for an eternity and that I'd better watch my back. Ha! I love you too, darling."

He sighed.

"I love you too—*CLICK!*"

29

Those Eyes

Spasms rippled through her beautiful frame as her body arched, then collapsed on top of him. The taste of his mouth was so much better than she had remembered. His kiss softer, his breath intoxicating.

He bit down on her lower lip, then scraped his teeth against the warmth of her neck. It sent jolts deep into her core and Teddy drank in the sweet mixture of his Old Spice and sweat. Suddenly, he lifted her hips up higher and higher and then slid into her again.

Oh my, a second round?

The saturation of the indigo pigment on her skin resembled a Cézanne painting. A bright red finger painted circles around her nipples, squeezing, pinching, torturing them until he took one in his mouth. His usual calloused hands were soft and warm as they brushed against her skin, lightly feathering her chills.

The sex felt different. It was slower, deeper, more passionate. She connected with him, meeting his moves, matching his need, feeding the insatiable hunger until the dizziness swallowed them up in a frenzy. Her eyes rolled back, her lips quivered, and then his piercing blue eyes locked onto hers, and she shuddered awake.

"Damn him!"

Her body hummed as she stared at the ceiling.

"Jesus, that was the best sex I've ever had," she laughed, and a spasm caught her by surprise. "Mmm, too bad, it was just a dream."

The rustling of the wall heater switched on and she kicked off the blankets. The toasty room felt heavenly on her bare skin. She looked at the clock on the desk.

Hm, it's four, and still no word from Cole…

Teddy stood up, and a sharp pain shot up her leg from her swollen ankle. With a grunt, she popped two aspirins in her mouth and headed to the bathroom for water.

Now why is this blue-eyed janitor invading my dreams? He is SO not my type! She hovered over the sink and took a sip. *Pfft, who am I kidding? He's gorgeous, that's why. And intense, which I LOVE, and a bit of a nudge, like Cleo—eww, erase that thought!*

She snorted and looked at the bags under her eyes, then winced. "The last thing I need is a man that is as much of a pain in the ass as my sister."

She returned to the bed and propped up her foot.

I need to focus on my beautiful Cole. The FABULOUS painter extraordinaire and the LOVE of my life. And, most importantly, the one whom I will be reuniting with tomorrow—but DAMN, that dream was SO hot!

Teddy cuddled the pillow.

Hmm, I wonder if he—and by he, I mean Kenneth, Mr. Blue-Eyes, is as good in bed as he was in my dream? She grinned. *I bet he is. He has that kind of swagger about him that a man gets when he knows he can please a woman. Heh, too bad he's not an artist. Ha, I'm so shallow, but he does have that tortured look in his eye. Hm, I wonder why—*

STOP IT!

She slammed her hand down, then looked over at the phone.

Oh, Cole, where are you?

She punched the pillow a few times and turned to her side.

Does a sex dream constitute as cheating? Her brows furrowed. *If it does, I'm screwed.* She closed her eyes and grinned.

Goodnight, Kenneth.

30

Jilted Lover

Friday, 8:45 am
Police Headquarters

Back in Tampa...

"Listen up, folks. It's been a busy morning, so this is gonna be brief," Captain Russo yelled. He was a stocky, dark-haired Italian with a thick New Jersey accent. He stood behind the lectern in front of an overcrowded briefing room packed with reporters, cops, and, to Agent Walters' surprise, Jeffrey Peters.

Hmm, what's he doing here?

Annoyed, Walters listened from the back of the room. He didn't like what he was hearing. Information was leaking to the press faster than he could access it.

"So, at O-three hundred hours, behind the old Tampa Theatre, a female body was discovered. The victim was in her early forties, killed by a single bullet to the heart. Her name is being withheld so that all family members can be notified. Until that time, we have nothing further to add. Questions?"

"Did the victim know her killer?" a male reporter shouted. "I heard it was a jilted lover," a woman interjected.

"An old-school crime, revenge, payback, a tumultuous love affair gone wrong." Russo let out a loud, sarcastic laugh. "At this time, it's anyone's guess—"

"I heard it was the Senator's mistress," a sexy blonde reporter sneered. "You know, the one from the video. Is that true, Captain?" The volume of the room went silent, then exploded into questions, and Walters glanced over at Peters, who was absorbing every single word with a satisfied grin.

"Settle down! Settle down," Russo shouted. He eyed the reporter. "Ya see here, Missy, it's our job to find the murderer, and it's your job to report what we tell you." Pissed, he turned to the others. "Now, if any of yous guys interfere with our investigation, we're gonna have problems, capisce?"

"But you haven't told us anything that we didn't already know," she rebuffed. "So, is it, or isn't it the woman from the video?"

"Oh, I'm sorry, am I boring you? As I told you already, her name is being withheld until we contact her family. I'm sure you Einsteins can understand that. So being that there are no more questions, we're done for the day." Agitated, Russo packed up his things and stormed out.

Stewart walked up to Walters, smirking, "Well, that was enlightening."

"What a waste of time. Any news on why Mrs. Kelly was there?"

"Nope, but I'm guessing blackmail."

"It does have that kind of stench."

"Yup, killed with a .38, and I'm guessing it's *that* .38. And I don't think it's a coincidence that she was shot in the heart. Her purse was still clutched in her hand, and her body sprawled out in the gutter with her legs spread wide open." Stewart shrugged. "The poor thing never saw it coming."

"Any witnesses?"

"Nope," he frowned. "None that are talking."

"Well, whoever did it was brazen enough to do it in public. It's almost as if the killer is toying with us. I'd bet my life he's here getting his kicks off, just watching us chase Prescott's ghost around." Walters scanned the room. "And did you see Jeffrey Peters over there grinning? I bet he knows something."

Stewart's brow rose, and he pointed to the blonde who had just finished talking to him and grinned. "I dated that hottie about a year ago—ha, she's fun. I'll go question her and see what she knows." He winked. "I'll meet you by the car."

"Good luck," Walters said with a nod, and he scribbled Anne Kelly's name to the bottom of a long list of names on his notepad and tucked it away in his jacket. He hadn't been an agent long, but he had good instincts and knew when something didn't feel right.

Another body added to the late Senator's Dead Friends Club. So much power around a single man. That kind of influence always leads to nothing but trouble.

From his early days on the force, he relied heavily on his instincts, but what really pissed him off was being played the fool—and with the way Mrs. Kelly had died, it felt like someone was playing him.

It's just too many coincidences for my liking, and any more than two screams cover-up. First, the gun is missing, then the note, a trail of dead business partners, and now dead lovers.

If the Senator was still alive, he'd be my first suspect, but he's not, so who then?

"Hey, Walters—Walters, wait up," Agent Jones called, rushing over with his arms full of folders. "I've got the documents you requested."

Awkwardly, he freed a finger to push his glasses straight. "Jones, when are you gonna get those fixed? Jesus, you're never gonna get laid."

"Yeah, I know," he laughed and handed him the folders. Walters looked them over and frowned, "There's nothing about Cole O'Keefe in here. Did you find his place in the Village yet?"

"No, nothing definite. The phone lines are still down, and he's been on the move. Plus, the lousy weather hasn't helped any."

"Shit—hey, by the way, what happened that day you tagged the gun at Prescott Manor?"

"Nothing special, just the standard protocol stuff."

"Anybody hanging around or asking questions?"

"Nope, just me and Grady."

"No maid or butler?"

"Well, Alpheus let us in and brought us drinks, but if he wanted to take anything, he could have done so before we arrived. He found the bodies."

"True." Walters nodded. "What about Bridget? Was she there?"

"No, I don't recall seeing her."

"Hm, good to know." Stewart pointed to the door, and Walters finished up. "Alright, Jones, I've gotta run, but let me know as soon as you find O'Keefe, okay?"

"Yup, will do, but who is this guy? Does he have something to do with the case?"

"Sort of, we're looking for his girlfriend."

"What's her name?"

"Theodora Hayes."

"Huh, interesting… very interesting. Well, keep your fingers crossed that it quits snowing up there, and hopefully, I'll find him soon," Jones snickered, and with a nod, Agent Walters headed for the door.

31

The Exes

From a dead sleep, Teddy jerked awake and grabbed the phone.

"Cole, is that *you?*"

"Good morning, Ms. Hayes. This is Arthur from the front desk. Will you be checking out today?"

"Oh, Arthur… sorry, I thought you were someone else. Yes, I'll be out by ten. Thank you." Groggy, she hung up and glanced at the clock. "Shit, it's already nine. I better hurry, but first, let me try Cole again." Teddy dialed, and when the phone rang, instead of waiting for him to answer, she hung up and laughed. "Nah, I think I'll surprise him."

She kicked off the sheets and was ready to start her day. Shockingly enough, she felt rejuvenated. She guessed it was from sleeping in a warm bed, but deep down, Teddy knew it was from her dream. With a pleasant shrug, she crossed over to the windowsill and grabbed her freshly cleaned clothes off the heater that she had left drying overnight, and headed into the bathroom. An hour later, she handed in her key and blew Arthur a kiss goodbye.

"Thanks for everything," she hollered as she pushed through the revolving doors and onto the sidewalk. It was chilly out, but the snow had thawed considerably, and the city was bustling with life.

The stroll down 7th Avenue was stunning as the sun peeped in and out of the tall skyscrapers, warming her face. The pain in her ankle eased up, but Teddy refused to accept that Cleo's ugly boots had anything to do with it and decided that she would have preferred the pain if it meant having her sexy heels back. Forty minutes later, she rounded the corner onto Minetta Street, and there stood Eni dressed all in black, smoking a clove.

"Now, who would have thought you'd be early, Ms. Hayes," she said with a wink, her German accent sounding more pronounced with each drag of the cigarette. "You seem ze type to sleep in." She flicked the butt to the ground, stomping on its cinders with her pointy-toed boot, and then blew a puff out the corner of her smile. Grinning, Teddy greeted her with a kiss on the cheek.

"Good morning, Enilika."

"Darling, did you get laid last night? You have that sexy glow."

"Oh, I ah, um, no…" Teddy flushed red.

"Ha, I'm just playing vith you. I can see why Cole likes you. You're absolutely yummy. Come on, let's go find lover boy."

"So, how do you know Cole?" Teddy smiled at her suspiciously. "Are you one of his girls too?"

"Nah, he's not my type." Eni pursed her lips, accessing the snow-cleared streets. "Over there, let's go that way." She charged through an alleyway, then dashed in and out of a couple blocks, turning back every now and again to check on Teddy and holler something.

"So, the phones are working," she said, crossing the street. "I called around, and it seems our illusive Cole has been couch hopping." She paused at a busy intersection and lit a clove. "Phyllis told me he's bouncing from place to place."

"But I left a message on his machine last night."

"Impossible. It's disconnected."

"Shit, maybe I dialed the wrong number—again."

"Again?" Eni's brow rose, and she waved her across the street. "It's this way."

"Heh, it's a long story and a boring one at that." Teddy let out a frustrated sigh and pulled her beanie down over her frozen earlobes.

"Well, SoHo is just around the corner. Are you ready to meet some of his exes?"

"Some of his *who?*" Teddy's mouth went slack.

"Cole's girls. Hopefully, he's vith one of them."

"Oh, no!" Teddy halted.

"What dear?"

"Ugh, I thought you were taking me to a friend's house—*NOT* one of his lovers! Fuck, this trip is getting worse by the second." She kicked the snow. "Geez, I'm so naive. Forget it. I made a huge mistake coming here."

"Theodora," Eni said softly. "What did you expect?"

"It's just that, Eni… well, I… um," she caught her breath and paused. "I just didn't expect this, okay?" She wiped a tear from her eye. "And what makes things worse is that if I don't find him, I have nowhere else to go."

"Ah, gotcha." Eni's face softened. "Relax, Schnuckiputzi. You can stay at my place. It's not much, but it's warm, and Michael will feed us."

"The *Michael* from yesterday?"

"Yeah, he likes you."

"No, he doesn't—he laughed at me and treated me like a lovesick schoolgirl!" Eni shot her a lopsided grin. "You mean you aren't?" Teddy frowned, "And he was thrilled when his mother told me off!"

"Yeah, he's a bit wicked that way, but he can be really sweet too. He's just a big ole bear, and he has a big ole crush on Cole, which, I'm sure made him very jealous of you." With her sleeve, she wiped Teddy's face dry. "Theodora, Michael *loves* drama, and Cole is drama with a cherry on top."

"He is, isn't he?" Teddy sniffled. "Huh, I guess some things never change—and how do you fit into all of this?"

"I'm his neighbor. A frustrated engineer by day who dreams about being a poet at night. Plus, I'm obsessed vith artists. The more tortured their soul, the more I fall in love vith them."

"Interesting, those are my weaknesses too." Teddy smiled. "I'm also a poet. Well, actually, I haven't written anything lately. I've been uninspired. Hey, recite me something, please?"

"No way… are you crazy?"

"Oh, come on, I'd love to hear one of your poems. Besides, it beats talking about Cole or one of his exes, don't you agree?"

"It sure does… I'll tell you what, I'll share one of mine if you share one of yours, okay?" Eni grinned. "Wait, even better— Theodora Hayes, I challenge you to a poetry-off!"

"A *what?*"

"I say two lines, you repeat them, and then finish off the poem, okay?"

"Oh, Eni, I'm not good off the cuff like that."

"Come on, Theodora. Just give it a try. It'll be fun." She gave her a naughty smile. "I promise I'll be gentle with you."

"Pfft, I doubt that," Teddy snickered as she loosened her scarf and exhaled. "I bet you're a poetry shark, aren't you?"

"I've been called worse," Eni chuckled. "Hey, let's do a limerick. They're easy. Now remember to listen, repeat, then finish. Got it? Here it goes, so…"

> *There once was a*
> *German lassie named Eni,*
>
> *Who frolicked in the cold*
> *vith the flatlander Teddy…*

Your turn—oh, and it has to be naughty and fun."

"Naughty *too?*" Teddy scratched her head. "Geez, you gave me the hardest part." She mumbled the lines to herself a few times, then smiled. "Okay, I think I've got it…

> *So, there once was a*
> *German lassie named Eni,*
>
> *Who frolicked in the cold*
> *with the flatlander Teddy.*
>
> *They searched high,*
> *they searched low,*
>
> *Through the towns*
> *and through the snow,*
>
> *For the painter's HOs*
> *are many!"*

"Ha-ha! Yes, they are! Bravo, Theodora, bravo!"

Teddy grinned. "Oh, that was such *CHEESE!"*

"I know! Ha-ha, but I love it!" Eni beamed with joy as she

walked up to an art gallery on the corner of an old five-story cast-iron building and peered in through the window. "So, this is our first stop, but I must warn you, she's a bit wacky."

"Who is?" Teddy looked over her shoulder, trying to catch a glimpse. "Quinlan, Cole's ex, but she's fun. Well, sort of, in a quirky way. So, let me do the talking because she can get unnerved easily." Teddy nodded and pulled off her hat. She looked as though she was about to throw up, and with a quick pull of the handle, they entered.

The place had a loft-style layout with high ceilings, pendant lights, a reception area, and rows of brightly colored works of contemporary art hanging on freshly painted white floating walls.

An attractive brunette in her forties stood in the center of it all. She was dressed in an oversized baggy red sweater that hung down low over her long white frilly skirt, followed by hot pink leg warmers scrunched at the ankles, drooping over her white sneakers. There was a crazed look in her eye as she swung wildly into the air. "That's our girl," Eni chuckled, and Teddy's eyes grew large.

"Bug!" she screeched, scurrying back and away from a big black flying critter that zigzagged around her head. In a panic, she panted, "Eww-BUG-bug-*BUG*-bug-BUG! Enilika, ew—*help ME!*"

Grabbing a magazine, Eni swatted, and in one shot, the fly dropped to the floor.

"Enilika, you're my savior! Oh, you're such a doll. I truly adore you." Her body shuddered, "Ooh, that little nasty thing, how it got in here, I'll never know." She beamed at Eni, and then her eyes narrowed on Teddy. "And who might you be?"

"This is Theodora Hayes. She's from Florida."

"During a blizzard, is she crazy?" She glared at Teddy, incredulous. "I know that face." Her brows rose, and she was just about to say something when Eni took her by the arm and led her over to a blood-red, monotone painting of a naked woman stabbed in the heart.

"Quinnie, darling, did you do something different with your hair? It's just fabulous. Oh, and I just love this artist you're showcasing. Is he your new toy?"

"Eni, you know me too well, and I've missed you so. Things have been so boring as of late. What brings you here today?"

"I'm looking for Cole. Have you seen him?"

"O'Keefe? Nah, I haven't seen that little shit since he borrowed money from me and took off. Last I heard, he was living with someone in Queens. One moment, let me ask Loretta. You know how she keeps track of everyone's business."

She cupped her mouth and yelled, "Hey, Lolo… is Cole shacking up with that woman from Queens?"

An older woman, reading a newspaper in the back of the studio, popped her head up and shouted, "Wadda you talking about? You're thinking of Joey, Joey the lip, the sax player. That lucky bastard hooked up with a hoochie mama who's rich. Her daddy owns hotels or something," she snickered. "I heard O'Keefe is banging Suzi, the one from the parlor."

Teddy went pale, and Eni shifted gears.

"Suzi on Sullivan, right?"

"Yup, that's the one."

"All right, ladies, thank you."

"Eni, darling, please stay a moment. I want to ask you something, but just the two of us, if that's okay with your friend?"

"Yes, of course. I'll just wait outside." With a wave and a strained smile, Teddy pushed out the door.

The city block was bustling with people, some shoveling snow while others darted in and out of the buildings. She sat on a stoop and played with the snow, trying to shake off her foul mood, but her stomach kept rumbling—she was hungry. It didn't help that she hadn't eaten all day or that the Italian restaurant down the street was scenting the entire neighborhood with delicious aromas.

"Take care, ladies," Eni said as she stepped out. "Ready to go?"

"Did he really sleep with that? I must be out of my mind, pfft…"

"And why is that love?"

Teddy grabbed a handful of snow and made a ball. "Eni, what am I doing here?"

"My guess ist you're crazy."

"I'm chasing a dream, aren't I?" Eni shot her a deadpan look. "Okay, so I am." Teddy threw the snowball and scowled, "I'm searching for a memory of a man that I don't even know exists anymore."

"Oh, he exists all right *and* probably better left as a memory if you ask me."

Teddy shook her head in frustration. "Can you make me feel any worse?"

"Aww, I'm just playing vith you. I know Cole cares about you."

"You do?"

"He told me so. Now let's get moving before the day is gone." She headed across the street, and Teddy stood there. "Eni, come on, tell me what he said."

"Move your tuchus, and I'll tell you on ze way."

"Oh, poo, you're no fun!"

"You're cute, Theodora. I'm crushing on you."

The words were music to Teddy's ears, and she sped up to catch her. The sun peered through the clouds, and she tilted her face to soak it in.

"He called you, and I quote, 'Girlfriend Zero'."

"A *who*—what does that *even* mean?"

"Darling, you're the one zat ruined him—"

"*NO!* He did *not* say *THAT!*"

"Ja! Da kannst du Gift drauf nehmen."

"*Heh?* English, *please*—"

"You betcha tuchus he did!"

"But I didn't." Teddy paused to reflect, "Did I? Hmm, I guess I did."

"Yup, and I'm sure that every girl we see today will know about you. They all saw your painting and heard ze tears, and I'm pretty sure they hate you—"

"*Moi?*" Her brows rose. "Toi, and ja! And the next place, well… Cole is a bit of a manwhore, so there might be several women he slept vith."

"Oh, that's just lovely." Teddy threw her hands up. "Wow, I just had a revelation!" Eni's brow lifted. "I've decided that men are *MUCH* more sexier when they are left as a mystery—*AND,* by the way, your accent is getting thicker."

"Heh, I'm hungry, and all dis valking ist exhausting."

They crossed the street and headed southwest. "Okay, so now it's your turn to lead. Maybe you could try one vith a little bit more *oomph*—like a haiku. You know, a three-line poem vith seventeen syllables. Do you haiku?"

"Yes, but it's been a while," she frowned.

"Oh, and it has to be the classic five, seven, five-syllable count."

"Give me a topic then." Eni waved at their surroundings. "Zis snow will do."

"Hmm, let me think," Teddy murmured, spreading her fingers wide as she counted and rambled on. "Okay, I got it…

Swirling folds of cold.
Dark haze covers the sun's light.
The snowbird dances. "

"Oooh, good imagery, Theodora, and the perfect syllable count too." Teddy bowed. "Okay, Ms. Smarty-Pants, it's your turn."

"Ew, I forgot how much I hate these." Eni bubbled her lips and laughed, "Die Daumen drücken…

Hush ze bitter white.
Clinging to ze cloudless sun.
Ring of breath rises. "

She curtseyed. "Voila."

"Wow, you're really good."

"I have my moments," Eni grinned, then she pointed to the beauty parlor across the street and sighed. "That's Suzi's place."

The salon was long and narrow and glowed in glossy whites and silvery fixtures with a splash of red for sizzle. Three female stylists, all in their early thirties, were gathered around the front counter, laughing, engrossed in a conversation.

"Ready?" Eni said, gripping the door's handle. "By the way, the blonde is Suzi."

"Oh, *great.*"

"Happy faces," she chortled and entered. "Ladies!"

"Enilika," they all cheered.

"Guten Tag!"

"We're bored," pouted Patsy, a fiery redheaded Southerner with green wingtip eyes. To her right stood Vee, a tall Asian beauty covered in tattoos. "Eni, this place is so dead that I won't be able to afford my rent this month."

"Well, don't look at me, darling. I'm poor," she teased.

"—It's you," Suzi interrupted, glaring at Teddy. "It's the *ONE* from the painting."

"It is her," Patsy gasped, and Vee's stenciled eyebrows rose.

"We've heard so much about you," Suzi sneered. "The sex, the lust, and all the itsy-bitsy things our charming Cole made us promise never to repeat." She gave the girls a mischievous smile. "We love our little secrets, don't we, girls?"

"Yes, we do," they giggled.

Aside from being a hot blonde with smoky eyes, Suzi had all the right curves in all the right places and the attitude to work it. Teddy managed a smile, and Eni interjected, "Suzi is Cole around?"

"No, dear, sorry he isn't."

"Do you know where he is—"

"Cole. Cole. Cole… my, that boy has more women than a girl can keep track of."

"Amen," Patsy thundered, and she threw her hands up in the air. "And he has more coming to Jesus moments than my pastor."

"Who are you kidding?" cackled Vee. "You don't have a pastor, and we both know you're going straight to hell."

"Sinners sin, baby… ha, sinners sin." Patsy winked at Teddy.

Suzi's face darkened, and she walked over to the nearest styling booth and threw a hairbrush into the drawer with a bang. The girls went silent.

"Hey Vee, don't you love that tormented look Cole gives when he wants sex?"

"Oh yeah, he does that pouty, sexy thing all the time, but with him, it's all work and no play."

"And who does the work, girls?"

"We do," they giggled.

"Still, don't ya just love a playful man?" Vee said in a dreamy voice, then she frowned, "Heh, but that's not our Cole. Nope, he's not playful at all—he's a tornado of torment."

"Yup, that's sooo him, babe." Patsy put a backward hand to her forehead and swooned, "Oh, my darling sweet Cole, don't cut off your little ol' ear for me."

Eni rolled her eyes, and the girls laughed harder. Speechless, Teddy leaned back against the wall and rubbed the knot in her temple.

Was he always an asshole?

"Cole just takes himself way too seriously. It's exhausting,"

Patsy said, twirling a finger in her hair, and Vee's eyebrows shot up. "You know, he's more emotional than I am, and that's saying a lot—"

"Oh, and that perpetual bored look," Suzi added, shaking her head. "Unless, of course, it's sex time, and then *WHAM*—he comes alive like Prince Charming!"

"Right on," cracked Vee. "Yup, that's the one," said Patsy. They were all laughing so hard that they forgot about Teddy, and she slipped out the door.

Ugh, I hate that look too!

The day's light was fading, and it was cold out. Teddy stood at the corner and tightened her scarf.

Thank God Cleo's not here to see this. She'd never let me live it down.

"Auf Wiedersehen, ladies," Eni yelled as she stepped out. "Heh, that was rough, but I did get another address." She lit a clove. "It's at the end of Perry. Shall we go?"

"Cole has turned into a real dog, hasn't he?"

"Yup, Romeo is a manslut." Eni laughed, but Teddy didn't find humor in it. Instead, her eyes welled up with tears.

"Aww Schnuckiputzi, don't be sad. The city moves fast. People don't have time to fall in love, so they just move on to the next warm body to keep sane." Teddy shrugged. "Still, it's like the universe doesn't want me to find him."

"Ya think?" With a crooked smile, Eni blew out a puff of smoke. "Don't worry, we'll find him, and when we do, I know he'll be thrilled to see you. And if we don't, you can stay vith me." She grinned. "Besides, I'm way more fun in bed—so, vat style are we doing next? We've covered limericks and haikus."

Teddy shook her head in wonder as Eni shifted gears and continued talking a mile a minute. She seemed to know just what to say to make her feel better, which wasn't easy to do. Yet, Teddy could tell they had some kind of connection, but what exactly it was, she hadn't a clue.

Maybe we were sisters in another life, or yikes, LOVERS? Oh, geez, ha-ha, bad, bad, BAD Theodora!

"What was zat look? I like it. I can tell it was naughty." Teddy flushed red. "You know, Eni, I do believe it's your turn… do something you've written recently. It can be a poem, a song, or anything—you choose."

"Ooh, I like zat." They turned onto Perry. "So, I was toying vith this the other day. It doesn't rhyme much, but it speaks to my heart. It goes something like zis…

Shades of confusion
color my mind,
mystified by deceptions.

Where there's nothing black,
nothing white, nothing but
illusions to dance with.

So if it's love your after,
empty you feel,
is loneliness your color?

It's just a finer shade of gray,
a finer shade of gray."

"Wow, great visuals."

"Thanks, darling—ha, I'm just a ray of sunshine." Eni stopped in front of a cluster of buildings and lit a clove. She looked left, then right, and pointed to the one in the middle. "I think this is ze place."

The white Spanish-style building stood out like a sore thumb in a neighborhood filled with industrial warehouses. They peered through the wrought iron gate and then up at the fire escape on the second floor.

"That's a painting, no?"

"It is." Teddy's face went pale. "Eni, can you go up and check? Because if I go and meet another girlfriend, I think I'll vomit."

"Scheisse," Eni chortled, shaking her head. "Wenn man dem Teufel den kleinen finger gibt, so nimmt er die ganze hand."

"Translation, please?"

"You don't vant to know." She tugged on the gate's handle. "It's locked. Let's go have pizza over there and come back later."

"Phew," Teddy said, relieved. It surprised her how much she dreaded seeing Cole at the moment but guessed it was due to hunger. Eni winked, "Oh, and Missy, it's your turn."

"Alright, so this next one is a tad depressing, so please refrain from throwing your popcorn at me, okay? So…

Knock me down,
take away my name.

Trapped with no power,
a pawn in your game.

You may have left me
helpless, needing, crying.

Darkened before I could walk,
cold, alone, and dying.

My eyes rise in search of you
on every street and every corner.

My heart breaks for you,
a denied, forsaken mourner."

"Whoa, that's intense and straight from the heart too." Eni

let out a long sigh, then balled her fist in the corner of her eye and wailed. "Whaaaaa! Boohoo *whooo!*"

"Oh, that's *NOT* nice, Enilika!" Teddy smacked her playfully on the arm. "Ha, you are so uncool!"

"Darling, you know I'm just toying, but I am curious…"

"Ja," Teddy mocked.

"Do you really think you can go back?"

"To where… Florida or Cole?"

"Either, darling—Cole… the love… your past?"

"Hmm, I don't know." Teddy pursed her lips. "I guess I've never really given it much thought. I usually just follow my heart wherever it takes me," she laughed.

"Man muss die Dinge nehmen, wie sie kommen."

Teddy stared at her, puzzled. "Enilika, are you flirting with me?"

"Ha-ha always, darling, but the translation means 'You have to take things the way zey come'."

"True, but honestly, I would have preferred it if you had said, du hast wunderschöne Augen."

Eni's face lit up. "Ooh, Theodora, I am very impressed, and yes, you do have beautiful eyes. Still, you said that like a true native. Do you know vat it means?"

"I do," Teddy said proudly. "I briefly dated this German sculptor who barely spoke a word of English, and every day he'd take my face in his hand and say, '*Meine Prinzessin, du hast schöne Augen.*' And, of course, with me not knowing the language, I thought it must've been something dreamy or profound, but instead, he was just talking about my peepers—pfft, so pathetic!"

She let out a hearty laugh, and Kenneth's rugged grin popped into her head, then she frowned. "Heh, and I guess since then, it drives me crazy when a man calls me princess."

"I imagine it would," Eni snickered. "So, whatever happened vith your sculptor?"

"The usual. I got bored and left." Then out of the corner of her eye, Teddy saw a man trailing behind them. "Hey, check out that guy."

"Where?" Eni Turned.

"Over there by the tree." Teddy pointed. "I think he's following us. Is he a boyfriend or something?"

"No, definitely not, but we should be careful." She grabbed Teddy's hand and led her into an apartment building, and they hid near the door, watching as he passed by.

"That was unnerving." Teddy gulped. "Should we be afraid?"

"Probably not, but this is the city, and it can be dangerous." Eni walked to the back of the lobby and lit another clove, then leaned up against the mailboxes. "He's probably some perv thinking he can get us in bed for a threesome." Teddy laughed."Really, how odd… have you had many?"

"Many what, threesomes?"

"Yes."

Eni grinned.

"I've had a—*CHRIST!*" Her face turned to fear. "He's got a gun!" She grabbed Teddy and spun her around, shielding her with her body.

BANG! BANG!

Their bodies slammed into the wall, then fell to the ground in a crumpled pile. Cautiously, the hooded man approached. His spit-shined boots stopped short of the blood trickling from their bodies. He knelt and pushed back his hoodie.

"Such a waste," Agent Jones said as he pulled a camera from his pocket and snapped a few photos.

Peters, you owe me.

32

Waiting Room

Back in Hollywood...

The hospital's ICU ward settled down, and all was quiet in the patient recovery area. The pungent sweet smell of disinfectants lingered in the air as nurses sat working at their stations. Mr. Hayes hovered over the front desk, tethered to the courtesy phone line, and huffed into the mouthpiece.

"Can't—*never* could I. She's madder than hell at you, and I don't blame her!" His tone, growing more agitated by the second, echoed loud down the corridor. One of the nurses waved a hand for him to bring down the volume, but the feisty old geezer just turned away and continued shouting, "Now you just hold your horses there, mister. That's my little girl you're talking about!"

Furious, Cleo rushed over and yanked the phone from his hand. "How dare you raise your voice at my father—"

"Oh, gimme a break," her ex-husband, Frank's voice bellowed from the receiver. "I'd rather shoot myself in the foot than have anything to do with you or your crazy family!"

To say the Bowens' marriage ended nicely was a polite way of putting it. Instead, their relationship could best be described as spiteful on good days and 'drop-the-pin' explosive on bad. Phone calls usually lasted minutes, and they almost always ended up with Cleo sputtering things like, "They're your kids too!" or "Where the hell is the alimony check?" But mostly, "Frank, you're such a fucking *ASSHOLE!*"

The thought of her beautiful marriage being reduced to such a volatile state of existence saddened her deeply. Cleo often struggled to understand how Frank could have left her and the kids without at least once trying to make things work.

At forty-one, her awkward, ultra-conservative husband seemed far too young to be going through a mid-life crisis. Yet, with the purchase of a blue Corvette and a bubbly bleach blonde on his arm, he sure did seem like the poster child for it.

Sexy RED cellophane??? What was I thinking...

It was early spring, a few months after their separation, and Frank's birthday was coming up. Cleo was feeling lost and a bit desperate. As much as she hated to admit it, winning him back was not as easy as she thought, so she decided the kids should throw him a party.

"It's your dad's birthday, and we need to show him what real love is," she screamed at the boys through their locked bedroom door, but they were still furious with their father for leaving and didn't want any part of it. Yet, Anna missed him terribly and loved the idea, so they hopped in the car and went on a shopping spree.

If it's shiny things he wants, that's what he's gonna get!

Cleo spared no expense, and on the way home, she stopped off at a party store for decorations. Anna rushed to the birthday section, but as Cleo followed, something on the sale rack caught her eye. Valentine's Day had just passed, and a barrel of red cellophane wrapping paper glistened under the lights.

Oooh, adding a little spicy something-somethin' to the equation could be just what I need to reel Frank back in—AND this totally screams HOT sex!

On the day of his birthday, piles of candy apple red gifts sat on the kitchen table. Cleo stood by the front window anxiously waiting. She was all dolled up in a sexy red maxi with four-inch stilettos. The kids sat restlessly on the couch, dressed to the nines, and much to her surprise, they were behaving.

The perfect family.

But Frank never showed—he didn't even bother to call, and the presents sat there for more than a week. And with each passing day, Cleo's heart hardened, and her mood turned from desperate to worry to 'how dare you' anger.

RING! RING!

On the tenth day, he called, and Anna rushed to the phone.

"Happy Birthday, Daddy! We've got lots of prezzies for you!"

"You do, honey? Oh, how sweet." Frank's cheerful voice made Cleo cringe. She was so angry that she could've ripped his eyes out.

"Daddy, why didn't you come to your party? I decorated for you." Cleo scooted in closer to hear.

"Aww babe, I had other plans—"

"Other *PLANS?*" Cleo grabbed the phone from Anna. "You could've at least called. We—I mean, the kids have been waiting all week to see you!"

He laughed, "What'd you buy me, Cleo... handkerchiefs, neckties, underwear?"

"Oh, *SCREW* you, Frank!"

Shaking with rage, she slammed the phone down.

"Aaarrrgggh—I hate *HIM!*"

And in one scoop, she grabbed all the presents off the table and charged out of the house. Anna chased after her. "Mom, where are you going? Those are Daddy's—"

"Not anymore," Cleo snarled, racing to the canal out back. She dropped the presents on the deck and stood at the water's edge.

"You *SELFISH* bastard!"

Then one by one, as if skipping stones, Cleo hurled back and tossed each present into the water, almost chanting in exasperation...

I don't *NEED* you—*SPLASH!*

I don't *WANT* you—*SPLASH!*

I don't *LOVE* you—*SPLASH!*

And as the last one flew, she held her chest high and roared.

"I will *NEVER* forgive you!"

"Why, Mommy, why?" Anna screamed, terrified.

Startled, Cleo snapped out of her rage and embraced her.

"Oh, honey, I'm so sorry. I didn't mean to frighten you. I'm just so angry with your father." She started to cry. "I tried to make it work, but your father wouldn't let me."

"Why doesn't Daddy love us anymore?"

"Oh, sugar, he loves you just fine. It's me he doesn't love."

"But why?"

"I don't know. Sometimes love just fades away."

"Will he ever come home again?"

"I... I ah..."

She stared out at the glistening presents dancing on the water's crest. They were floating downstream in a single file line, and softly she smiled, "I don't think so, honey. Your father wants a different life."

As the words left her mouth, a sense of relief swept over her.

It's over—

"Dammit, Cleo! Are you listening to me?" Frank's voice screamed through the receiver, and she snapped out of her head and laughed. "Yes, I hear you just fine—*One thing's for sure, this fucker's days of intimidating me are over*—Frank, you're taking the kids for a few days."

"But this is my weekend off!"

"Mom is in ICU, and Teddy's in trouble—"

"Teddy's always in trouble! I'm tired of her shit."

"Well, lucky for you, she's not your problem anymore. However, my sister is missing, and I have to go find her. So, whatever plans you have this weekend with your little girlfriend, cancel them."

"Dammit, Cleo!"

"I'll see you in an hour."

"But—"

CLICK!

Oh, that felt so fucking good!

Cleo exhaled, and the elevator doors opened. Agent Walters stepped out. "There you are," he said with a tone that was more concerned than he wanted to show. "I've been looking everywhere for you."

"Did you find my sister?"

"No—is your mom okay?"

"Yes, but barely."

"What happened?"

"I don't know. I found her passed out and covered in blood."

"What about your dad?"

"No—he'd *never* hurt my mom!"

"Jesus—I meant, is he okay?"

"Oh… he's fine." Flustered, Cleo pointed to the waiting room. "He's watching TV with Anna."

"Okay, good." Walters looked down at the blood on her shirt. "Did you get hurt?"

"No, it's not mine." She crossed her arms to cover it up. "It's my mom's. I didn't have time to change. I must look like hell."

"Actually, you look quite good—better than expected."

"Oh, thanks," Cleo said awkwardly as she ran her fingers through her hair. "It's been a rough day. My nerves are shot."

"Yeah, I can imagine." He gave her a warm smile. "So, did your mom fall?"

"We don't know. I mean, there was broken pottery on the ground, things were moved from their usual spots, and all sorts of papers were missing.

"What was missing?"

"Some of Teddy's things—hey, my mom said there was a female agent at the door earlier in the day before I got there."

"That can't be. We don't have any female agents working on the case." He scratched his head. "Was she a brunette?"

"I don't know. My mom just said she was pretty."

"Hm, interesting…"

"Oh, and there was this other woman, a blonde. She was seated in the back of a cab, and they almost hit us. Anna said she was a friend of Teddy's, but I doubt it."

"And why is that?"

"She's not her type."

"How so?"

"She looked sophisticated."

"Do you remember which cab company it was?"

"No, sorry, I don't."

"No problem—hey, let's go to your mom's house. I want to have a look around."

"I can't leave now. My mom will have a fit if I'm not here when she wakes. Plus, I have Anna with me, and she's been through hell."

"Can't your father watch her?"

"No, he's not good with kids, and I'm worried about him too."

"Well, give me the key then."

"No way, are you *crazy?*"

"It's not like I'm going to steal anything."

"Oh, I don't know…"

"Trust me, I saw the place, and there's nothing I want to touch, much less take." He rolled his eyes, and Cleo laughed, knowing her parents weren't the cleanest people on earth.

"Okay, but promise you'll put everything back where you found it." She pulled the key from her chain and hesitated. "My mom will freak if something's out of place or missing."

"I promise."

"You know, she'll probably call the cops on you."

"I bet she will," he laughed, remembering the first time he met Abby. "Your family is very colorful, Ms. Hayes, but don't worry, she won't even know I was there. Oh, and another thing… your son told me you're leaving for New York."

"Ooh, that little traitor," Cleo snipped, furious. "Agent, don't ever have kids. They'll rat you out the first chance they get."

He laughed, "Either way, you can't go—at least not now."

"But I have to—"

"You're not going." His face went stern. "It's too dangerous."

"So, you lied to me?"

"No, I didn't."

"You said there was no danger!"

"Oh, come on! I didn't know then what I do now." He shook

his head, frustrated. "You're driving me nuts. Will you just let me do my job?"

"Well, then do your job," she shrieked. "My *MOTHER* almost died! There's *BLOOD* everywhere! Anna is scarred for life, and where, oh *WHERE* is my sister, huh? You don't have a clue—*AND* now you tell me it's dangerous and expect me to be calm. Are you crazy?"

"Listen, I don't know where Teddy is yet, but I promise we will find her. One of our guys is in New York looking for her as we speak."

"You promise?"

"Yes."

"Agent, I hate broken promises."

He looked her square in the eyes. "I never break mine."

Cleo studied his face. There was something about him she liked. He was strong, handsome, and direct to the point—or maybe she was just feeling *a little horny?*

Walters tapped the elevator button.

"The danger level has just gone up a notch, especially now with the possibility that your mom was attacked. I'll assign a security detail to protect you and your family. Is that okay with you?"

"I guess," she frowned.

The doors slid open, and he stepped inside. "Promise me you'll stay put?" He held the door, waiting for a response.

Her face went blank, and she bit down on her lip, contemplating what to say. Cleo hated to lie, but she also didn't want to argue. So, she twisted her mouth into a smile, and with a shallow breath and two fingers crossed behind her back, she promised."

"Great! I'll bring the key by in the morning." His brow lifted, and a slight smile appeared. "Oh, and I like my coffee black."

As the elevator doors closed, Cleo stared at her reflection in the stainless steel and smiled, then she primped her hair.

Is that a date?

33

911

"What's your emergency?" the female dispatcher asked.

"I *NEED* an ambulance! My friend's been shot." Teddy cupped the phone tight to her mouth.

"What's the address?"

"Fifty-third Greenwich Avenue, just off the corner of Perry. She's in the hallway dying—please hurry!"

The sun went down, and the streetlights were systematically turning on one by one. She was huddled in the payphone outside the lobby from where they were shot. Her clothes were drenched in blood, and she was freezing.

The neighborhood was eerily quiet with no one else around, and then out of the corner of her eye, she saw a shadow of a man step up to the street's edge.

Oh, God, is that him?

She slid to one side so he wouldn't see her.

Fuck, I can't tell.

Her vision was blurred from the concussive blow to the back of her head when she hit the floor.

"Is your friend conscious?"

"No, I don't think so, but she was breathing."

A chime rang across the street, and she went still as the man entered the pizzeria.

"Ma'am, are you hurt?"

"Um, yes, I was shot." Teddy lifted her jacket, revealing a flesh wound under her shirt, blood trickling out.

The chime rang again, and the man stepped outside. He walked to the corner and lit a cigarette under the streetlight. As the smoke rose into the brisk air, he reached behind his head and lifted his hoodie.

"Oh, God, it is *HIM!*"

"Who, ma'am?"

"The killer—he's here." In a panic, Teddy dropped the phone.

"Ma'am? Hello, ma'am, are you there?" the dispatcher's voice rang out, and Jones' ears perked up. He glanced over in her direction, then the pizzeria's door opened, and the cashier waved him inside. As soon as the door shut, Cleo's voice in her head started screaming.

"Get the hell out of there—*NOW!*"

Full throttle, Teddy took off running. Excruciating pain shot up her ankle, straight to her temples. Absolute fear drove her faster and faster through the streets. She wasn't about to stop for anything until she heard the sirens—

ARRRRR! ARRRRR!

The ambulance whizzed by, and it hit her like a brick wall. She collapsed to her knees, crying as shame and guilt swept over her. She turned to go back but couldn't. Fear wouldn't let her, and so, numb, she continued on. She needed to be around people—*her people,* the musicians.

Instead of entering Penn Station from the main entrance, Teddy took the side street and went in through the taxiway. But unlike the underground maze of the train platforms, this section was a vast, wide-open rotunda that looked more like an upscale shopping mall with people everywhere, a ticket booth in the center, and luxury retail shops.

Embarrassed by her appearance, she rushed down the escalator and into the bathroom. The reflection staring back at her from the mirror wasn't a pretty sight. Wads of hair were stuck together. Gingerly, she pressed a finger to the gash on her stomach and then to the bump on the back of her head.

OUCH!

She doused a paper towel in hot water and tended to her wounds, then attempted to clean her jeans, but it was useless. Blood was everywhere.

That fucker almost killed me!

Her brows furrowed.

Kenneth did say the city was dangerous, but still, he didn't take anything. What did he want?

An hour later, she leaned against the ticket booth with her foot propped up on her backpack and stared out at all the people. The view was surreal. Musicians stood to her left, ready to perform, and groupies, stranded travelers, and the homeless were scattered about to her right. Suddenly, she shot upright.

I wonder if he's here?

Applause sounded, and the sultry female singer stepped up to the microphone. "This next song goes out to all the lonely hearts in the room. It's called 'When I'm Needing Someone'."

Disappearing into the drone of the guitars, Teddy closed her eyes as the singer lamented…

> *Ode to the fire in my soul,*
> *Give me the strength*
> *to be on my own.*
> *It's a comfort to have you,*
> *when I'm alone.*
> *When I'm needing someone.*
> *Ode to the calm in my heart,*
> *Help me from losing control.*
> *'Cause oh, how I feel you,*
> *I want to touch you—*

AAYEEES!

A harsh male voice shouted from above, and everyone looked up. The hooded man, a blur of an image, rushed down the escalator two steps at a time. He was determined, full of purpose, as he stepped over the bodies to get to her.

Fear grew in her eyes.

Oh, GOD, it's HIM!

"Help!" she tried to scream, but nothing but air came out. She scurried back against the booth, trying to claw herself away.

He lunged at her.

NO—please don't!

Her hands shot up.

THUMMPPP!

He landed inches from her.

"HAYES!"

Teddy's eyes went wide as his hoodie skewed, revealing his intense blue eyes. "I've been searching everywhere for you. Holy shit, is that *blood?"*

"Kenneth," she gasped.

"Are you hurt?" He knelt down, running a hand over the dried blood on her jeans.

"How'd you find me?" she muttered in shock, and her mouth went slack.

"I had a feeling you were here."

"You *did?"* Complete confusion sat on Teddy's face as he lifted her chin up. "Is that your blood?" he grimaced, and a nervous jolt shot through her.

"I ah…"

Don't tell him. He'll freak!

"Um, no, it's a friend's." He frowned, then several baseball fans shouted his name. "Do you know those people?" she said, looking over.

"Yeah, kind of—hey, are you crazy? This place is worse than the airport. Why didn't you call me?"

"I, ah," she stuttered as her mind went blank. "I, um, lost your *number?"*

"What? How could you lose it? I wrote it on your arm." He reached down and grabbed her stuff. "Come on, we're going."

"We *are?*"

"Don't try me, Teddy. I'm in no mood." He went to help her up. "Okay, just give me a second while I put my boot on."

"What the FUCK is that?" His eyes rounded on her foot. It was very swollen and very purple. "What happened to you?" His face twisted with guilt.

"Nothing, just an accident."

"What do you mean, and what's with all this blood?"

"Look, I'm not ready to talk about it." Flustered, she put on her sock. "Just let it be, would you?"

"Jesus, you're stubborn."

"How so—"

"You could have waited."

"I *TOLD* you I needed to go—" She was just about to rage but stopped when she caught the helpless, worried look in his eyes, and her face softened.

"Oh no, Missy… don't look at me that way. I'm mad at you."

"What'd I do now?" she laughed.

A sudden rush of emotions swept over him, and he looked down to regain control.

"Well, Kenneth?"

The little twinkle in her eye screamed *OWNED,* and he scowled back at her.

"Well, nothing, Missy… you scared the shit out of me, that's all." He headed for the escalator. "Come on, let's get out of here before it snows."

"More *SNOW*… does this stuff *EVER* quit?"

Up the escalator, he went two steps at a time, shaking his head. *Be tough with her. If you're soft, she's gonna eat you alive!*

"Wait up, O'Connor—*WAIT!*" Teddy hobbled faster. "I'll come with you, but first, you have to take me to see my friend."

"No way, not tonight." He kept moving. "The weather is going to turn, and I don't want to be on the road when it does."

"It'll only take a moment."

"No."

"O'Connor!" She abruptly stopped. "Either you take me, or I'm staying here!"

"You're kidding me, right?!" He spun around, ready for a fight but was disarmed the second he saw the tears welling in her eyes—*God, she's beautiful.* Frustrated, he threw up his hands. "But why, Teddy?"

"I have to say goodbye."

"To who—and can't it wait?"

"No. I'm afraid it's now or never." She wiped her tears with her sleeve.

"Can't you just call—"

"*KENNETH!* This is not a discussion. I need to see her," Teddy's voice broke. "Please, it'll only take a moment, I promise."

Exasperated, he looked up at the flurries falling in the darkness, then at her. "Alright, let's do this, but let's make it fast, okay?"

"Thank you."

"And don't think that being all sweet will make me forget." He quickened his pace. "I'm still mad at you, Hayes."

"You have no right to be," she huffed, following closely behind him. "Says you," he barked as they reached the black Rover parked in the taxiway, and he opened the door for her. "You know, O'Connor, I think you like being mad at me."

He bubbled his lips in annoyance and shooed her in, then closed the door. Settling into the leather seat, Teddy stared up at the shiny buildings that were stabbing into the night and wondered if her friend was still breathing.

Eni, please hold on 'til I get there...

34

Brooklyn

It was after midnight when the Rover drove down the posh neighborhood of Brooklyn Heights. Buried under a fresh layer of snow, the streetscape had rows of elegant brownstones with large windows, fancy gates, and stoops.

Kenneth parked out front and hurried over to the passenger side to help Teddy get out, but when he reached in, she waved his hand away. "I can get out on my own."

Shaking his head, he stepped back and watched as she wrestled from the car, then almost tripped on the curb and wobbled up the stairs, clutching the railing as if her life depended on it.

"No, *Kenneth*, I don't *need* your help…" he mocked in a high-pitched voice. "No, *Kenneth*, I don't want *your* hot chocolate… no, *Kenneth*, just stop. I can *do it* myself!" He snickered, incredulous. "Hayes, you're impossible."

With a pinched expression, Teddy crossed her arms and said nothing. "Have you ever let a man take care of you?" He unlocked the front door and pushed it open.

"Pfft, never found a man that could." She brushed by him with a counter-snicker and entered. Immediately, her mouth dropped, and she almost laughed out loud but refrained.

"Like *SPORTS* much?"

Her eyes traveled around the room in disbelief.

Virtually every wall, shelf, door, windowsill, and crevice was filled with photos, books, balls, helmets, gloves, bats, rings, flags, and sports posters. One especially *UGLY* mosaic hanging by the front door caught her eye. It was made from old baseball cards and had a big red 'K' scribbled at the bottom.

"Did you make this?"

"I did," he grinned. "In the seventh grade, my creative years."

"Interesting." Teddy couldn't resist the urge and had to touch it. "It's almost Warhol-like."

Kenneth's tastes ran from comfy leathers to gunmetal blues. In the middle of the room sat an enormous TV, surrounded by a huge manly couch and an oversized loveseat. Facing the window was an old, worn-out leather recliner.

Disneyland for jocks, she thought as she scanned the various knick-knacks on the shelf. *Take away all these tchotchkes, and this place could be stunning.*

It was evident that no Mrs. O'Connor lived there.

Pfft, no woman EVER would!

Kenneth raised an eyebrow, grinning at her displeasure. He went into the kitchen and opened the fridge. "Beer?"

"Yes, I'd love one, please." Teddy approached a shrine of photos on the mantel above the fireplace. "How old is this place?"

"It was my grandfather's."

"It's beautiful."

The old brownstone had the original white wainscoting panels, wide-plank pine floors, and a gorgeous wooden staircase that ran up three stories along the wall.

Teddy was shocked at how clean he kept it. And even though the sports decor was a bit much, she had to admit it was quite impressive.

"This has to be the largest man cave that I've ever seen."

"Nah, I wish it was bigger," he pouted, handing her the beer.

"Thanks—So, *no* wife?"

"Nope. She left and took the dog." He smiled and took a swig.

"Hm, with all this…" she waved her beer around. "I can't imagine why?"

"Beats the hell out of me." He scratched his head and shrugged. "I guess I just have a bad picker."

"Is this you?" She studied a photo of a man in a Yankees uniform. Amused, he shook his head, then she examined it closer and gave him a once-over. "It looks like you."

"Ya think?" he grinned.

"Why do you say you have a bad picker?"

"My therapist mentioned it." He enjoyed watching her analyze the pieces of his life. "She says I have a Superman complex or something silly like that."

"Huh, interesting." Teddy thought about it for a moment, then picked up a signed baseball and searched for his name.

He's very playful. I bet he's fun in bed—STOP it, Theodora!

She blushed.

No naughty thoughts!

He cocked his head and smiled. "Yeah, Dr. Nancy says I like women that are broken, you know, so that I can fix them."

"And do you?" Teddy replaced the ball and locked eyes with him. "Hell no, they break me more than I fix them."

"Yeah, I can see that, especially with your caveman ways."

"Hey now… be nice, Ms. Hayes."

"I meant that in the nicest possible way, Kenneth. An evolved caveman, of course. One that goes to therapy—I'm very impressed." She struggled a smile. Exhaustion was written all over her face, and a pang of guilt gnawed at his gut.

"Well, this caveman thinks it's past your bedtime. Follow me."

He grabbed a few towels from the hall closet and handed them to her. "For your bath, Madame." Then he led her up a flight of stairs and to the last room at the end of the hallway and waved her in. "It's not much, but it is warm and comfy."

"Wow," she said, stunned by the simplicity of the room. "Were you robbed, or did you just run out of sports paraphernalia?"

"Very funny, Missy." He stood in the doorway and reached up, grabbing hold of the door's frame above his head. "This is my mom's room. She's like you—she hates anything to do with sports."

"Like me, huh? Now *that's* interesting." Teddy sat on the bed and surveyed the room. Colored in whites and pastels, it had lace ruffled-bedding, pink florals, and a single painting of a ballerina in a Croisé Devant pose that hung over the headboard. "This is lovely, Kenneth. Thank you for letting me stay here."

With a kind smile, he pointed. "The bathroom is over there. Mom loves to take baths, and she has a bunch of crystals and soaps for every mood, so help yourself."

Teddy nodded, eyeing his sculptured physique through his sweater as he directed her to the closet. "Nightgowns, t-shirts, blankets." He continued around the room, her eyes followed, and her thoughts wandered—*he's so intense, so strong, and SO not my type! But there is something about him… something so familiar—*

"Are you hungry? I can make you a sandwich."

"No, I'm good." Softly, she smiled, and he instantly regretted not feeding her. "Seriously, if you need anything, just holler. I'm down the hall."

"Will do."

"Goodnight, Theodora."

As he grabbed the door handle to leave, she jumped up and screamed wait, then gave him a kiss on the cheek.

"Thanks for everything."

"It's the least I could do." He touched his face and then smiled. "Sweet dreams when you get there."

"Yeah, you too."

The door shut with a click, and she leaned back against the wall. The weight of the day suddenly crashed upon her, and panic crept in.

Whoa, RELAX!

She closed her eyes, trying to calm the anxiety that was building, but instead, the gunshots rang out in her head, and Eni's body jerked from the bullets.

Oh God, don't let her be dead!

Shaking uncontrollably, she slid to the floor.

Don't cry, please don't...

But the heartbreak was too much for her and she lost control. She held her hand over her mouth, muting the sounds, then wrapped her arms around her knees and rocked. The beautiful image of the ballerina bowed before her and helped to unleash the pain. Teddy cried until the sobs went silent, and then slowly, she stood, catching her reflection in the mirror.

Disheveled and raggedy... who could ever love this?

Stripping out of her bloodstained clothes, she headed into the bathroom. It was painted in soft pinks and white and had wall-to-wall mirrors. She turned on the facet, grabbed a bottle of Kenneth's mother's bath crystals, and sprinkled until the water turned a violet swirl of lavender.

Looking in the mirror, Teddy assessed each of her bruises. There were a few more than expected, but the one oozing on her ribcage concerned her the most.

Three inches up, and it would've been me dying in a pool of blood—STOP IT!

With a loud exhale, she dipped a hand in the bath to see if it was ready, then slid into its warmth. Her wounds were on fire, and she winced until the pain eased, then darkness consumed her.

Times like this scared the shit out of her. Her past was a grenade she wore around her neck, always fearing that the day would come when she'd give up and pull the pin. She inhaled deeply and completely submerged into the purplish cloud, holding her breath, hoping the heat would heal her thoughts, but Eni's face kept appearing.

Where was she?

There wasn't a trace of her when she and Kenneth arrived at the building. There was nothing to see—no cops, no ambulance, not even a speck of blood.

Did they take her to the hospital or the morgue, or did he bury her somewhere?

Teddy's adventures were always on the wild side, but this one was dangerously different. The thought of not finding Cole and the loss of Eni raged in her heart, ravaging her soul. It left her teetering on the edge of sorrow. She tried to force herself to believe that Eni was all right, but deep down, she knew she wasn't.

Life is so dark...

She held her breath a little longer.

So destructive...

35

The .22

The good ol' Tampa air…

It was late when Agent Jones retrieved his car from the airport's parking garage. The humidity was high, smothering even, as he rolled down the windows on his drive home. The ride was easy. Hardly anyone was on the road, and he lived just a few miles away in a tiny one-bedroom flat.

Damn, it's good to be home. That cold weather chills you to the bone. The sooner I get paid, the better I'll feel. I can't believe Peters barked at my price—that cheap fuck!

"Now, don't get greedy on me, Jones. You're in this for the long haul," Jones mimicked Peters' voice, and he laughed.

Like hell I am! As soon as I get my money, I'm out of here.

He felt anxious. He didn't trust Peters one bit, and the thought of having to wait until he got off work on Monday to get his money made him uneasy.

I'll meet him at six, my flight is at nine, and then I'm off to Costa Rica to spend my days riding waves and picking up babes—hell, yeah!

Smiling at the thought, he jiggled the key in the lock of his front door, but it was stuck and needed coercing. So he forced it in, and then with a quick turn of the knob and a heave from his shoulder, he pushed the door open and entered.

A halo of a man stood in the hallway, waiting in the dark. His arm raised, then a muscle in his cheek twitched.

BANG!

The bullet fired into his forehead. He had no time to think, no time to blink, the body fell backward, and his polished black boots went easterly westerly.

He was dead.

Mills holstered the .22 and gazed down at the body before him. The death stare fixated on the ceiling, locked in surprise.

"Amateur."

He picked up Jones' bag and stepped over the body, careful not to get blood on his Allen Edmonds.

Another mess, cleaned.

36

Cleo's Ride

Back in Hollywood...

She woke up determined.

So help me GOD, this is going to be Theodora's LAST adventure—EVER!

With direct orders from Agent Walters telling her to stay put and a security detail watching the house all night long, Cleo slipped out the back and into a cab that was waiting for her two blocks away.

She was unrecognizable, wearing her mother's short dark wig, granny glasses, and her floral muumuu. "Can you please hurry? My train leaves at six," she told the driver, and he hit the gas.

The taxi pulled into the Amtrak station with a few minutes to spare. She threw him a twenty, grabbed her bags, and rushed on board. Instantly, she regretted not booking a private sleeper because the train was full.

Cleo made her way to the back and sat in the last available seat by the window. As the train departed, a man in a dark suit ran alongside on the platform, glaring into each of the compartments, and she hid her face to avoid being seen.

Sorry, Agent Walters, but I'll have to give you a rain check on that coffee—and oh boy, are you going to be pissed when you find out I left!

She chuckled.

Oh well, I guess I'll just have to make him dinner instead. I bet he'd love a delicious steak on the grill and maybe a little wine and candlelight too.

Cleo smiled at the thought and took her mother's wig off, then slipped out of the muumuu—she was fully dressed underneath.

Okay, enough of this kissy-kissy stuff. I need to concentrate. The trip will take about twenty-six hours, and that'll bring me to Penn Station on Sunday morning around eight. So, do I get a hotel room first or just go looking for her? She pulled a map of New York City from her bag and frowned.

Is it considered kidnapping when you drag someone home by their hair—especially when they're kicking and screaming that they don't want to go?

She stared out the window for a moment, contemplating.

Dammit, I don't care how much Teddy cries… she's coming home with me!

Her anxiety level was peaking in the red zone, and to say that Cleo was overprotective of her little sister was putting her nudge factor mildly. Maybe it had something to do with never knowing her own parents, or perhaps the instant love she felt for Teddy the day the Hayeses brought her home, but the bottom line was that no amount of snow—*or danger,* could ever stop her from making sure Teddy was safe. She closed her eyes and settled into the ride.

Girl, you were such a handful…

An image of her ten-year-old sister sitting on the neighbor's roof flashed in her memory. Cleo had just come home from school, and Abby was in the living room complaining to Henry that Teddy was making them the laughingstock of the neighborhood.

"I've had it with that one," Abby yelled.

Growing up with the Hayeses wasn't easy, especially for Teddy. Her independent spirit drove them nuts. Abby, more than Henry, tried to control her, which made Teddy lash out even more. She took pride in embarrassing them. If they said no, she'd say yes. If they said don't go, she went. She didn't care if they were right because everything they represented felt wrong.

"Jesus is my Lord, but he never prepared me for a child like this one." Abby picked up the phone and started dialing. "That's it, I'm sending her back—"

"No, you can't," Cleo screamed. "If Teddy goes, then I'm leaving too!"

"Over my dead body!"

Abby tried to grab her, but Cleo ran past her and into the kitchen. She opened the fridge, threw some food into a bag, and ran out the back door. As she neared the end of the block, she could see Teddy doing cartwheels on the neighbor's roof.

"Theodora Hayes, stop that right now! You're *SCARING me!*"

Teddy peered down the one-story ranch with the biggest kitty cat grin and snickered, "What took you so long?"

"Get down now!"

"Nope. I won't."

Teddy took hold of the ladder and held it against the house. "You come up."

"But I... well, you know I hate heights. Just come down, please?" With a devilish grin, Teddy challenged, "First, prove to me you're not a chicken." Cleo's face squished into an angry little ball, and she scowled, "Fine. I will!"

Determined, she pushed up onto the ladder, and it wobbled—she almost fell off but steadied herself. Then slowly, she continued up one shaky step at a time, chirping, "Don't let me fall, don't let me fall!" Then when she reached the top step, she made the mistake of looking down.

"Yikes, it's too high—Theodora Hayes, you come down now!"

"Pfft." Teddy shook her head.

"Don't *pfft* me! What are you doing up here anyways?"

"Don't ask, Cynthia Marie—"

"Hey, that's not fair!"

Teddy looked at her, curious.

"What's not fair—*your* name?"

"Yes, you know how much I hate it." The ladder wobbled, and she held on tighter. "Yours is so cool, but mine sounds stupid."

"Well, if you hate it so much, then change it."

"You can't change a name."

"Why not?" Teddy twirled.

"Mom wouldn't stand for it."

"Oh, forget her... so what do you want to be called?"

"I dunno," she shrugged. "I've never thought about it before."

"Well, let's see... blonde hair, green eyes." Thinking, Teddy tapped a finger to her lip, then blurted, "How about Wilhelmina?"

"Ew, that's gross—be serious."

"Okay, okay, no more jokes," Teddy snickered. "Let me see, girls like you are usually called Barbie or Chrissy—oh wait, what about Meryl, or *oooooh, Marilyn?*"

"Uh-uh, no M's."

"How about Ms. Picky?" Teddy giggled and did a pirouette near the ledge.

"No—*AND* you're gonna fall!"

Bubbling her lips again, Teddy searched the skies.

"I've got it—what about Cleopatra? I learned about her in school today." Her eyes brightened. "She's just like you—fearless, a risk-taker, and ruthless!"

"Ack, that sounds nothing like me—that's totally you!"

"Okay, it does sound more like me, but she's *FAB,* just like you, and we can call you Cleo for short, which is sort of like Cynthia, so Mom won't freak too much." What do you think?"

"Cleo-*O*... hm, it does have a cool ring to it."

Then her face lit up.

"Oh, Teddy, I LOVE it!"

"Me too!" Teddy danced over to her and tapped her on her head. "I now declare you, Cleopatra Cynthia Marie Hayes, the Egyptian Goddess of Dania Beach!" The sisters burst into laughter, giggling with joy, and then Teddy pointed to the bag in Cleo's hand.

"Whatcha got there?"

"I brought you some food." Cleo tossed it to her, then rested her chin on the ladder. "So, are you going to tell me why you're up here?"

"Heh, the usual… Mom and Dad don't like me very much."

"They like you bunches, but you just drive them bonkers all the time. Mom worries sick about you."

"I doubt that—she wants to send me back and rent out my room. Pops says they need the money."

"So what… you can stay with me in my room." Teddy opened the bag and squealed in delight. "THIEF! You *STOLE* Pop's Mallomars!"

"Yup, I *DID!* Ha-ha, but so what—he's harmless."

"Yummy!" Teddy popped one in her mouth. "You want one?"

Cleo shook her head.

"Look, Teddy, who cares what they want? I want you, and that's all that matters." Her eyes filled with tears. "I can't imagine my life without you, and until the day I die, I'm gonna follow you to the ends of the earth!" In a heartbeat, Cleo pushed up from the ladder and onto the roof and pulled her younger sister into the biggest hug.

"Theodora Hayes, I love you—"

SCREEEEECH!

The train arrived at Penn Station. Anxiously, Cleo grabbed her bags and readied herself for whatever insanity was about to come her way. With a long exhale, she stepped out of the compartment and followed the other passengers all the way up to street level, and then rode the escalator to Seventh Avenue.

BRRRRR!

"Damn, it's cold here," she shuddered, looking for street signs. "So, how do I get to Cole's?" Her face lit up when she saw a cop standing by the ticket booth. "Sir, whoa, sir," she called out, slipping on the icy pavement.

"Careful there, Missy," he said.

"Officer, which way is the Village?"

"Greenwich Village?" he scrutinized her. "Looking for a boyfriend, are you?"

"Well, no, but funny you should ask because I am looking for my sister who was, well, um… looking for her boyfriend."

"Dammit! I knew she'd get lost." Furious, he threw up his hands, and Cleo's eyes widened. "Did you see my sister?"

"Dark brunette with great eyes?"

"Yes, that's her!"

"Geez, I saw her the other day. She looked lost. I warned her not to go, but she wouldn't listen, and I haven't seen her since. Hopefully, she found him."

"I don't know. I tried calling many times but couldn't get through. Can you show me which way she went? I'm worried sick, and I need to find her." Looking down the icy street, he turned back to her and said, "Let me go get my car, and then we'll look together, okay?"

"Really?"

"Yeah, we'll find her." He winked, "And don't worry, you're in good hands with me, so just wait here, and I'll be right back."

Was that a flirt? Cleo watched him strut to his car. *I guess being single is not so bad...*

The patrol car pulled up to the curb, and he opened the door. "Hop in—Val Finn's the name." She beamed at him, "Are all cops as helpful and nice as you?"

"Nope, just me." He grinned, and her eyes twinkled.

And this adventure stuff is kind of fun too...

"Hi, I'm Cleo... Cleopatra Hayes."

37

The Mansion

A Tribute to My Love
by Sarah J. Jenkins
the 26th of January 1961

Farewell, my beloved,
even in slumber.

I am sad that I must abandon you,
tho, not in heart, nor spirit, nor soul.

You will always be my one true love,
as you sleep under the ashes,
way below the heavens above.

The loss, the beauty, the outcry, the toll,
for which I will forever be broken.

Farewell, my beloved,
even in slumber.
Without you, darkness is my home.

● ● ●

Prescott Manor, with its turret, portico, and wraparound porch, wasn't the typical three-story house you'd find in Tampa. The Victorian beauty was built in the fall of 1865 by Jubal himself after the war and stood just blocks away from the old fort. It had sat there for almost a century until Blake's obsession with his family's legacy led him to uproot the entire home and transport it by barge to five acres of land just across the river.

It was after nine, and Bridget stared at the faded poem she found lying on her mother's desk next to a single wilted daisy in a tiny bud vase. She had guessed her mother changed out the flower daily in memory of this mysterious person but still hadn't a clue who he was. Curiously, she reached in her bag for her father's diary, and as if being willed, the journal opened to the page with the house fire, and she checked the date.

January 23rd... hm, very curious. Mom wrote this poem just days after the fire.

Leaning back in her mother's beautiful leather chair, she pondered the poem's meaning. She shifted, trying to get comfortable, and let out a small laugh, reflecting on how stiff it was, and decided that it suited her mother's personality perfectly. Then suddenly, she winced.

'I knew what real love was!'

Her mother's last words screamed in her head. Bridget had never seen her so passionate about loving anyone—not her father, and definitely not her.

So, who is this person?

Her eyes darted to the closet.

I wonder what other curious things Mother has hiding in there.

Exploring, she noticed that tucked behind her mother's

favorite parasol hid the floral treasure chest.

'Don't Touch My Things!'

Bridget looked down at her hands; they were shaking. Her mother often rapped the colorful umbrella across her knuckles whenever she didn't behave—and as if it had just happened, she rubbed them. Then, careful not to disturb anything, especially the parasol, she grabbed the chest.

Mother could be so mean...

Trying to rid herself of the dark memory, she closed her eyes tight and then remembered a time when her father kissed away her pain.

Thank you, Daddy...

With a flip, she dumped the contents of the chest onto the desk. It was filled with letters. Some were old and yellowed, but many were recent. Most were from her father confessing his love when he was younger, others were from family and friends, but none looked to be from the mysterious beloved.

Heh, and why are there so many letters from Jeffrey Peters?

Annoyed, she opened one and cringed. "Ew, you're so pathetic!"

With each letter of his that she read, Bridget grew angrier. Most of them were full of promises of undying love, loyalty, and of a wonderful life filled with everlasting bliss. Yet, Peters also detailed all of her father's illegal dealings and infidelities, making it clear his intention was to corrupt her mother's thoughts.

Ugh! This horrible, conniving, deplorable man tempted Mother and turned her against Father! He destroyed our family—

The doorbell rang, startling her.

"Alpheus, someone's here!"

The old butler glided down the staircase, and he instantly recognized the man's silhouette through the frosted glass. "Madam, it's Mr. Peters."

Speak of the devil and he rears his creepy self!

Hurrying, she tossed the letters in the box and returned them to the closet. Her hand lightly touched the parasol, and she jerked back as if it had burnt her.

"I'll be right there," she yelled, her tone brewing with rage. After years of watching her mother put on the perfect facade, Bridget glanced in the mirror, blew out the venom she felt towards the man, and calmly fixed her hair. Then with cold, steely eyes, she made her way to the stairs.

"Why, Mr. Peters, what a coincidence. I was just going over Mother's things. I didn't realize that the two of you were so close."

"You?" he gasped, realizing that she was the blonde woman hugging Mills at his restaurant. "Well, my dear, your mother and I do go back a long way. And yes, our friendship has indeed grown closer over the years."

"I see." She clutched her neck and gave him a polite smile. "Let's go talk in Father's library."

Leather-bound books covered the walls of the stately room. It was an impressive collection but one that was entirely for show. Bridget knew that her father had never read any of them, much less opened one. "Please have a seat," she said, gesturing for Mr. Peters to sit on the oversized Chesterfield sofa in the middle of the room, which made him look insignificant. Then she proudly walked over to the fireplace mantel and stood in front of photos of her father and famous world leaders, knowing it would irritate him. "Tell me, Mr. Peters, what brings you here at such a late hour?"

"I was in the neighborhood and thought I'd check in on

you." He stroked his mustache and offered a kind smile. "How are you doing?"

"As well as can be expected after such a horrible tragedy." She sighed and adjusted one of her father's picture frames on the mantel.

"Yes, indeed it was. I can't imagine what you are going through. If there is anything I can do to help, please do not hesitate to ask."

"That is very kind of you."

"I heard you visiting family down south."

"No, just friends." Her eyebrow arched as she watched him cross the room. He was fixated on a younger picture of her mother. He picked it up, and sadness grew in his eyes. Gently, he caressed Sarah's face, then returned it to the shelf.

"So, Bridget, do you think it wise to stay here all alone?" He turned and locked eyes with her. "You know, so soon after their deaths?"

"I'm not alone," she scoffed. "Uncle Paddy is here for me as well as Alpheus." She followed his gaze as he looked around the room. "Mr. Peters, is there something that I can help you with?"

"Yes, actually, there is." He walked over to an end table and picked up a set of keys, scrutinizing them, then placed them back down. "Bridget, I was wondering if you've stumbled upon an odd-looking key or relic. It would be one from your great grandfather Jubal's days. Have you seen it?"

"Sorry, can't say that I have."

"Well, have you ever seen your father with anything like that?" Bridget laughed. "You know my Father, he loved those antiques, and this house is full of them." His eyes brightened as he scanned the room again. "Yes, I was just noticing that. If I could just have a look around—it won't take long."

"Not tonight, Mr. Peters. It's been a long day, and I am exhausted."

"But it'll only take a moment—"

"I said no." Her tone was stark, and his eyes darkened. "Young lady, you do not know who you are talking to here." Bridget sneered at him, "Actually, Mr. Peters, I know *exactly* who I'm talking to."

"Your father is gone because of his reckless behavior, and now it is up to me to pick up the pieces." He hovered over her, trying to intimidate her, but the anger she felt screeched out, "Like hell, you will!" The look she gave him could have cut him in two. "My parents are dead because of you—I know it was you who sent the video to the television station. And you who sent the photos to the press, but more importantly, I read your pathetic love letters!"

"I loved your mother!"

"You sabotaged my family!"

"I spent my life devoted to her! Every single goddamn day was spent trying to ease the pain caused by that cheating bastard!"

"You filthy liar! Mother never wanted you. You did it for yourself!"

"I did it for love."

"Your so-called love killed my parents. You drove my mother to murder, and your lies drove her to take her own life. Now get out and never come back! Alpheus, show Mr. Peters to the door!"

The manservant rushed in from the hallway. "Sir, please, Madame has asked you to leave." He took him by the arm, but Peters pushed the old man aside.

"I'm not going anywhere!"

"Leave, or I'll call the police." Bridget picked up the phone, her fingers hovering over the dial as the tone buzzed loud.

"This isn't the end, young lady," he shrieked, bolting out the door. "I'll get what I need, and when I do, you'll be sorry!" His voice trailed down the driveway. "I've paid my dues—this is my time!"

Furious, Bridget threw the phone at the wall and then rushed into her father's study. "How could you leave me this way?" She shouted at his portrait, then paced back and forth, trying to make sense of it all. "What am I supposed to do here? I don't know anything!" She collapsed into his chair.

"I need your guidance…"

Crying, she reached for a tissue and saw a book on the top shelf of her father's file cabinet.

THE FIRE STARTER
INCINERATOR MANUAL

Instantly, she pulled it down and flipped through the pages, then gasped, "It's Father's diagram…"

Sobbing in relief, she picked up the phone and dialed. "You've reached the office of Patrick Mills. Please leave a message."

BEEP!

"Uncle Paddy, Jeffrey Peters was just here and said that if I didn't give him what he wanted, he'd make me pay! Please don't let him hurt me—"

CLICK!

Bridget wiped her tears.

"Goodbye, Mr. Peters."

38

The Kiss

Icicles dangled from the neighbor's roof, glistening in the moonlight. It was late, and the house was quiet as Kenneth sat alone in the dark. He took a swig from his warm beer and continued staring out the window, lost in thought.

She hasn't come out of that room all day—no food, no drink, not even a peep. I hope she's okay... He looked at his watch. *It's been twenty-four hours. Enough of this madness. I'm going up!*

He rocked forward, catapulting out of the recliner, and headed straight for the staircase, then abruptly stopped inches from the first step as if some invisible hand was holding him back. He looked up in trepidation.

I bet Mount Everest is less of a challenge than she is.

With a flick of his hand and an *oh fuck it mumble*, he returned to the recliner and gazed at the lazy snowflakes floating across the windowpane.

Covered in blood, bruised, and battered—what happened to her? And why the hell didn't she call me? Flustered, he swigged his beer. *Oh, who am I kidding? Teddy would've never listened to me anyways.* Pulling the lever, he tilted back in the recliner and took another sip. *Feisty. Stubborn. Reckless… and who was that girl we were searching for?*

"It's none of your business, O'Connor. Just leave it at that," he said, mimicking her voice, which brought him back to the day she left the airport.

Dammit, I should've bopped Lebowski in the nose for telling her how to get to the city, but still… why did I even let her go?

Teddy's careless determination to blindly go somewhere she had never been for something she desperately wanted was admirable—*BUT never seeing her again was unacceptable!* So, a half hour after she left, Kenneth hopped into his Rover and tore out of the airport, heading straight for the Village.

After all, how hard can it be to find her? The thought lingered as he remembered sliding into the turn and then frantically pumping the brakes to avoid hitting the highway barrier—*but just barely.*

The icy roads were treacherous, and the sporadic snowfall didn't help much. Stranded cars hid under snowdrifts, waiting for unsuspecting drivers to careen their way, but Kenneth swerved, skidded, and plowed through with enough luck to avoid the traps. He was determined to get to the city before nightfall.

I'll find her. I know the city like the back of my hand, and the Village is just a beeline from the station, so I can't miss her!

But by the end of the second day, Teddy was nowhere to be found. News on the radio said a cold front was coming in. Defeated, Kenneth turned the Rover around and started home when a detour led him to the Penn Station taxiway.

Nah, it can't be?

He parked out front.

"What are the chances she's in there?" He tapped a finger on the steering wheel. "Slim to none, but maybe, just maybe, I'll get lucky." So, chanting under his breath, "Hit hard, run fast, and go left all the way 'til ya get home," he bolted out of the car, stormed into the station, and then stood perched at the top of the escalator, staring down at the people below. Yet almost all of their faces were hidden by scarves or hats, but then—*WHAM!*

"HOME RUN!"

There she was with her eyes closed, swaying to the music.

My heart exploded—

CRACK!

A frozen tree limb snapped outside the window, and he jumped. "Damn, I hope she's okay?" Suddenly panicked, he looked around the house, but it was still. "She wouldn't do anything to harm herself, would she?" He chugged his beer and wiped his mouth on his sleeve. "Fuck it, I'm going up."

Ejecting out of the recliner, he went into the kitchen, grabbed a plate of food off the stove, and then a beer from the fridge.

"Christ, what if she's dead?"

With the feeling of foreboding doom, he rushed up the stairs. It was dark. Only a small light lit his path as he contemplated what to say. Then he put an ear to the door and listened for any sign of life.

Nothing… heh, maybe I shouldn't? Oh, STOP being a pussy!

Lightly, he tapped. "Princess… hey, princess, are you awake?"

No response, his brows furrowed.

TAP-TAP!

"Teddy, it's K—you in there?"

In the tenebrous room with the window cracked for air, she whisked awake from her dream.

Ummmm... Cocooned under several layers of blankets, she opened her eyes. *Huh?*

"You up?" Barging in, he flipped the light on.

"OUCH—Kenneth!" Teddy screeched, disoriented.

"Oops, sorry," he said with a laugh, relieved. "There you are…"

"Where else would I be?" She pulled the blankets over her head. "Go away. I'm still sleeping."

"I brought you some food." He put it on the side table and sat next to her. She squinted, dipping the blankets just enough to see him. "What time is it?"

"After midnight."

"You woke me to *eat?*" She rubbed her face.

"Yeah, you must be starving—"

"Jesus, Kenneth, it's the middle of the night—are you *crazy?*" She kicked off the blankets and charged into the bathroom.

His eyes grew wide.

She's wearing my FAVORITE JERSEY! Oh, that's so hot—

The door slammed shut.

Oops... he let out a happy sigh. *Well, at least she's alive.* It surprised him how much seeing her quickened his heart rate. *I could watch her all day.* The toilet flushed, and the door swung open. Teddy was fully dressed. She grabbed her boots and put them on. "What—where are you going?"

"Catching the train."

"Noooo, you are not!"

"I have to find my friend." She threw her stuff in her backpack.

"At this late hour?"

"I saw a station down the block."

"Uh-uh, you are not leaving. I won't let you! Plus, you haven't eaten—"

"Oh, not that again, O'Connor—"

"I said no, no, and triple NO!" He grabbed her backpack, trying to take it from her, but she held tight.

"STOP it—*let* go!"

"You are NOT going anywhere!" He pulled the bag harder.

"Oh, *YES,* I am!"

"Not a chance, Hayes." A shit-eating grin grew on his face, and he tightened his grip. "I should've done this the other day."

"I'm warning you, O'Connor!" She stared him down, and he let out a hearty laugh. Then her face twisted, and her arms flailed.

"Give *ME*—tug—*BACK*—jerk—*MY*—tug, jerk, tug, jerk, tug—*BAAAGGG!"*

RRRIP!

In shreds, the seams of the backpack split apart, sending all her stuff, as well as both of their bodies, crashing onto the bed. Quickly, Kenneth climbed on top. "I win! Ha-ha-haha," he shouted with his arms up in the air.

"You brute, you *BROKE my BAG!"* She smacked him on the stomach, and he yelped, then laughed harder as he grabbed both of her hands, pinning her down.

"I gotcha!"

"Get off of me," she bucked.

"Nuh-uh, no way, princess. Ha-ha, it's never gonna happen."

"Kenneth! I'm warning you—" Her body jerked. "Get off me!"

"Keep fighting, and let's see who wins this battle." His face went stern. "You're not going anywhere, so I'd suggest you settle down."

"Says YOU!" She struggled harder. "Now *GET* off *ME!"* She kicked up, almost throwing him to the floor, but Kenneth just smiled and rode her, tucking her legs under his. "Whoa, settle down, princess, settle down."

"Don't call me *PRINCESS—"*

"Or what? Whadda ya gonna do? He shifted his weight, and a pained expression appeared on her face. "Ouch, Kenneth, you're hurting me. Please get off—"

"I'm not falling for that old trick. Promise you'll eat, and then maybe we'll talk."

"Never!" She bucked wildly. "I'd rather starve to death, argh!"

"Don't try me, princess." He tightened his grip. "Either you eat, or I'll tickle the shit out of you."

"You wouldn't dare!"

"Try me."

"I'll bite you so hard that you'll cry like a baby."

"Ooh, don't tease me like that."

"I'm *NOT* playing Kenneth! I've been known to draw blood."

"Is that a dare, Ms. Hayes?" The happy devil in him shined, and he inched his lips closer to hers. "Ready then?" he winked. "On the count of three…"

"No, Kenneth, please don't!"

"One…"

"Stop!" Her hands fisted, trying hard to pull away.

"Two…" He held his lips within biting range, and she snapped. "You better stop! I'm not kidding—I'll hurt *YOU!*"

"Two and a half," he chuckled, collecting both arms in one hand. "O'Connor, don't you even think about it—I *HATE* to be tickled!"

"Two and three-quarters…" He brushed his nose against hers. "Eskimo kisses?"

Furious, Teddy darted her face left and right to avoid his touch, which made him laugh harder, and then his finger rose.

"STOP! Don't *you* dare!"

"THREE …"

As the words left his mouth, Teddy lunged up and bit him hard. A trickle of blood appeared on his lip, but he didn't flinch. Instead, he melted into her taste, and then shocked by her own desire, Teddy captured his lips in hers—kissing deeply as her head swirled in his hungered passion. His breath was deliciously intoxicating. Her fingers dove into his curly hair, pulling him in closer. She could feel herself giving in to his touch—

"NOOO!" she screeched.

Startled, Kenneth pulled back.

"I, ah—"

"It's not going to happen, O'Connor!" She took a deep breath, trying to calm her racing heart. "I came to New York to fix things, not make them worse!"

"Sorry," he said gently, then planted a kiss on her forehead. "I didn't mean to complicate things. I just wanted you to eat." A rugged grin stretched across his face, and he grabbed the plate of food. "I made you a BLT—try it. It's delish."

"Dear God, you are worse than my sister." She rolled her eyes and took a big bite. "Happy now?"

"Yes, very—oh, and one last thing…" he walked to the door. "Promise me that you won't leave in the middle of the night."

"But I have to find my friend."

"I know you do, but just stay until the morning, okay?"

Reluctantly, Teddy held up three fingers. "I promise—"

"Wait, you were a Girl Scout?"

"Are you insinuating that I don't look the type?"

"Well, just a little… wait, wow, I just had a vision of you wearing the green skirt and the little slash full of badges—oh, that is sooo hot!"

"Perv…"

He let out a hearty laugh and turned to leave.

"Wait!"

"Yes…"

"I'm sorry for biting you."

"I'm not," he grinned. "It made my night. Now eat up and get some rest. Sweet dreams, Theodora."

"Goodnight, Kenneth."

The door closed, and he whistled down the hallway. Teddy pursed her lips, laughing, then gently touched them—they were throbbing.

Mmm, better than my dream...

39

Death of a Hitman

Red walls, drenched in blood, toppled over one by one as she ran to the car. Her swan embellished satin wedding pumps were stained scarlet. She looked up at the ceiling, and it erupted into flames, then down at the floor as the heat rose from the vents below—she was trapped. Quickly, she wrapped her arms around Russell, his body lifeless and blue, and gently kissed him on the lips. A tall, dark shadow of a man stood in the corner, watching.

Uncle Paddy... is that you?

The alarm rang, and Bridget woke.

● ● ●

The early morning sun rose as Jeffrey Peters waited in his Jaguar behind a wall of evergreens that lined the driveway of Prescott Manor. He was listening to country music with a gun on his lap, and his eyes fixated on the front door.

"Where the hell is she? I need that key—and where the fuck is Jones? He should have been here, not me, goddammit!"

He glanced down at the clock.

"It's already six-thirty. She was supposed to leave for the gym by now. I'm gonna kill Jones next time I see him. Ooh, I love this song!"

He turned up the radio.

As he hummed to the salty tune about loose women and beer, the tall emerald bushes behind the car parted, and Bridget stepped onto the driveway. Careful not to make a sound, she aimed the .38 revolver.

Daddy said hold it firm and steady... then squeeze—

BANG!

Peters' head jerked forward, and blood sprayed across the windshield.

"So…" With a twisted smile, she stared at the gurgling corpse. "After all these years manipulating Mother and backstabbing Father, I guess you didn't see that one coming, did ya, honey?" Her eyes shifted to a large satchel on the passenger seat. "Oh… and what do we have here?" A map of Tampa lay on top with an address circled in red. Bridget reached in and grabbed it, then headed over to the limo as Alpheus pulled up the driveway.

"Enjoy hell, Mr. Peters."

She blew a wisp of hair from her face.

"Mother would have never loved a repulsive creature like you—*ever.*"

• • •

"Jesus Christ!" Paddy Mills watched from the servant's entrance in shock. "She just blew his fucking brains out!"

The very last drop of innocence he had left in his soul evaporated as the car's windshield blew red. He had been up all night worrying that Peters might try to do something, and he raced to the mansion at first light to warn her. Still, he couldn't believe his eyes and staggered back to the car, his mind reeling.

"She's turned into a cold-blooded killer. Dammit, this is all my fault!" He punched the steering wheel, then spun the car around and raced after the limo. "Why did I wait? I should have taken him out sooner—fuck, what have I done?"

BEEP! BEEEEP!

The streets were filled with Sunday morning churchgoers. Mills sped through the town and hopped onto the highway, weaving in and out, trying to catch up. The limo swerved across three lanes doing ninety, then got off at the next exit. Mills followed, veering south into a rural farming community.

The sun was up, and the skies blue. He feared she might recognize his car, so he slowed down, keeping at a safe distance. Ten minutes later, the limo turned onto a dirt road that led to the entranceway of a colossal old mansion that was surrounded by acres of withering citrus groves.

I've never been here before.

The limo vanished behind a wall of silos, and Mills parked behind a rusty shed close to the house.

What is this place?

It appeared to be vacant.

I better be careful.

He reached into the glove box, grabbed his gun, and got out.

VROOOOM!

A plume of dirt shot up into the air, and the limo sped off to the main road. Mills checked to see if Bridget was in the back seat but couldn't tell. Curious, he returned his attention to the tattered mansion.

"It looks like a plantation."

The three-story structure was asymmetrically balanced with a set of double-curved staircases in the center, a projecting wing to the right, a curved bay to the left, and tons of shuttered windows.

Maybe it's the vaults?

He climbed up the steps which led to the front door and knocked, but there was no answer. He tried the handle, but it was locked.

Following the porch around, he located the service entrance, and his eyes grew large—one of the doors was propped open by a rock. The hairs on the back of his neck stood as he cautiously approached. He raised his gun, pushed the door open with his foot, and entered.

"Hello?" Cabinet doors dangled from the hinges in the disheveled pantry. "Bridget, are you here?"

From the kitchen, he moved into the spacious, towering living room, which seemed more fitting of a hotel lobby than a home. Faded sheets draped over torn furniture, and tattered rugs covered the hardwood floors. What paintings were left hanging on the walls were destroyed by mold and mildew. But underneath all of the decay, Mills could tell that the house was once stunning. He imagined the place must've been something in its heyday with its vast staircase that swerved to the left as it reached the second floor and all of the beautiful crystal chandeliers that still dangled from the ceilings. His ears perked up at the faint sound of laughter coming from behind the wall, and he walked over.

"Bridget?"

There were three doors down at the end of the hall. All were closed except for one. Mills raised his gun, pulled back the hammer, and then with slow, methodical steps, made his way down the stairs.

"Here it is, Father. I told you I'd figure it out," Bridget laughed.

The basement was divided into two compartments. The first section was a small control room with an observation window and a console that flashed yellow and green lights. On the wall next to it was a big red button covered by white tape that read DO NOT TOUCH.

The second chamber was as vast as the mansion above and was filled with rows of wooden cabinets that traveled all the way to the back of the room. A steel door with no handles connected the rooms.

As Mills stepped down onto the last tread, a loud crack sounded. "Alpheus, is that you?" Bridget questioned without looking up. Her eyes were fixated on the console before her, comparing it to her father's notes. "Hello, Bridget."

Startled, she jumped.

"Uncle Paddy?" Her eyes narrowed on the gun. "What are you doing here?" she said with a nervous laugh and slid the diagram under a stack of papers as she stood.

"I saw you kill Peters."

"You what?" Her heart skipped a beat. "It wasn't my fault! He was waiting there to kill me—he wanted Father's key."

"Why didn't you tell me you found it?" Mills said furiously, and fear grew in her eyes. Bridget had never seen him like this before. He was filled with rage.

"I was going to—"

"It was you!" He stepped closer, the gun still aiming at her heart. "You killed Mrs. Kelly, didn't you?"

"Of course not." She turned away from his penetrating glare, but he angrily grabbed her by the arm and spun her back around. "Don't lie to me, Bridget! I saw her go into the theater after you."

"How dare you," she hissed, jerking free. "For all you know, it could've been Peters. He wanted to kill everyone Father ever loved—even you, Uncle Paddy. I had to kill him. I did it for Father, for you… I couldn't stand losing you too."

Tears pooled in her eyes.

"You're my only family now."

Her words tore his heart in two, filling him with grief, angst, and guilt, but mostly love. "Dear God, what have I done to my little girl?" He put away his gun and held her tight in his arms. "I'm so sorry. Can you ever forgive me?"

"Of course, Uncle Paddy, and honestly, I was going to tell you about Mrs. Kelly, but with her death and all," she shrugged. "I didn't want to worry you."

"I know, I know," he said as he cupped her chin and kissed her on the forehead. "But please promise me that there will be no more surprises, okay?

"I promise." Her head dropped in exhaustion, and her father's diagram peeped out from the papers, and she remembered why she was there.

"Are we good?" he said, locking eyes with her, and held out his hands, inviting her to hold them.

My handsome hero… Father's best friend… someone who I have adored my whole life—and yet, he came here to kill me…

With a sad smile, Bridget placed her hands in his and squeezed.

"Yes, Uncle Paddy, we're good."

"Trust me, Bridget. Everything is going to work out, I promise."

A flashing green light caught his eye, and he pointed to it. "Hey, what's that?" Intrigued, he stepped over to the console, then peered into the chamber. "So, is this the vaults that everyone's been asking about?"

"It would appear so." Bridget took out her compact mirror from her purse and dabbed at her tear stains. "And it's filled with all the Prescott family secrets."

"How'd you find it?"

Returning the compact to her bag, she saw her father's gun and paused.

"Bridget, are you okay?"

"Um, yes, Uncle Paddy. I'm fine… it's just been an intense morning, that's all." She took a deep breath and rubbed at her temples. "I found the directions in Peters' bag. I guess all he needed was Father's key, and he would have ruled the Order."

"I told your father to watch out for him, but you know your father, he wouldn't listen to me. He was too busy wanting to be President."

"You felt that Father shouldn't have run?" Her eyes narrowed.

"It was pretty ambitious for someone who acted so recklessly. Hey, what's this for?" He pointed to a large square handle with a downward arrow.

"Don't know, but I think this button opens the door. Do you want to go in and have a look around?"

"Sure, I'd love to."

Bridget pushed the green button. The hydraulic lever activated the steel doorway, and a breeze of perfectly cooled, humidity-free air rushed in. Mills smiled and entered the chamber. "You coming?"

"In a bit, you go first. I'm still figuring this out. I don't want us to get locked inside." She smiled.

"Yeah, good thinking."

There was a sense of thrill in the air as Mills traveled down the aisles. He eyed the nameplates on each of the cabinets, then stopped at the Ws and pulled the drawer open. His fingers flipped through the names.

"Holy shit, your dad had the goods on Old Man Williams." He stared at a racy photo and let out a long whistle. "Oh, you dirty dog."

Realizing it was now or never, Bridget picked up her father's diagram and turned it over. A note was scribbled at the bottom:

In case of emergency,
type in 012361,
and activation will begin.

Emptiness filled her heart, and with a deep sigh, she hit the green button, and the door started to close. Mills turned, and she hurried, typing the numbers into the flickering black screen, and then the generators kicked on. He looked confused and rushed forward, but it was too late. The door clicked shut.

"What are you doing?"

"You know, Father always said you weren't very bright." She let out a knowing laugh. "The funny part is that's what he loved most about you. He said you never asked questions. You just did as you were told—the good soldier."

"Come on, Bridget, stop playing games and open the door. It's getting hot in here." He loosened his tie.

"I'm sorry, but I can't." Her eyes were flat, her voice cold.

"Why are you doing this?"

"You lied to me, Uncle Paddy."

"I have never."

"You always have."

Her eyes darkened, and she hit another button.

"Uncle Paddy, did you know that Father loved fire? It excited him. He said the man who could control fire would control the world."

"He what?" The temperature gauge on the wall read ninety-seven degrees. "Come on, please, just open the door."

Scrutinizing the sweat dripping down his forehead, Bridget wondered if he was afraid.

"Father's greatest fear was that someone would find this place. He said it would ruin the family name. At least that's what he wrote in his diary." She shook her head. "Such a pity too. He hated the thought of anyone knowing his secrets." She shot him a look. "Even you, Uncle Paddy, he didn't trust you much."

"He trusted me with everything, including his life!"

"And yet, you failed him."

"No—you can't blame his death on me! I wasn't even there."

"Exactly, but back to his love of fire... guess what Father did with this place?" Panicked, Mills looked down at the vents and then up at the ceiling.

"Yup, he rigged it to burn at the push of a button—*POOF!* And everything turns to ashes," she let out a childish squeal. "And all without destroying the building. It's quite brilliant, don't you think?"

"Bridget, come on, please."

"You shouldn't have followed me, Uncle Paddy." She stepped within inches of the glass. "Oh, and I'm curious, what were you planning on doing with that gun you had pointed at my heart? Were you going to shoot me just like Peters wanted to do?"

"No, of course not. I was just being cautious."

"Lies... and I know it was you who killed my Russell."

"No, I didn't! He was dealing drugs, and your father told him to stop, but he wouldn't. So, your father hired someone to make it look like an accident."

"More lies... Father would never betray me like that. He knew Russell was the love of my life."

"Goddammit, he was cheating on you!"

Mills punched the glass, and she staggered back, clutching her heart as if he had hit her.

"You shut your lying mouth! Russell loved me, and I'm pregnant with his child. And now, because of you, my baby girl will never know her own father!"

"I swear, I didn't!"

"Father never killed anyone—you did. You killed that family in the house fire, you killed my Russell, and then you killed Father."

"But I wasn't even there!"

"Well, you should have been."

"Bridget, please, don't do this! What about my wife, my kids—"

"Enough," she screamed. Her eyes went flat, and Mills gasped. He knew that look. "What's the matter, Uncle Paddy... do you see a ghost?"

The innocent little girl who used to light up every time he walked into the room now bore deep in his soul with eyes as cold as her father's.

"Oh, and yes, I did kill Mrs. Kelly—that bitch deserved to die for destroying my family." She typed in the last of the code. "And for the record, I killed all the others too." She turned to the red button and ripped off the tape. "I guess Mother was right. I am just like my father."

Bridget gave him a sad smile, remembering how much she idolized the man standing before her, then pressed the button.

"Goodbye, Uncle Paddy."

The incinerator kicked on.

"Tell Father I love him."

Searing flames dropped from the ceiling, and he scurried back. He pulled out his gun and started firing, but the small .22s ricocheted off the glass. He begged for his life, but she just stared at him as the fire devoured him whole.

The limo waited outside. Alpheus stood with the door open, and she collapsed into the back seat. Her father's diary lay on the floor next to his pen, along with her to-do list. Crying, Bridget picked up the list and angrily scratched off Uncle Paddy's name over and over until the pen tore through the paper. Then she leaned back and stared at the last remaining name:

Theodora Hayes

40

Wake Up

Some colognes are so familiar that it doesn't matter if you know its name or not. You just remember the way it made you feel. However, Teddy knew this scent too well. She had only known one other man who wore it—her father, Henry, but never before had it had such a tantalizing pull on her.

Deeply, she inhaled its fragrance. Her head swirled as she drank it in with such need, such desire, such wanting. Her fingers knotted into his hair and pulled him down so that his lips were inches from hers, and she demanded a kiss.

Kenneth complied, parting her lips just enough to slide his tongue over hers.

Such tormenting pleasure...

A burst of cool air brushed over their naked bodies as they stood by the window. His hardness pressed up against her back as he scraped his teeth along the nape of her neck and slowly dragged downward, nibbling, biting, and leaving a trail of goosebumps glistening in the moonlight.

"Umm-mmmmm," she hissed. "This is just what I needed." Kenneth grinned, knowing she was his to own, but for now, his

only thought was that of pleasing her.

"May I?" his throaty voice asked as he took one of her nipples in his mouth and sucked long and hard, and Teddy squirmed in delight.

He lifted her onto the bed and straddled between her legs. His mouth, thirsting to taste her. He slid his tongue deep within, twirling, teasing, caressing until her body arched and went rigid—

"Theodora... hey, princess, it's time to get up!" Kenneth's voice rose up from the floor below, and Teddy woke.

Noooooo—Oh, come on!

"Breakfast is almost ready!"

"Damn him!" With a shudder, she threw off the blankets. "Theodora, are you coming?" Teddy stared at the ceiling and sighed. *I was...* then she yelled, "One second, Kenneth, I'll be right down!"

Shivering, she rolled out of bed.

Fuck, it's cold.

Too groggy to see straight, she fumbled through his closet looking for something to wear and grabbed one of his sweatshirts and put it on, then dragged on a pair of his sweats. Quickly, she paused by the mirror, primping her hair just enough to remove the "I had an *AMAZING* sex dream" look, and was ready to go.

"Morning," he said cheerfully, sitting in the kitchen nook, finishing his eggs.

"Don't even look at me," she thundered, heading straight for the coffee pot.

"What'd I do?"

"You and those piercing blue eyes." She waved a dismissive hand. "And that damn smile—pfft, it's nothing but trouble."

"Who me?" he said with a devilish grin.

"Uh-huh." Teddy's insides tightened, then she cocked her head and let out a small laugh. "I bet that's the look you give all the girls to get them in bed."

"Ms. Hayes, is that an invitation?"

Her eyes drifted to his mouth, unaware that she was touching hers. "Just making an observation," she said, perplexed. "So, I was wondering if you could drive me to the train station this morning."

"Actually, I have bad news—"

"Don't you *DARE* say snow!"

"Bingo—everything is down and won't return until tomorrow."

"Fuck. Fuck. Fuck!" She slammed her hand down on the counter. "How do you people live like this?"

"Hey, one more day won't kill you. Plus, we have electricity, and the TV works."

"I don't watch TV." Incredulous, Teddy pulled the kitchen curtain open and cringed at the whiteness of everything. "Jesus, does this stuff come in *any* other color?" Grinning, he shook his head.

"And while we're on the subject of things you love... the game's on today, and the guys are coming by to watch. It'll be fun, that is, if you like football." His eyes locked with hers, and his smile softened. He was happy to see that her cheeks were less hollow and that she had a bit more coloring than the night before. "You look rested. Did you sleep well?"

"I did, thank you." She made her coffee and smiled. "Good, you needed it." Kenneth sensed something different about her— she seemed less cocky, softer, kinder, and more beautiful. He kept on talking, and every now and again, she'd nod, but he could tell she wasn't listening. "Theodora?"

"Ah… yes, Kenneth?" Her cheeks blushed pink, flashes of her dream kept popping in and out of her thoughts, and she couldn't focus.

"Is something wrong?"

"Oh, no, not at all. I'm just enjoying my coffee." Her fingers wrapped around the mug, and she moaned. "Mmm, so good."

"I see." He eyed her curiously, knowing she was side-stepping the question, but that was okay because at least she was there with him and not lost in the city.

"Kenneth, I saw a romance novel on your mom's bookshelf that I've been dying to read. So if it's fine with you, I'd like to pass on the game today, okay?"

"Sure, whatever you want."

"By the way, do you have a needle and thread I could use? Some madman tore my backpack to pieces," her eyes rolled. "And it needs a little repairing."

"A little?" he laughed. "I think that bag is a goner. However, I do have a black leather one down in the basement that will go nicely with your jacket. It's yours, that is, as long as you promise to eat."

"Really, O'Connor?" She looked at him, puzzled. "You are such a nudge and *sooo* familiar too."

"Is that a bad thing?"

A peaceful feeling swept over her, and she sat down next to him.

"So, what's for breakfast?"

41

Betrayal

AARRGGHHH!

In a fit of rage, Bridget stormed into her mother's study. Flashes of her Uncle Paddy begging for his life—his hair and skin melting off his bones—rattled her thoughts, and she bellowed out in anguish.

"Why?"

There was a crazed look in her eye as she prowled around the room, searching for something. She wasn't sure what but knew she'd find it.

Her eyes narrowed on her mother's parasol, and she scowled. It was sitting all alone in the rack, just laughing at her—at least, that's what she thought when she picked it up and started furiously beating things with a vengeance.

"I know you're hiding in here. Now where the hell are you?"

Mascara streaked down her face as she swung wildly at her mother's treasures, destroying everything in sight. Then her mother's belligerent voice shrieked, "How *DARE* you touch my things!" Bridget froze, and then, once again, the memory of the parasol rapping across her knuckles flashed before her eyes.

"Father, help me!" she screamed as if she were five, but this time the air depleted from her lungs, and she gasped at the sad reality. "He can't... *he's gone*... forever."

Staggering to her mother's desk, she wept uncontrollably, knowing she was truly alone—*everyone I love is dead!* A porcelain music box sat open on the ledge, she cranked it, and her mother's favorite song played. With a ferocious primal scream, she raised the beautiful umbrella high above her head and smashed down upon it. "I hate you," she cried. "I hate you! I hate you! I hate you!"

Over and over, she pummeled until a letter fell from its hold. Her breath hitched, and Bridget unfolded it.

My Beautiful Theodora,

You came to me
in my dreams again,
I sang you a lullaby.

Time and distance
don't mean a thing,
when I'm rocking you in my arms.

Fly away,
let's go together,
let's make a clean getaway.

You and I will be
happy ever after,
If only for—

"Mother, how could you!"

42

She's Wanted

"Hey K, bring me a cold one, would ya? This one's done—"

BUURRRPPP!

At the sound of his own long disgusting belch, DM Jones sunk back into the couch and burst into a fit of laughter.

DM was Kenneth's best friend since elementary school and lived down the block. He was a burly man with dark hair and kind eyes and had a big smile and an even bigger beer belly that jiggled every time he laughed, which was often.

"I gotcha covered," K yelled from the kitchen, then he kicked the fridge shut and headed back into the living room with his arms full of beers, two bags of chips, and a large bowl of onion dip. It was Sunday afternoon, the Pro Bowl was on, and the score was tied at sevens.

"GO! GO! GO!"

Upstairs, Teddy put down the romance novel and shook her head.

Has it really only been six days since I left Florida—

"TOUCHDOWN!"

Geez, it feels SO much longer—

"YESSSSS!"

DM lunged at the TV from the couch, following the ball as it passed through the goalpost for the extra point, and he screamed, "It's going in, fellas—it's going in!"

"Sit your FAT ass down!" CeeCee yelled from the recliner. He was a wiry Irish boxer in his late forties who smoked like a fiend and had a few teeth missing, which he wore like a badge of honor. "I can't see a shittin' thing!"

"Is that so?" DM winked at K, then he wiggled his big butt in front of Cee's face and let one go—

RIPPP!

"Oh, *GROSS!*" Cee gagged, and then DM busted into laughter.

"WINNING!"

Pulling the blankets over her head, Teddy cupped her ears to block out the sound.

UGH! Is there no escape from this MALE testosterone MADNESS?

Totally beside herself, she threw off the covers and jumped out of bed. Then she stripped on the way to the bathroom, deciding a steamy hot bath was her only getaway. There was a biting chill in the air, so she cranked the faucet to hot, tossed in a handful of sweet calming crystals, and then slid down into the luscious smelling sanctuary, immersing her head deep within its bubbles.

Oooh, my savior—

"THEODORA!"

Kenneth's muffled voice rose up through the pipes, and

Teddy went still.

Seriously?

"Quick, Teddy, come down!"

Annoyed, she climbed out and grabbed his mother's robe off the hook, then hurried to the stairs. "What?" she yelled, hanging her head over the railing.

"You're on TV!"

"I'm *what?*"

Rushing down two steps at a time, Teddy charged into the living room. The guys stepped back to let her by, gawking at the beige silk clinging to her wet curves. "Holy shit, it is her," DM uttered, nodding approval to K.

"Nah, it can't be," Cee doubted, swinging his head back and forth from the girl on the screen to Teddy. "This one's way hotter."

She ignored them both and stepped closer to the TV, staring in disbelief at her driver's license photo that took up the entire screen, along with the words MISSING PERSON and the phone number for the Crime Stoppers hotline.

"The Florida woman—"

"Hey, babe, you from Florida?" Cee interrupted, flashing his toothless grin. "My grandmother lives there. She's a great cook— you cook?"

Incredulous, Teddy said no.

"Authorities are asking for anyone who has seen or heard from this woman to call Crime Stoppers or contact the NYPD Police Department—"

"Whatcha do, doll, rob a bank?" DM let out a hearty chuckle.

"That's enough, guys—and you, come with me." Kenneth grabbed Teddy by the hand and dragged her into the kitchen. "What's this all about?" he said in a hushed voice so the guys couldn't hear.

"I don't know," she looked at him confused, then turned back to the screen. "Wait, my stuff was stolen… maybe it's about that?"

"Nah, I don't think so… I don't think they do this for missing IDs. Let's call them."

"Right *now?*" she shrieked. "Can't it at least wait until tomorrow morning?"

"No," he said, frowning.

Glaring at him, she blew out a frustrated huff, then grabbed the phone and dialed, mumbling a few incoherent expletives under her breath.

"*Pain in my ass—*"

RING!

"Operator, how can I help you?"

"Hi, my picture was on TV, and it said I needed to call this number."

"Your name, please?"

"Theodora Hayes."

"One moment…"

Tension filled the air as they nervously waited, then the line clicked over.

"Hello, Ms. Hayes. I'm Agent Walters from the FBI." Teddy's eyes went large, and Kenneth leaned in closer to hear. "Sir, are you looking for me?"

"Yes, we are, Ms. Hayes." Walters exhaled, relieved to finally hear her voice. "I don't mean to frighten you, but a situation has come up and we need to speak with you in person. Are you still in the city?"

"No, I'm in Brooklyn."

"Oh, good, that's not too far from here. Can you meet us tomorrow morning at ten? If you need a ride, we can pick you up."

"I'll drive you," Kenneth said, and Teddy nodded, relieved. "No, thank you, sir. I have a ride."

"Great, I'll see you then, Ms. Hayes."

CLICK!

43

O' Malley's

"Hayes!"

The game was over, the guys had just left, and Kenneth's hand barely let go of the doorknob when he rushed to the stairs and shouted, "Are you going to tell me what the hell is going on or what?" Fully dressed, Teddy came down, side-stepping past him, and headed straight for the front window and peered out. "Didn't you say there was a pub around here?"

"O'Malley's, and don't try to change the subject."

"I'm not." She grabbed his jacket off the banister and handed it to him. "I just want a drink. Let's go."

• • •

The crowded Irish bar sat at the end of the block. It was his dad's favorite hang after a long day's work. His mom hated the place. She'd complain that it was too loud, too dingy, and always full of boozers. But K loved it—the smell, the locals, the vibe. It was his home away from home. Everyone knew him, which was good on most days but not today—

"Hey K, how's it going?"

"K, where you been?"

"K, did you catch the game?"

Voices in every direction called to him, but he just charmed them away with a wink or smile and headed straight for the bar.

"Well, aren't you Mister Popular?" Teddy laughed, surprised by all the greetings.

"I grew up here—Hey, Flynn, give me two shots and a round of Stouts."

"Sure thing, K," the gray-haired bartender said with a wink, and Kenneth grabbed Teddy's hand and guided her to a small table in the back by the kitchen.

"Is this okay with you?"

"For a drink, I'd sit anywhere." She scooted in, and he sat across from her—their knees accidentally knocked. "Sorry," he said and instinctively ran a warm hand over her leg. The suddenness of his touch caught her by surprise, and she shuddered.

"Ticklish, are ya?" said the twiggy Irish barmaid with red hair and curious green eyes as she stepped up to the table. "Crack on, Kenny-K. What brings you here on this miserable day?" She sent a kind smile to Teddy while she divvied up the drinks. "And who's the stunner?"

"Yeah, who's the stunner?" chimed the regulars at the bar. Embarrassed, Kenneth looked around and realized all eyes were on them. He stood on the bench and waved a hand to quiet the room.

"Hear ye, hear ye… this is our new friend Theodora Hayes. She's visiting us from Florida and has been stranded due to the snow in this lovely place we call our home." Sympathy calls bounced off the walls, and he placed a hand on his heart. "So, please treat her kindly, and maybe she'll come back and visit us on a finer day." He winked at Teddy, then shouted, "Next round is on me!"

The room filled with cheers.

"Feeling generous, are ya, O'Connor?" the wiry old boozer at the next table piped. "Wud ya get outta that garden?" The words barely left his mouth when his wife slapped him upside the head and yelled, "Oh, you hush your filthy mouth. Can't you see he likes her?" Then the bar broke out into joyful laughter, and Kenneth's face turned a shade of red.

"Don't pay any attention to them," Shannon quipped. "They passed go a couple of hours back and are wired to the moon." She let out a hearty laugh. "And besides, I can think of plenty of places worse than K's to be stranded at, if you know what I mean?" She sent Teddy a naughty look.

"That'll be enough, Shannon. And you," Kenneth pushed a shot into Teddy's hand and lifted his glass. "Stop stalling, and let's drink—Antifogmatic!"

"What?" Teddy said, confused.

"ANTIFOGMATIC!" the patrons at the bar yelled, and Shannon whispered in her ear, "It takes the fog away, my dear."

"DRINK! DRINK! DRINK!"

Pounding on the tables and stomping their feet, the patrons roared in excitement as Teddy lifted the glass to her lips, and Kenneth shouted, "O'Malley's finest!"

DRINK! DRINK! DRINK!

"Cheers to foggy no mores," Teddy said, gulping hers down with a gag. Then Kenneth threw his back with a shiver—Sláinte!

The room burst into cheers as the burning warmth of the whiskey tingled down her throat. Teddy melted into the chair, enjoying the moment, and watched as the folks faded into their worlds. A content smile sat on her face, and she wondered if she'd ever fit into a place like this.

"Um, Ms. Hayes…"

"Yes, Kenneth?" His piercing blues furrowed, and he locked eyes with her. "So… do you have something you want to tell me?"

"Ew, do I have to?" she winced. "Can't we just get happily drunk and deal with it in the morning?"

"Come on, Theodora, just tell me why the cops want you."

"Want me? Yikes, you think that they want *me?*"

"Of course, they do. The FBI doesn't put your face on TV unless you've killed someone or know somebody who has. Either way, they want to question you."

"Hmph, that's not good," she frowned, picking at her beer label, then shook her head. "Honestly, Kenneth, I don't know—"

"Oh, bullshit, Teddy… it's about your boyfriend, isn't it?"

"Who, C*ole?*" she laughed. "No, at least, I don't think so."

"Well, who then?"

Alarms screamed in her head.

DON'T tell him about Eni.

"Oh, come on, you still don't trust me?"

AND don't mention being shot.

Her mouth turned into an "O" as she contemplated what to

say, and then she stared deep into his eyes. *They're so blue… so intense… so caring—Ugh, and he's just like my damn nudgy sister!*

"Oh, alright, Mister-Pain-In-My-Ass, if you must know, I think it has something to do with my girlfriend."

"Your *who?*" Kenneth choked. "You have a girlfriend?"

"No, not that kind of girlfriend, perv—*GEEZ!*"

"Oh, good," he smiled, relieved.

"Eni, the one we were looking for." As the words fell from her lips, she covered her mouth. "Oh, God, I hope she's not dead…"

"Dead?"

"Yeah, she was shot—"

"Shot?"

"Stop it! You're freaking me out."

"BUT—"

"But nothing… where's Shannon? We need more drinks?" Her hand waved in the air, and he frowned. "Teddy, I'm worried about you."

"Oh please, O'Connor… you worry too much."

"When I found you at the station, you looked so frightened, like a captured animal trying to escape."

"That's because a *CRAZED* madman rushed down the escalator, jumped over dozens of bodies, and lunged straight at me." She shot him an incredulous look. "Jesus, what were you thinking?"

"Yeah, well, that wasn't my finest hour, but at least I found you."

Taken aback at the reality that he had rescued her, Teddy's lips bubbled into a smile. "Hmm, I guess you did, didn't you…"

"So, did you find your boyfriend?"

"Seriously, O'Connor," she cocked her head. "Are you going to ask twenty questions, or are we gonna drink? My buzz is fading." The look on her face told him there was only one option.

"Heh, I guess we're drinking then." And with a twirl of his finger, he gestured to Shannon for another round. He shifted into her gaze, noticing she looked well-rested and relaxed, happy even. *It's probably the shot kicking in,* he figured. "So, Theodora, what would you like to talk about?"

"Hm, I don't know, let's see… hey, how about you?" She stuck out her tongue and then threw back her head, laughing. "So, did your wife really leave and take the dog?"

"It was my girlfriend, and yes, she took the dog along with everything else."

"Your heart?" Teddy smirked. "No, she never had that. That's probably why we split." His eyes widened. "How about you, ever been married?"

"Hell no," Teddy frowned.

"Why not? Are you against marriage, or you just haven't found the right mate?"

"Heh, not sure. Maybe a bit of both." Teddy played with a lock of hair. "It's probably too conventional for me, you know?"

"Yeah, same here." He held up his beer. "Here's to being single."

"Single, you? Ha, you could have fooled me, O'Connor." She clinked her bottle to his. "Every ounce of you screams the marrying type."

"Is that a proposal?" His brow rose, hoping for a nod but instead got a shake, and he laughed. "So, Teddy, when you're not stranded, what do you do for a living?"

"I waitress, sometimes I model, and, oh yeah, I make costume jewelry—but basically, whatever pleases me, really. So, what's up with you being a janitor? How did you land that gig?"

"A detour, I guess."

"How so?" Teddy could hear the hesitation in his voice, and her eyes widened in curiosity. She could tell he was holding back something really good. "What's the matter, O'Connor, feeling shy?"

"Never with you, Ms. Hayes."

"Well, then, spill it," she demanded, giving him a taste of his own nudge-ness.

"I have to warn you that I get cranky talking about this stuff, so it's best if I just give you the highlights, okay?"

"Duly noted but ignored. Now fess up, O'Connor!" She sat closer to hear, and he cleared his throat. "Ahem… so my career, my life's dreams kinda came and went, and I lost myself in a bottle of booze, then woke up surrounded by cops, and instead of doing time, they gave me the midnight shift—end of story."

"Dreams of grandeur?"

"More like delusions," he mumbled begrudgingly into his beer and swigged it.

"Heh… O'Connor, those are a whole lotta words for saying a whole lot of nothing, so stop stalling—*SPILL IT!*"

"Okay, okay," he threw up his hands playfully. "Well, in case you haven't figured it out yet, I'm a baseball player."

"Aha, I knew that *was* you in the photo!"

"Yes, indeed it was," he winked. "So, a couple of years ago, there was a baseball strike between the owners and players. It lasted about a year or so, and the whole season was canceled. Many players struggled to get by, so one by one, they started to cross the picket line." Kenneth took a long swig from his beer and shrugged. "And you know me," he laughed, locking eyes with her. "I'm way too proud, way too set in my ways to cross, and then—"

WHAM!

He slammed the table.

"They fired me." He looked down, defeated. "And that, my dear, is my story. I lost everything—"

"Every*thing*?"

"Yup, just like that." He snapped his fingers. "No more dreams, no more career, no more life that I knew—poof, it was all gone."

His fingers gestured to nothing.

"Wow, I'm so sorry… that's so tragic." She took a sip of beer, and her thoughts wandered. Warmth spread over her, she wasn't sure if it was the alcohol or Kenneth, but she knew what it meant—*PASSION!*

I can't believe I didn't see it. It was right there in front of me this whole time, all wrapped up in all of those beautiful, sexy thingies—

"Teddy, are you okay?" Kenneth's brow raised. "That must have been some thought because your face just flushed red."

"Nah, it's just the shot kicking in." Her smile went devilishly crooked. "We need more drinks *AND* some music to liven up the mood, don't you think?"

"We do," he said softly, loving how she could just turn his mood from the darkest of spaces. "They have a jukebox. What do you want to hear?"

"Anything with a soul."

"Well, that narrows it down," he laughed and headed over. Teddy watched as he sauntered to the machine and dropped coins in.

Wow, they fired him—her face flushed—*Jesus Christ, Theodora, stop looking at his ass! He just lost his whole world, and all you can think about is horndoggin!*

"Here you go, luv, shots for my girl." Shannon offloaded the drinks and winked. "Ooh, yummy." Teddy grabbed one and threw it back. "Whoa, that bitch burns."

"Hey, you'd better pace yourself, or else K's gonna be peeling you off the floor. Those bitches can sneak up on ya—"

"Whoopsies." Teddy threw back another and giggled, "Too late."

The bite of the whiskey rose like delicious needles, tormenting her skin, and then the room blurred. She ran a finger over her bottom lip. It was still tender from the kiss the night before.

Mmm, it feels so good.

Her eyes honed in on his broad shoulders, hovering over the jukebox. Kenneth had on a long black turtleneck, tightly fitted faded blue jeans, and a long, gray scarf dangling loose on his neck. She laughed, thinking he looked like one of those models she had seen on a giant billboard in the city.

He's truly gorgeous.

A sudden throb of need swept over her, and she realized that her buzz overruled all logical thought. Her eyes were glued to his purposeful hands.

SWOOSH!

The red-painted finger from her dream flashed in her memory, twirling around her nipple and making her throb down there. Then without warning, Kenneth looked up. His intense blue eyes stared deep into her soul, and she shuddered.

Oh, fuck...

Her heart nearly stopped when she heard the sound of a slow, sultry tune come humming from the speakers. By the look on her face, he knew his selection pleased her, and he headed back. Her eyes locked in on his purposeful left-right fluid gait. It sent a pang ringing in her groin, and she clenched her legs together. Then in one swift jerk, he pulled her up on her feet and onto the dance floor.

"Oh, my," she swooned. "Who would've thought you could dance?"

"I have Sister Mary to thank for that."

He pulled her in close, and she melted into his arms with a shudder. Her nose nuzzled into the nape of his neck, and she inhaled deeply, closing her eyes. Cradling tighter into his hold, they connected like the perfect puzzle piece.

Oh, fuck, I want him.

She pulled back.

"Kenneth, let's go?"

"But I just filled the jukebox."

"I wanna go now."

"But—"

"I want to go to bed," she said, her voice husky.

"But, we—"

"With you, Kenneth." She bit down on her lip. "I want to go to bed with you."

"You do?"

"Yes," she murmured, her words barely a whisper.

For a dizzying moment, he stared at her swollen lips. The hunger, the need that he had felt since they met, aching in his gut. Gently, he took her lips in his and kissed her with such passion that she swayed, and he pulled her in tighter.

"Yummy," she murmured. "Can we please go?"

O'Malley's faded away, and the bedroom door kicked open with the help of his foot as he carried her to the bed. Naked, they tumbled down. His fingers laced into hers, dragging them high above her head. Thirsting for her lips, he retook her mouth with a need he had never known, and she let out a deep groan.

The dark cavernous room glowed from the halo of streetlights shining through the windows. Teddy attempted to climb on top, but there was no way Kenneth was going to let her take control.

"Not today, Hayes," he murmured, his voice low and husky. And with something of a growl, he spun her on her back, pinning her down under his weight.

"Mmm… very good, O'Connor. You passed the first test." Her voice was soft, sensual, a bit daring, but mostly playful. He grinned.

"Are you schooling me?" he crooned, retaking her mouth before she could answer. He knew he could never get enough of it. The caring look in her eyes caught him by surprise, and he felt an overwhelming need to satisfy her—*to blow her mind.* Then his simple kiss morphed into possession, trailing down her neck.

"Mmmm, deliciousness," she groaned with a shiver. Her hand reached down to touch him, but once again, he grabbed the throttle.

"What's the hurry?" he hissed, pinning her hands away from his loins. He pressed up against her stomach, and she cooed.

"I feel you..."

"And I, you." He cupped a hand against her warmth; she was wet. He bowed his head down to drink in her taste and let out a deep moan.

At first, her body shuddered from the heat of his lips, and she locked her fingers into his hair, riding his skillful mouth. But when he slid his middle finger gently over her folds and pushed two inside, she threw her head back in pleasure.

"Oh, God, yes," she panted, struggling for consciousness.

Kenneth's tongue twirled slowly around her clit with such torment. His fingers, sliding in and out, gliding over her wetness. Her body began to stiffen. He could feel she was close, and with a thrust, he sent her over the edge and into his arms.

A flood of emotions swept over him as her heart lay beating with his. Teddy stared into the blue of his eye. The smell of her scent still lingered on his lips, and she inhaled deeply as if it was her last breath. Then she dug her nails into his back, pulling him into her possession—she was done debating.

And the heart unwinds...

The violence of need exploded, and tiny chills rose up on her skin as his talented fingers glided over her delicious curves, exploring, caressing. His teeth scraped down her neck to her nipples. He took one in his mouth, biting, sucking, tugging, then shifted to the other, tantalizing her with such sweet torment. His long, hard cock slapped against her stomach, just aching for attention.

"I want you…"

His eyes darkened, and quickly he drove his penis into her. The pain was so sweet, so deliciously sweet, as he lifted her hips to the heavens.

With each thrust, she writhed against his body, twisting as he pounded violently deep. His cock throbbed. He was close, but he held back, waiting for her. Higher and higher she went, her eyes closing, her body arching. *She's ready!* He held her tight as he pumped himself into her, pounding deeper, faster. In unison, they screamed, crashing into spasms.

44

Morning After

Damn, those shots!

She plopped her head back down on the pillow and squeezed her eyelids shut.

Ugh, what DID I do?

The warmth of the morning sun came in through the blinds, and her naked skin, still buzzing from Kenneth's touch, soaked it in.

"Pfft, what's an adventure without a little fun? Besides, I sooo needed it."

Exasperated with herself, Teddy kicked off the remaining covers and glanced around the bedroom.

The blue and gray walls gave off a manly vibe, which she had expected, as did Kenneth's massive bed and leather chair that sat in the corner covered in clothes. There were a few inspirational posters on the walls, but that was it, no other imagery. A long dresser was pressed against the wall with a tiny, itty-bitty mirror above it. She scowled, thinking no woman could possibly use it.

Gingerly, she touched her lips.

Ooh, ouchies…

They felt so tender and tingled.

Mmm, he was WAY better than I had expected. More loving. More intense—ugh, and way more passionate. Pfft, I'm so screwed.

Quietly laughing, she shook her head in disbelief.

Cleo's going to kill me!

The sweet smell of cinnamon wafted in the air.

"Theodora?" Kenneth's light-hearted voice beckoned through the floors. "For the third time, you need to get up, or else we'll be late."

"Ewww, the FBI… fuck, fuck, *FUCK!*" Grunting, she punched the pillow, then turned on her side and whined, "I don't want to go…"

"Teddy, did you hear me?"

She let out a whimpering cry, then jumped up and popped her head out the door.

"I'll be right down!"

Rushing into the bathroom, she brushed her teeth, fixed her makeup, and with a pucker, decided her lips didn't need any color, just a bit of gloss due to their perfect shade of bruise. Finally, she primped her hair, pulling down a few strands so they cradled her face, and she smiled. "You gotta love sex curls."

Pfft, I say screw the FBI and let's spend the whole day in bed making love. No Eni, no Cole—oh shit, I forgot about him!

Quickly, she threw on her clothes, grabbed her new backpack, and headed down.

"There you are," he beamed. "Wow, your hair looks great."

"Thank you." Her insides tightened as her eyes dropped to his deliciously kissable mouth, and her stomach growled. "I'm hungry, O'Connor."

"I see," he said, grinning, and pulled her into his arms, capturing her swollen lips.

"Mm, cinnamon," she moaned. "Can't we just stay home today?"

He pushed a curl from her eyes.

"I wish, now stop tempting me. We're late. We gotta go."

"But I'm hungry."

"We'll pick you up something on the way." He grabbed their jackets and dragged her out the door.

"But I want pancakes—"

• • •

A half-hour later, worry filled the air as they drove in silence through the slush-filled streets of Manhattan. Teddy nibbled on a bagel, but the thought of being interrogated by the FBI made her nauseous, and she packed it away.

"Don't worry, it's going to be fine, I promise," Kenneth said with a reassuring smile, but then the memory of her face, all bloodied and bruised, flashed before his eyes, and he wondered what all she wasn't telling him.

The dashboard clock read a quarter to ten as he pulled up to the curb in front of the FBI Manhattan field office and put the car in park. "Well, we're here and right on time too," he sighed. "You ready?"

Teddy stared up at the tall, gloomy-looking building with its impenetrable windows and shook her head. He reached over and gently caressed her cheek with his thumb, and her eyes softened. "You go in, and I'll park the car. I'll meet you inside, okay?" Clutching her backpack, she nodded and hopped out.

The sun was shining, but it was chilly out. Teddy pulled up her collar and hurried to the entrance. A blonde woman stood by the glass entrance doors, watching as Teddy approached. She had on a black fur hat and was wrapped in a bright pink fur coat with her hands tucked deep inside the pockets.

"Theodora Hayes," she called out in a harsh tone.

Teddy turned a startled look, and her eyes went wide. The woman rushed forward, her hands jerking free from her pockets, and Teddy gasped. A familiar golden lock of blonde hair fell from the crazy hat that sat crooked on the woman's head, and in an instant, Teddy's cat-shaped eyes filled with tears of joy.

"Cleo, is that *really* you?"

The two sisters crashed into each other's arms, both sputtering a million incoherent words a second with tears streaming down their faces until finally, Teddy pulled back and screeched, "Cleo, what the *HELL* are you *wearing?*"

"It's crazy Abby's," she sighed with a laugh and pulled her sister in for another hug. "Oh, Theodora, I thought I'd never see you again."

Just then, Kenneth rounded the corner, and Cleo sputtered, "Oh my *GOD*, it's him!" Quickly, she patted her face dry and pulled off the hat. "It's K, and he's coming over here!"

Teddy did a double take.

"You know *him?*"

"Of course I do, silly. He's a great baseball player." She reached out to shake his hand. "Hi, I'm Cleo. I'm your biggest fan."

"Cleo-*O!*" Teddy swatted her hand away. "Stop being such a groupie. Kenneth, this my older sister."

"Your what?" His bright blues darted back and forth between the two strikingly different women, trying to absorb that they were related, then flashed a huge grin. "It's a pleasure to meet you—"

HAAYEEES!

A male voice shouted from the building, and they all turned. Agent Walters charged out the door and headed straight for Cleo. "What the hell are you doing here? I thought I told you to stay put!"

"As if," she snapped, crossing her arms defiantly.

"Cleo, you know this man?" Teddy said, baffled.

"Clearly, I do," she huffed. "Agent Walters, this is my sister, Theodora."

Walters shifted his annoyance to Teddy. "You're a hard one to find, Ms. Hayes."

"Sir, how's Eni*?* Is she okay? Please tell me she's not dead. "

"What? Who's *dead?* " Cleo sent Walters a frantic look, and he shook his head. "Enough, ladies, not here. Let's go inside. Agent Stewart is upstairs waiting for us." He headed to the entrance and held the door open for Cleo, then Teddy walked through, and when Kenneth crossed, he pulled him aside. "Hey K, I'm a big fan of yours, but this is official business. You can't come—"

"But he's my ride."

"Don't worry, Ms. Hayes, we'll get you a driver."

"I don't want another driver!"

"Sir, I'll just wait here in the lobby if that's okay?" Kenneth sent him a pleading look, and Walters cracked his neck, clearly agitated. "Fine, but it's going to be a while, and the heater is broken." Then he headed over to Cleo, who was already waiting by the elevators with her arms crossed.

"Oh, this is such bullshit," Teddy muttered, annoyed beyond belief. She watched as Walters approached her sister, and the look on Cleo's face said it all—*Ewww, she likes him... pfft, and he's sooo her type too!*

Teddy let out a puff of deflated air and turned back to Kenneth. "Look, I completely understand if you want to go home."

"No fucking way, screw Agent Stuffy Pants. I'm not leaving."

"Really?" A chuckle slipped from her lips, delighted.

"Yes, I mean, if that's okay with you?"

"Of course, it is," Teddy beamed. "And besides, you did promise me pancakes."

"I did, didn't I?" he grinned.

"Yes, O'Connor, you owe me." Lightly, she poked his chest and the memory of the first time they met floated in the air.

"Who me?" he gushed playfully. "Yeah, you buddy—you," she laughed and poked him once more, but this time, he caught her finger and pulled her in for a kiss. "Mmm, yummy," she groaned. "Wanna guess where I felt that?"

"Theodora Hayes," Cleo's voice thundered. "Stop the flirting and get your ass in this elevator now!"

• • •

Five hours later, the waiting room was empty, and Kenneth sat leaning forward, blowing heat into his hands for warmth. The elevator doors slid open, and the sisters stepped out. He jumped up to greet them, and his eyes went wide as soon as he saw Teddy's tear-smudged face.

"That good, huh?" he uttered in despair. "What can I do to help?" Teddy gave him a soft smile and nodded as if to say nothing.

DING!

The adjacent elevator doors opened, and Agent Stewart stepped out. "Here you go, Ms. Hayes, your boyfriend's address that you asked for." He handed Teddy a slip of paper and quickly hopped back in. "Oh, and we're still looking into the other matter." The doors closed, and she tucked the note in her pocket.

"Sweet Jesus," Cleo muttered, exasperated as she saw the confused look on Kenneth's face. Then she marched towards the exit. "Come on, Teddy, let's get out of here. I'll go and get the car. Say your goodbyes—oh, and K, it was nice meeting you. Come and visit us in Florida." She waved a backward hand at them, then pushed through the glass doors.

●●●

Outside, the brisk day had turned wet, and Kenneth and Teddy stood under a bus stop, waiting for Cleo. The tension was thick. She could see the hurt in his eyes and her face twisted into a ball of guilt. "Look, I'm not going back to Florida, okay?"

"Teddy, I'm a bit lost here… I thought you were coming back to my house. I wanted to make you pancakes." The innocence in his voice caught her by surprise, and in a beat, she dug her fingers into his tousled hair and pulled him into a deep kiss with her tongue sliding over his, needing to taste him, to feel him, to have him.

BEEP!

"Oh, not now, Cleo-*O*!"

"Come on, Theodora, let's go!"

BEEP! BEEEEP!

"Stop it with the goddamn horn, would ya?" Teddy rolled her eyes, and Kenneth's brows jerked up, surprised at the feistiness between them. "She's just worried about you and wants you to be safe." He pushed a curl from her eyes. "I know the feeling."

"You do?" Teddy glanced at her sister and then back at him. "You know, O'Connor, something tells me you are going to be trouble." And with a tiny head shake, she laughed. "Can I get a rain check on those pancakes?"

"Absolutely, and I'll throw in some bacon too, if you'd like?"

"Ooooh, I *LOVE* bacon."

Cleo pounded on the horn again, and embarrassed, Teddy shook her head. "I better get going before she breaks that thing." She gave him a quick kiss and ran to the car. "I'll call you later."

"Great," he smiled, waving goodbye. The door slammed shut, and the rental took off. The horn blared all the way up the block.

Crazy Floridians—Kenneth thought with a laugh as he crossed the street without looking. A taxi swung around the corner and barreled into him. His body flew up and over the hood like a rag doll.

The yellow blur sped off.

45

Sisters

BEEEEP!

"You didn't even ask about your birth mother."

"Pfft..."

Teddy pulled down the visor and primped at her hair. "So, what's up with you and Officer Stuffy Pants? I don't know if I approve of him yet, but it's nice to see you all sparkly again."

"It's Agent Stuffy Pants, and don't change the subject. Aren't you at all curious about her?"

"Have you slept with him yet?" The little devil in Teddy snickered when her sister's face recoiled in embarrassment. "My guess is you haven't because I could feel the unsatisfied sexual tension building up in that tiny little room. I didn't know whether to grab popcorn and watch, or smoke a cigarette."

Cleo gripped the steering wheel tighter, then pressed down full palm for a long, nerve-wracking honk and swerved into the left lane. Teddy grabbed the roof handle and laughed, "Jesus, would ya get laid already before you kill us!"

"Theodora, this is not a game. That woman was your mother,

and it's time for you to consider all of the implications of what's going on here."

"Oh, lucky me," Teddy's words dripped with sarcasm as she stared out the window. "Hey sis… did you know that most serial killers are adopted?"

Cleo waved a hand to shoo away her silliness.

"No, it's true," she insisted. "I read it somewhere. In fact, Ted Bundy was adopted, Son of Sam, the Hillside Strangler, the Boston Strangler, and even the Eyeball Killer." She dabbed on lip balm and muttered to herself, "Hmm, I wonder what he had to do to get *that* name?"

"And your point is?"

"Well, maybe being a killer wasn't their fault. Maybe it's in their genes or something. You know, like the fat gene?"

"Seriously, Theodora, I don't think there's a serial killer gene, and if there is, I don't think you have it—if that's what you're getting at."

"You know, for as long as I can remember, there hasn't been a day that I haven't wondered about my mother. Millions of thoughts, trying to guess who she was, what was she like, do I have her eyes, but mostly, I dreamt about finding her." Teddy gave Cleo a warm smile. "I've even fantasized that one day we'd live together." Her lips thinned, and she looked down, pained. "And then today, I find out she's a murderer and that my sister wants to kill me."

She flipped the visor shut.

"How fucking lovely is *that?*"

Cleo swallowed hard. The meeting with the agents was rough. And while Teddy seemed to dismiss everything Walters had said as if it didn't pertain to her, Cleo knew it rocked her to the core.

"Fuck those people, Teddy!" She punched the steering wheel. "You don't need them. You have me, and I'll beat the crap out of that creepy bitch if she comes anywhere near you!"

Tearful, Teddy grabbed Cleo's hand and kissed it. "Always my protector… I'm the luckiest girl in the world to have you. You are my family, and I don't need anyone else." A single tear rolled down her cheek and she held Cleo's hand tight against her chest and hummed a beautiful melody.

Aside from the blaring horns of rush hour traffic, the city was peaceful. The beautiful winter's sun had returned and sat hovering over the Hudson. They stopped at a red light, and Teddy glanced over at a clock in a window display.

"Holy shit, Cleo, it's late. It's after four. It'll be dark soon. We gotta go!"

"What—*where?*"

"To the Village," Teddy uttered, reaching in her pocket for Cole's address, then glanced over it. "It says he lives on Perry, east of Greenwich—hey, I've been there before. Well, the good news is that it's not too far from here."

"Are you crazy? I'm already dreaming about being in a warm bed, eating cheap Chinese, and watching a crappy night of TV."

"Oh, that does sound amazing, but it'll have to wait. First, we have to find Cole."

"Uh-uh, no way." Cleo's head zigzagged. "I'm still angry at him."

"But you promised."

"He almost got you killed!"

"I told you it wasn't his fault."

"Would you stop making excuses for him? He left you there!"

"No, he didn't!" Furious, Teddy slammed back against her seat. "Cole did *NOT* leave me *ANYWHERE*—he didn't *KNOW!*"

"What?"

"I didn't tell him I was coming—"

"You mean you lied to *me?*" Cleo shot her a piercing look. "Just fucking great… and to think I believed your sob ass story about you coming here to settle down and have kids. Shit, you even called me Auntie—so much for that fantasy!"

"I didn't lie—I left a message on his machine!"

"Enough of your *INSANITY!*" Cleo hit the brakes. "You said he was going to pick you up with *FUCKIN'* bells on!"

The car skidded sideways, missing a fire hydrant, and slid into a parking spot.

"Dammit, Theodora!" She vaulted out of the car, spewing a litany of cuss words that turned into puffs of cold mist as she marched back and forth along the ice-scattered sidewalk.

"Cleo, stop it! You're going to fall!" Teddy jumped out of the car with her hands up and almost slipped herself. "Whoa, this shit bites!"

"Oh, screw you, *Teddeeeeeeh*—"

WHOMP!

"Ouch, my *FUCKIN'* ass!"

Teddy laughed so hard that she thought the sides of her jacket would split. "I told you so." She reached down to help her up, but Cleo knocked her hand away. "Ooh you, I am so pissed at you! You slept with him, didn't you?"

"Who, Kenneth?" Teddy pulled her up. "Yeah, so what if I did?"

"Sabotage," Cleo scoffed, rubbing the sting from her backside.

"You're kidding me, right?"

"It's what you do. I've seen it a million times. It's like you feel you don't deserve to be loved, so you destroy it before it destroys you."

"Oh no you don't, Cleopatra." Her finger and head were wagging in opposite directions. "This is not my fault. It's called a nor'easter—the blizzard of the century, and I had *NOTHING* to do with it!"

"Well, maybe not, but I hope you do know that you just blew your *ONE* chance at happiness with this fabulous artist of yours."

"Say *what?*" Teddy's mouth dropped as she realized her sister was right. "Fuck, Cleo!" Then she threw her hands up over her head, blanketing her eyes. "You have no idea what I've been through these last couple of days. It just happened."

"Oh really?" Cleo crossed her arms. "So, you just happened to fall into his bed naked?"

Teddy peeped an eye out.

"Kind of…"

"Jesus, Theodora, if that isn't sabotage, what the hell is?" Fuming, Cleo turned away but then swung back. "Why did you come here?"

"What?"

"You heard me. Why did you come to this godforsaken place for a guy you dumped years ago?"

"I don't know." Teddy shrugged. "Who knows why I do

half the things I do."

"Oh please, would you just stop it with the goddamn clueless shit!"

"No, you stop!" Teddy's voice broke. "Stop trying to make me think of things I don't want to."

"Oh Christ, Teddy, grow up! I lost my parents too, but you don't see me running away every time life gets difficult."

"Your parents died for you!" Teddy's eyes burned into hers. "Mine didn't want me, and every *FUCKING* day that passes, the gloom of knowing they left me behind on some stranger's doorstep gets darker—I leave because I have *NOTHING* to stay for! And no, I did not lie to you!" Angrily, she wiped her tears. "Cole told me that he wanted me back, so I bought a ticket, and here I am. I didn't tell him because I wanted it to be a surprise. Is that so bad?"

"You could've told me."

"Would you have let me come?"

"No fucking way," Cleo snickered and pulled her into a hug. She was mad at herself for not being able to take away her sister's pain and even more furious at those who caused it. Then she searched Teddy's eyes. "But still, Theodora… you do know that this is not love, right? And even if it was, you don't do it like this." She waved at all the snow. "Because this is the chaos that follows."

"I know, you're right." Tears welled in Teddy's eyes. "I guess I'm in love with the idea of Cole. He's broken like me, you know?"

"You are not broken! Maybe a little too adventurous, but that's a good thing for such a beautiful spirit like yours." Teddy's eyes softened as Cleo blotted her tears. "And what about K?"

"He's sooo not my type, but he's breathtakingly beautiful, and he makes me feel things I've never felt before." Teddy pursed her lips and smiled. "And surprisingly, I feel safe when I'm with him."

"Is that so?" Cleo let out a happy sigh. "Now him, I approve of."

"I figured you would, especially since he has all those damn thingies everywhere, but Cleo…" Sadness trembled in her voice. "Maybe you're right. Perhaps, I do sabotage everything." Teddy shrugged. "Ever since I left Florida, I've had this gnawing feeling that I have to see this through with Cole, or else I'll regret it my whole life. Does that make any sense to you?"

"Yes, in a crazy way, it does."

"Plus, I have to see my painting."

"Your *what?*"

"My portrait—it's this semi-nude, realistic painting that Cole did of me when we first started dating. It's really beautiful and oh, so hot."

Laughing, Teddy closed her eyes, remembering the day he painted it. "I was half-dressed, wearing nothing but my red silk robe and just sitting there on the corner of his bed, pulling off my stiletto." Her breath hitched. "Afterwards, we made love for hours. It was quite magical, but what makes the painting so special is that he mixed our blood into the paint and said that by pouring our love into its creation, we created an everlasting life bond between us."

"Eww, that's creepy," Cleo shivered.

"That's art, my dear sister—and you are freezing, so let's go." Teddy threaded her arm in Cleo's, and they headed to the car. "Oh, and Cole also said that as long as he kept my painting…"

She stopped short, and her brows furrowed.

"I will forever belong to him."

46

He's Hurt

"He's been hit!"

A nurse shouted to a group of construction workers as she dashed across the street to Kenneth, who was lying face down in the snow.

"I need assistance—you," she barked, pointing to one of the men. "Quick, help me turn him over. I think he's suffocating." She held Kenneth's head steady while the man tucked an arm under his stomach. "Be careful," she urged. "He might have broken something. Now on the count of three, you ready?" The man's wrinkled forehead knitted together, and he nodded.

"One—two—*THREE!*"

In one heave, they flipped Kenneth on his back, and he lay there motionless as a crowd of people gathered around him. "Hey, isn't that K?" someone shouted, and everyone drew in closer.

Suddenly, Kenneth jerked awake, gasping for air, and the construction worker screamed, "Get back, you frigging idiots. Can't you see the man's trying to breathe?" He pulled a rag from his back pocket and pressed it to K's bloody forehead.

"Hey buddy, are you okay?"

"Get me up," Kenneth said, trying to focus, then he hissed, "We have to find Teddy."

"Sure thing, pal." The worker turned to his friend, "Hey Tony, you take his arms, and I'll get him from behind, okay?" His friend nodded, and the crowd began to chant K's name as the men got into position. "And when I tell ya to lift, you lift, okay?"

"Yeah, I gotcha."

The chanting grew louder.

"What the hell is this?" Agent Walters said as he stepped up to the window on the second floor of the FBI field office and stared down at all the people gathering in the middle of the street.

"Ready now?" the construction worker said, and Tony's brows furrowed. "And... one, two, three—*LIFT!*"

The crowd roared.

Holy shit, is that K?

Walters' eyes went large.

Oh, fuck—

"Stewart, we gotta go!"

47

The Studio

It was just after five when the rental rolled into the West Village. Cleo's foot hovered over the brake pedal as she scanned one brick building after the other, looking for Cole's address.

"Sweet Jesus, you drive worse than Abby." Teddy flipped down the visor and stared in the mirror for one last primp. "I look like hell."

"Oh please... you're gorgeous," Cleo said as she jammed down on the brakes in front of a white two-story building. "Well, I think this one is it."

"Holy crap, I've been here before." Teddy flipped the visor shut. "This is the last place that Eni and I visited." Cleo's mouth went dry, and she gawked at her. "Please tell me it's not the building where she was *shot?*"

"Oh, no, thank God." Teddy shuddered and glanced up at the second floor to see if the painting was still there, but it wasn't. "This is the place his creepy ex-girlfriend sent us to, but we couldn't get in, so we left." She let out a long contemplating sigh. "I guess it's now or never..."

"I say never." Cleo shot her a sideways look.

"Oh be nice… so, are you coming up with me?"

"Hell no," Cleo laughed. "No offense Teddy, but I'm not in the mood to see lover boy. Instead, I'm going to get myself a steamy hot cup of coffee from that deli over there." She put on Abby's hat and climbed out. "Do you want anything?"

"Yeah, get me one too." Teddy grimaced. "Will you be gone long?" Cleo let out a hearty laugh and tightened her scarf. "Shit, I'm going to take my sweet ass time. Have fun." She crossed the street, and Teddy pouted. "Pfft, she is so uncool…"

The frosted leafless ivy that clung to the old facade was probably gorgeous in the late spring, Teddy thought as she grabbed her backpack and climbed out of the car. She headed over to the entranceway, and to her surprise, it was open. The wrought iron gate was tied back against the wall with bungee cords, and a couple of empty moving boxes sat nearby, but no one was around.

A curious red flower caught her eye, and she bypassed the mailboxes and the bulky wooden staircase that led up to Cole's place and headed straight into the backyard to have a better look at it.

Wow, how can you thrive in such cold weather?

The scarlet camellia sat alone on a snow-covered table in the center of the square. Tiny icicles dripped from its green leaves. Delighted at such beauty, Teddy spun around to take in the rest of the hidden courtyard.

A row of three-story apartments enclosed the square with an eclectic mix of French windows and fire escapes that crisscrossed all the way up to the rooftops. Yet, aside from a few bicycles chained to the back gate, the place looked deserted.

"It's awfully quiet in here," she muttered as she returned to the staircase and headed up the riser. It was steep, and a loud crackle of wood snapped, startling her. Teddy clutched the handrail for safety. Then, when she reached the top landing, she turned to knock on the door but stopped midway.

Wait!

She took out her lipstick.

Just a little gloss, a little hair primp, and then girls—she cupped her boobs and lifted—*tits up!*

She placed an ear to the door listening for movement.

Oh, screw this—

RAP—RAP—RAP!

The door swung open.

"Um, *hello?"*

The scent of linseed oil mixed with a bit of body odor greeted her. Cautiously, with her fingertip, she pushed the door open further.

"Anybody *home?"*

It was dark. Teddy flipped the light switch on, but it was dead. She propped the door open with a rubber wedge that she had found lying on the floor, and it took a moment for her eyes to adjust. The only other light came from the front windows. Rays of sunset poured in through the glass and reflected off the studio's tin-foiled walls and ceilings, illuminating the room with an eerie mirrored glow.

This place looks like a tornado hit it!

Off to the left was a small kitchen with its cupboards open and bare. To the right sat a four-seater table covered in empty beer bottles and a pizza box. The flat seemed more like an industrial office space than an apartment. She picked up a half-eaten slice of pizza and wiggled it.

Hmm, it's about a day old.

Teddy tossed it back in the box and walked over to a pile of papers on the floor.

Ah, here we go—bingo!

A Valentine's Day card lay open. It had a big juicy red lipstick kiss planted at the bottom, followed by the words, 'Cole, my beating heart is yours forever. Love Suzi.'

Pfft, what an asshole…

Disgusted, Teddy made her way into the next room. It was a storage room with tubes of paint and unfinished canvases everywhere. Some were stacked on tables, while the larger paintings leaned against the walls. In the back was an adjourning door, and a tiny floral hung on its face.

Hey, I know you…

She lifted the happy little flower from the door's hold, remembering the day Cole painted it, and then in a beat, hurled it, pissed off.

Fuck you!

The little fresco glided into the main room and hit an easel that stood alone by the front window. Its portrait fell to the floor face-down. Teddy's eyes grew large with curiosity, and she walked over. The canvas was taller than wide. Duct tape was strewn across its back, bandaging over deep slashes that cut through its skin. Her eyes focused on the writing in the corner:

The girl with the cat shaped eyes
Cole O'Keefe
September 1987

"There you are..." her voice quivered as she turned it over.

Even torn, the painting was breathtakingly beautiful. Teddy struggled to catch her breath. Her tears were falling fast. The love she came to find was no longer. She let out a deep sigh, kissed her fingertip, and traced his signature.

Goodbye, Cole.

48

Illusions

The clickety-clack of heels climbing up the wooden staircase grew louder. Teddy wiped at her tears with the back of her sleeve.

It's Cleo… I'd better hurry.

Quickly, she pulled the painting off its wooden frame and carefully tucked it into her backpack. "I'll be right there," she yelled, zipping it up. She headed into the hallway and froze midstep—a .38 revolver was nonchalantly aiming at her head.

"Hello, Theodora…"

Dressed all in black, wearing a long wool coat with hood and ruffle, Bridget stepped into the light. Her knee-high boots clicked to a halt, and she tugged at her hoodie. It slid down to her shoulders, revealing her stark platinum cut.

"Well, if it isn't Mother's favorite," she hissed.

Amused by the look of shock on Teddy's face, Bridget prowled. "So, this is your boyfriend's place, huh? It appears to be deserted, tsk-tsk." She gave Teddy a knowing smile and winked. "I bet people leave you all the time, don't they?" She let out a snarky laugh, then paused before a stack of Cole's sketches on the floor. "Ooh, what do we have here?" With the tip of her patent leather toe, she separated the drawings. "Hm, I'm impressed. This painter of yours is quite good." She sent Teddy a steely look. "You have Mother's eyes, did you know?"

"No," Teddy uttered with more air than tone.

"Oh, silly me, how could you?"

"I'm sorry about your parents."

"Are you?" Bridget's eyes narrowed, and her arms crossed with the gun dangling, just twitching in her hand. "Yes, of course I am," Teddy said nervously, and she cleared her throat. "I mean, I feel sorry for your loss—"

"How *DARE* you feel sorry for me!"

BANG!

The bullet struck Teddy in the upper arm, and she fell backwards into the storage room and kicked the door shut. Frantically, she reached up and locked it, leaving Bridget ranting on the other side. Blood oozed out from where the bullet had entered and passed through. It was on fire. Quickly, she searched for something to stop the bleeding, and then everything went still. A tiny hissing breath hovered at the door.

TAP! TAP!

"Theodora," Bridget said in a sweet sing-song voice. "Did I hurt you, my love? I'm so sorry. You know that I was only joking, right?" She pressed her head against the door and drew a heart with the gun's barrel. "I've always wanted an older sister. Come out, and let's play." And with a wicked laugh, darkness crept into her eyes.

• • •

The clock on the wall read a quarter after, and the deli was busy with locals enjoying the last of the early bird specials. Cleo stood second in line at the food counter. Her eyes kept darting over to a little two-seater table by the window, hoping she'd get there before someone else did.

"Who's next?" shouted the balding deli clerk. He was dressed all in white with food stains on his belly and a manager's name tag that read Ernie on his chest.

"Me," Cleo chimed.

"Nice hat," he grinned. "Whaddya need, hon?"

Suddenly aware of her appearance, Cleo tugged off the crazy fur and ran her fingers through her matted strawberry blonde locks until they were free and flowing, which delighted him. "I'll take two coffees with cream and sugar and this cheesecake here." She pointed to the dessert display and smiled.

"Anything for you, doll," he said with a wink, then yelled to the crew. "Gimme two light and sweets and one of New York's finest for the pretty lady in pink." Laughter erupted, and her face flushed red. Cleo glanced over at the table. It was still available. Quickly, she paid and headed over.

"Oh, it feels so good to sit," she groaned and sunk down into the seat. The coffee smelled delicious. She wrapped both hands around it and took a small sip.

Mmm, just what I needed.

She tilted her face towards the sun's rays pouring in the window.

Brrr, I miss Florida… this place is way too cold for my liking!

She took another sip and stared down the street. The neighborhood was quiet, and the sky a clear blue. She angled her head a bit further, hoping to see Teddy standing by the car, but she wasn't.

Hmm, I wonder how she's getting on with lover boy? Hopefully not good—ha, and wouldn't it be great if he was fat and balding too?

She snickered.

Now, K, on the other hand, he's gorgeous—

"Hey, Ernie… did you hear about that girl who was shot down on Bleecker?" said a man standing at the counter, and Cleo's ears perked up. "Supposedly, it was a bloody mess—I tell ya, this frigging neighborhood is going to hell."

Suddenly, a wave of panic swept over her, and she gasped, "What was I thinking letting her go up there alone?" Then in two big gulps, Cleo finished off her coffee, tossed a dollar bill on the table, and rushed out the door with the boxed cheesecake and Teddy's coffee in hand.

"So, what are the odds she's ready to go?" Heading across the street, Cleo sidestepped an icy patch—her butt was still stinging from the earlier fall, and she subconsciously rubbed it, then made a beeline for the car. "Zero, Teddy never does anything fast, and if I had to guess, I bet she's confessing her love to him right now. Shit, aside from K, she has the worst taste in men!"

Cleo opened the back seat door and placed the cheesecake on the floor. Then she took a few steps toward the building and stopped.

Eww, what if they're having sex?

Freezing, she put on Abby's hat and zeroed in on Teddy's coffee.

You're mine now.

Popping the lid, Cleo took a sip and stared up at the second-floor window, then gasped.

"Oh no, it's the blonde—"

BANG!

● ● ●

The bullet shattered the antique crystal knob, and the door opened. "Theodora," Bridget softly called as she pushed into the room. It was dark. Only a hint of light trickled in from the hallway, and she could see that the door in the back was cracked slightly open.

"Are you hiding from me, my love? Tsk-tsk… come out, come out, wherever you are." She shoved the gun under a desk, then behind a painting. "That phrase is so cliché but so appropriate, don't you think?"

Tin cans tumbled to the floor in the outer room, and her eyelashes fluttered in delight. She rushed to the connecting door in the back but hesitated. Cautiously, she raised the gun, then jerked it open.

Tall shadowy figures surrounded her, and she jumped back— her gun swinging wildly at each of their faces until she realized it was just a group of mannequins stacked by the doorway with their silhouettes rising up to the tin-foiled ceiling above, swaying with the dimming of the sun's light.

Bridget let out a stream of breath to recalibrate, and then continued.

"You know, Theodora, I've always wanted to play hide and seek, but Mother would never allow it. She could be such a drag at times. Lucky for you that you didn't have to live with her."

She let out a snarky laugh and headed over to the front window in the center of the room to take in the studio's layout.

"Mother was always such a mystery to me…" Bridget paused at the fallen easel with a sad, musing gaze. "Heh, I guess it took her death for me to see who she really was—eww, Theodora, your boyfriend's place is gross!"

She kicked the wooden frame and scowled.

"It's disgusting in here!"

Garbage lay everywhere, along with spent paint supplies, broken wall dividers, and an assortment of theatrical props wedged in and out of crevices making the large room feel diminutive, claustrophobic even. Giant portraits of teary-eyed girls graffitied the walls, unnerving her with their heartbroken stares.

Shimmering lights danced above her head, and she looked up. A glittered paper-mâché hand twirled from the air of her movements, causing a tinge of nausea to set in. Bridget leaned against the windowsill, waiting for the feeling to pass.

"So, where is this secret hiding place of yours?"

Directly before her stood two large workstations covered in rags and empty paint cans. To her left was a couch blanketed in fabrics, a broken loveseat, and a coffee table stacked high with newspapers. And on her right, in the back corner by the brick wall, was a tiny bedroom filled with cardboard boxes.

Yet, Bridget's eyes fixated on the door next to it—*hm, it's closed.* She had guessed it to be either a bathroom or a closet, or better yet… she smiled.

The perfect hideout.

Heading over, Bridget's ears perked up, and she stopped. A subtle noise sounded on her left, and her eyes darted to the couch.

"Tsk-tsk, lil Theodora, the poor bastard child of Sarah…" she sneered, enjoying the nerve-wracking sounds her boots were making on the undressed concrete. "Left alone in this cruel world to fend for herself. Ha, it almost sounds biblical if you ask me, don't you think?" Shell casings dropped to the floor as she emptied the gun's chamber and reloaded.

"Well, at least you weren't left floating down the river like the baby Moses." Bridget stepped up to the couch and scowled at the pile of fabrics.

"You know, up until a week ago, I didn't even know you existed. Heh, I doubt Father knew either. If he had, I'm pretty sure that you wouldn't be here… and yet, here you are."

She snapped the cylinder shut.

"Goodbye, Theodora."

BANG!

Fragments of linen dusted the air, and Bridget ripped off the sheets.

"Where *ARE* you?!"

With her heart pumping in her ears, Teddy pushed back further into the tiny cubbyhole indented in the bricks. Her arm was on fire, and without thinking, she tugged at the twine tourniquet that was wrapped around it to relieve the pressure, and a slight groan slipped from her lips.

Bridget spun in its direction.

"Now, before I kill you, Theodora, you should know…" She paused at the front window and stared out at the dying sunset. "Our mother was no saint. She was a sinner." A single tear rolled down her cheek, and she walked to the closet door and aimed. "And you, my love, her sin—"

BANG! BANG!

The bullets blasted through the wood veneer with what sounded like a small explosion, and Bridget kicked the door open with a grunt. A white ceramic sink lay shattered in pieces on the floor.

"You're a clever little kitty, aren't you, Theodora?" Once again, her eyes searched around the room but this time with more urgency, knowing that it would be almost impossible to find Teddy when the sun went down. But just then, the courtyard's lighting system clicked on, and it sent a steady beam of light bouncing off the tin-foiled walls and ceilings, brightening the room.

Bridget sighed, "Thank you, Father," and a loving smile warmed her face. "I know you're here with me. I feel your presence." She pulled a handful of bullets from her pocket and reloaded again.

"Now, where was I... oh yeah, our sinner Mother." Suddenly, Bridget didn't need to rush anymore as she strolled around the room, laughing, exploring, and telling family stories. She wanted to relish in the moment and make Teddy pay for every injustice that ever happened to her, make her pay for every loveless moment that her mother showered upon her as a child, but most of all, she wanted to make her pay for just being born.

"To be honest, I never quite understood what Father saw in Mother. He was such a passionate man... so handsome and sooo unbelievably smart."

Bridget's eyes narrowed on a fluffy tan boot sticking out of the wall. Her smile crinkled in satisfaction and then darkened.

"But Mother was cold... hard... and so unloving." She sidestepped a broken divider, then raised the gun up. "And what infuriates me the most is that it was you who she loved." With a furious snarl, she pulled the trigger.

BANG!

The bullet ricocheted off the outer bricks, inches from Teddy's head, and a shot of adrenaline raced through her veins. A whirlwind of images flashed before her eyes, but oddly enough, it wasn't memories from her past.

Instead, time floated in space, lingering in muted silence, and Kenneth's beautiful face appeared. With a loving smile, he pulled her in for a long kiss, and as if feeling his warm lips upon hers, Teddy closed her eyes and recited the poem that she had written on the glass at the airport. "Dreamiest eyes of the bluest seas… your beautiful smile calls to me—*HOLD ON*, this wasn't about Cole! His eyes aren't blue, they're *green*, and his smile is *crooked!*"

Teddy let out a laugh, realizing she had written the poem about what she wanted, not what she already had. "I wasn't supposed to be with Cole. I just needed a taxi to get away and start living again." Suddenly, a peaceful calm swept over her, and she exhaled, "The angel lady was right… I found what I was looking for—"

BANG!

"Excuse me, Theodora, am I interrupting you?" Bridget cackled, and Teddy snapped back to reality. Desperately, she tried to climb out of the cubbyhole, but her legs wouldn't move. They were dead from being cramped up for too long.

NOOOOO—I don't want to die being surrounded by Cole's leftover crap!

Panic rose in her eyes as the walls closed in around her. For a split second, she considered her options but quickly realized there were none. She was trapped, and Bridget stood just feet away, toying with her, ready to blow her brains out.

FUCK!

Teddy punched her legs, trying to get the blood circulating— sharp needles tingled, but still, they wouldn't move. She slammed her head back against the wall in frustration, and regret sank in that she didn't get to say goodbye to anyone. She took a deep breath and closed her eyes, blocking out Bridget's tormenting chatter.

Think of love…

She wrapped her arms around her legs and pulled them in tight against her chest. Softly, Teddy hummed.

With a simple touch, my heart unwinds... oh, Kenneth, my dreams were trying to tell me that you were the one all along, but I didn't listen—

SLAM!

The front door closed, and everything went completely dark.

"Who's there?" Bridget called.

Silence filled the air, and disoriented, she stumbled through the clutter, swinging the gun left and right. She heard a crunching sound in the hallway and quickly turned, and then, out of the darkness, a golden blur lunged.

AAAHHH—You PSYCHO bitch!

• • •

"Get back—FBI here!"

Agent Walters jumped out of the SUV and wrapped an arm around Kenneth. He led him into the back seat of the car.

"Hey K, are you alright?" he said, assessing the bruises on his face, then climbed in next to him. "He needs medical attention."

"No hospitals please," Kenneth hissed, struggling to focus. "I'm good, really I am, but we need to find Teddy. I think she's in trouble."

"What—*is* Cleo with her?" Walters shot Stewart a panicked look. "Stew, you got that boyfriend's address on you?"

"Yup, it's in my bag." He spun the car around. "His place is in the Village." He hit the gas. "We'll be there in ten minutes."

"Make it five," Walters huffed as he grabbed a towel off the floor and pressed it to Kenneth's face. "Jesus, you're a bloody mess."

"Ouch—quit it," Kenneth bellowed, pushing his hand away. "That shit hurts!"

"Stop being a baby and quit moving! You're getting blood all over the car." Walters grabbed a water bottle from his bag, wet the towel, and tried again, but this time with a softer touch. "Now tell me exactly what happened."

"Oww—I don't know... one second, I was kissing Teddy goodbye, then—*BAM!*"

Pissed, he pushed Walters' hand away and stared out the window.

"Oh, wait... there was a taxi." He rubbed his forehead. "A blonde..." Confused, Kenneth's brows knitted together. "She was laughing at me."

Walters' eyes grew large.

"Stew, are we there yet?"

● ● ●

UGH—YOU BITCH!!

In the darkness, Cleo's pain-filled cries reverberated off the walls and into the cubbyhole where Teddy cowered, rocking back and forth.

Get up, Teddy... Get up, Teddy...

The numbness in her legs was gone, but with each of her sister's cries, Teddy's thoughts got fuzzier, more disorganized. She was fading into catatonia.

"You're weak, Hayes!"

Bodies crashed into the wall, and a large glass object shattered upon the floor. Teddy's breath caught. The horror of Eni's lifeless body lying on top of her flashed before her eyes, and she rocked faster.

Get up, Teddy... Get up, Teddy...

"You're just as useless as that sister of yours!"

OUCH!

Cleo stomped on Bridget's foot and clawed at her face, slashing deep into the soft flesh of her cheek. The pain seared like a hot iron, and Bridget shot back, drilling her fist into Cleo's gut.

"Oww—help me, Teddy!" she cried out, doubling over.

Her entire life was reckless, and never before did she worry about dying because Cleo had always been there to protect her. Yet now that the roles were reversed, and her sister needed her the most, Teddy found herself cradled like a child, lost in fear.

"Ha! Don't waste your breath on that pathetic sister of yours. She won't save you. She's just like her selfish mother!" Bridget swung the gun at Cleo's head, trying to knock her out but missed. And while she was taller and faster than Cleo, Cleo had her in weight.

Then with a ferocious screaming heave, Cleo rammed her into the pointy edge of the desk, and the gun dropped to the floor—

BANG!

All went silent.

"Cleo-*O?*"

Teddy sat up, her eyes blinking rapidly in the void. She listened hard for any sign of life coming from her sister. Then at once, in a thunderous crash, the two women dove into the clutter.

"Where the hell is it?" Bridget screamed as she swept the floor with one hand, searching for the gun. She saw Cleo reaching under the desk, and she dove at her. "Oh no you don't," she screeched, yanking her back by the hair and slamming her face into the ground.

Flashes of light danced in Cleo's eyes as she struggled to get up, but Bridget shoved her back down and climbed on top, straddling her waist, and blind with rage, she pummeled. The first punch grazed Cleo's chin, and Cleo tried to block the second one with her palms, but Bridget just punched through with more force until Cleo's hands fell away, and she went unconscious.

"I'm going to enjoy killing you," Bridget hissed as she tucked Cleo's hands under her knees and braced herself. Her smile twitched as her fingers tightened around Cleo's neck, and then slowly, she tightened, strangling the air from her windpipe.

With a buck, Cleo woke, her eyes bulging, her body lashing. "It's like riding bareback," Bridget cackled and held steady, clenching her teeth while her fingers dug in deeper.

The lights dimmed in Cleo's eyes, and Bridget exhaled, satisfied.

"One Hayes down and one to go—"

AAAAAAAAAHHHH!

"Get your fucking hands off my SISTER!"

Charging full force, Teddy dove at her, knocking her off Cleo and into the wall. Then crazed with fury, her arms flailed, legs kicked, fingers clawed, and teeth bit, leaving Bridget howling like a wounded animal. And with her last ounce of adrenaline, Teddy picked her up and tossed her at the desk.

Bridget crashed to the floor and crumpled up, winded. Her eyes fluttered as she focused on the shiny object lying under the desk. Quickly, she reached for it, and her hand closed over the gun.

• • •

"Ew, you're such a pig!"

Walters pulled a moldy half-eaten sandwich out from Stewart's overstuffed briefcase as he looked for Cole's address. "I know you said the upper pocket, but it's not there—Jesus, what the hell do you have in this thing? Shit, is this the Peters file that I've been looking everywhere for?"

"Here, give me that," Stewart scoffed as he pulled the car over.

"I betcha anything, it's on that messy desk of yours!" Walters scowled.

In throbbing pain, Kenneth blew out a frustrated breath. The agents' bickering was getting on his nerves, and the only thing keeping him from toppling over was the thought of finding Teddy.

Why didn't I just listen to her this morning? We could have spent the whole day in bed making love…

He closed his eyes, remembering the warmth of her kiss.

And I promised her pancakes!

"Found it! I told you it was in here." Stewart flashed the address in Walters' face, then pointed up the street. "It's about four blocks from here. My guess is it's the white one in the middle."

"Thank God," Walters sighed and sat back. Then he turned to Kenneth. "Now, K… I know Teddy's your girl, and you want to protect her, but you're gonna have to stay in the car while we go get her, okay buddy?"

"Like hell I do!" And even before Walters could roll his eyes, Kenneth hopped out of the car and hobbled as fast as he could, racing towards the building.

"Man, he's got it bad for her," Stewart laughed and threw the car in gear, following after him. "Yeah, he does." Walters reached for his gun and checked the bullets. "Those Hayes girls sure do know how to drive a man crazy." Stewart let out a chuckle, knowing that his partner was smitten.

"All right, so you go get him, and then I'll go up and get the girls, okay?"

"Gotcha."

49

The Lie

The bullet splintered the top of the door frame as Teddy ran out. The sudden burst of light temporarily blinded her, and she stumbled down the wooden staircase, then tripped over the last step, flying head-first into a mound of snow.

With a wicked smile, Bridget leaned over the railing and aimed.

"Well, this is no fun. It's like shooting apples in a barrel." She snarled and pulled the trigger. The bullet dusted by Teddy's foot, and she bolted to the courtyard.

Run, Theodora, run...

Two blocks away, Kenneth heard the loud crack and stopped short. "Was that a *gunshot?*" Panicked, he rushed toward the building's entrance and saw Bridget walking into the backyard with the gun leading the way. "Oh, fuck," he gasped. "It's her!"

Frantically, he tried to open the gate, but it was locked. He shook it, then looked up and saw an opening at the top. "Shit, that's at least ten feet up, and I'll have to get over those sharp metal spikes without impaling my balls, fuck!" Sucking in air, he stepped back and made a running jump for it.

OUCH!

And as he crashed to the floor, Teddy ran past the scarlet camellia. "How the *HELL* do I get out of this *place?*" she clamored in exasperation and ran down a side alley. She cried for help, but no one answered. It was a dead end.

Quickly, she rushed back to the main square in search of another way out. She saw the bicycles by the back fence and charged for them.

BANG!

The bullet whizzed by Teddy's head, and she tapped back in the snow. "Ha, Mother said you were a dancer, but this is just delightful," Bridget laughed. "Who would've thought that I'd have such a talented sister?"

Desperate, Teddy scrambled to the back gate, but it was tied shut. *FUUUCCCK,* she screamed out in frustration and tried to climb over the fence, but her ankle was too weak to hold her weight.

"Tsk-tsk, my love." Bridget cooed, walking up. "Nice try, but all the gates are locked. I made sure of it earlier in the day."

"Why are you doing this?" Teddy shrieked, and she turned to face her. Her hands were clutching the fence as she braced for the bullet.

Bridget stared at her sister's terrified eyes, contemplating her words. After a week of heartbreak and death, she was seconds away from checking the last name off her list. Yet, something was stopping her from pulling the trigger.

For the first time since her parents died, Bridget felt torn. Everyone she had ever cared for was dead, and her life no longer had meaning. Only a little heartbeat of love remained growing inside her, but even the promise of having Russell's baby no longer mattered.

"What do you *WANT* from me?"

"Everything," Bridget said in almost a whisper as she looked down at the gun and then back up at the sister she had never known. "I must do this—"

STOP!

Kenneth rushed into the courtyard and charged at her. Laughing, Bridget spun around and aimed the gun at his heart.

"Say goodbye to your ballplayer—"

NOOOOOO!

With a voracious roar, Teddy lunged at her, struggling for the gun, and it went off.

BANG!

The Agents entered with their guns raised.

BANG! BANG! BANG!

50

Breathe

The steady rhythm of pings and beeps hummed in the hospital room as Teddy's eyes slowly opened. She looked out the window. The sun was rising on the horizon.

Cleo was in the ICU recovering on the second floor, and Kenneth was fast asleep by her side, crumpled up in a chair with his arm in a sling and his feet resting on her bed. He had been there for the last two days, refusing to leave. Bridget passed away from her wounds.

So much loss… so much destruction…

The memory of the bullet entering and exiting her body was now a dull, aching kind of feeling that left her wondering why she felt at peace. After all, she had been shot twice in one day. Kenneth snorted, startling her, and she grinned.

I want pancakes…

The swelling on his face came down, but his lips were still puffy.

Mmm, and still kissable.

Feeling grateful, she watched him sleep. His jacket was propped behind his head, a sweater was blanketed over his lap, and she smiled at his chest muscles moving up and down under his tee.

I could get used to those.

He snorted again.

That's right, O'Connor, I took a bullet for you—you OWE me!

Teddy stared out the window, trying to make sense of it all. She felt conflicted about Bridget's death, especially since the woman tried to kill her multiple times, but still, she thought it would have been nice to have a younger sister.

Speaking of sisters, I better go check on Cleo before she wakes.

Quietly, she climbed out of bed, tip-toeing over to her backpack, and her eyes widened. A brown leather satchel was stuffed inside. Teddy pulled it free, and a small note dangled from its drawstring.

Show this to no one.
—Alpheus

51

The Letter

Dear Theodora,

You don't know me, but I am your mother. I remember the day you were born as if it were yesterday. Oh, what a glorious day that was... and from the very moment I saw your beautiful face, I just knew you were the love of my life.

Heartbroken, Teddy wiped the tears from her eyes. This was the fifth time reading her mother's letter, and still, she couldn't believe it to be true. Her emotions were raw. Yet, oddly enough, there was a tinge of happiness rumbling around in her soul. It didn't make sense, but she guessed it was because, for the first time in her life, she felt truly loved.

The day was the sunniest blue she had ever seen, but it was way too cold to be sitting on a concrete ledge on the hospital's rooftop. Her butt was frozen stiff, and the blanket wrapped around her was way too thin to keep her warm, but she just pulled it up to her chin and continued reading.

Theodora, please know that I never meant to leave you. To this day, I still do not know what happened. All I remember is that one moment I was holding you in my arms, and the next, you were gone.

The words caught in the back of Teddy's throat, and her lip quivered.

From that moment on, my world turned dark. I had even tried to end my life a few times with the help of Mother's painkillers, but I failed at that too. My therapist said I was suffering from a broken heart. Mother swore it was a nervous breakdown, and Father... well, he just figured he'd buy my happiness, and he spoiled me rotten.

Still, I couldn't get you out of my thoughts, and I became obsessed with finding you. I hired a private detective, but years of searching turned up nothing. It was as if you were wiped from existence. And then, out of the blue, I received an invitation to a dance recital. Attached to it was a note: 'Come and see your beautiful Theodora's first dance - Abigail Hayes.'

"Huh, go figure… only *crazy* Abby would do such a thing!"

Then when you stepped onto that stage, my heart exploded with joy. I could not believe my eyes... there you were, my little baby girl, all grown up and so beautiful. I just wanted to hold you in my arms and never let you go.

Tears streamed down Teddy's face.

But instead, I left and promised never to return. Selfishly, I knew that if word got out that you were my daughter, everything I've worked so hard for all my life — all of Father's dreams would have been ruined. And the truth is, Theodora, I am not a very nice person. The choices I have made in my life have left me bitter and cold.

"Enough!" Teddy shrieked. "Why is life so messy?" Irritated, she threw the letter back in the satchel and pushed it away. "Okay, so the woman was a little bit flawed." she blew out a puff of frustrated breath, "Heh, but then aren't we all?"

Teddy stared out at the city.

"Clearly, I take after my father's side," she laughed. "And how about that crazy Abby calling me beautiful? Ugh, I've been so hard on her and way too much of a brat to see all the good she's done for me. I guess I owe her a *BIG* apology."

A calmness settled over her, and she let out a long sigh. "I miss Henry. I wonder what he's gonna say when he meets Kenneth—ha, probably that he's a keeper!"

She tilted her face up towards the sun.

"Wow, it blows my mind that my real mother came to see me dance—*AND* that last part… could it really be true?" She grabbed the letter again and turned it over.

P.S... For many years, I believed your father to be dead. I was told that he perished in a fire. However, yesterday, I learned that he survived. If so, then you must find him for me, and when you do, please tell him that he was my one true —

"love…" Teddy uttered the last word and looked down, confused. "How can I be so much like someone I've never known?"

SLAM!

The rooftop door banged open, and Teddy leaned forward to see who was coming, but no one was there. Then a familiar sweet aroma wafted in the air.

"Is that… *cloves?*"

She stared in disbelief.

"Aw, schnuckiputzi…"

Eni blew a puff of smoke out of the corner of her smile, and Teddy started to cry.

"Why all the tears, my love?"

"Is it really you?" Teddy jumped up, grabbed her into a bear hug, squeezing her tight, then she pulled back, laughing. "And what the *hell* are you wearing?"

Eni had on her short black leather jacket, a white hospital gown that was flapping wildly around her skinny legs from the wind, and hot pink bunny slippers. She gave Teddy the most beautiful pirate smile and cooed, "Darling, the nurse has an adorable crush on me and keeps bringing me presents."

"Oh, Eni, I thought I lost you."

"Aw, Schnuckie, you saved me."

"I *did?*"

"Yes, you did." Eni lifted her face and nodded. "If the ambulance hadn't gotten there when zey had, I would have been a goner."

And with soggy smiles, they camped on the ledge. Teddy covered the blanket over their legs and rested her head on Eni's shoulder.

"Seeing you makes this crazy world beautiful again." She held her tight, and the two of them sat there in silence for a while, staring out as the skyline turned gray. Then Teddy pulled back and shot her a playful look.

"So, whose turn is it, yours or mine?"

"Darling, you go first," Eni cracked a smile. "Oh, and I want something flirtatiously naughty or downright deliciously lewd but nothing too drudgingly deep—my brain still hurts, so make it cheery too."

With a chuckle, Teddy let out a happy sigh, "Well, I guess it's gonna be flirtatiously naughty then."

"Ha, Theodora... I'm crushing on you."

To be continued...